# A Tale
# of Four
# Tall Tails

A Tall Tails Mystery

~

*A Tale of Three Tall Tails*: Book 1
*A Tale of Four Tall Tails*: Book 2

# A Tale
# of Four
# Tall Tails

## Adrienne E. Schabel

A TALE OF FOUR TALL TAILS

*A Tale of Four Tall Tails* is a work of fiction based on memories. The animal characters are real, but except for public figures, the human characters are imaginary. Businesses, locales, and events are products of the author's imagination. For the purposes of the story, some historical events are shifted slightly in time, and the town of Cumberland, Maine, has been moved closer to the Portsmouth Naval Shipyard.

Independently published

Printed in the United States of America

First Printing, 2020

ISBN: 9781670399342

To those who gave their lives in World War II to preserve our freedom.

And to Molly, who decided to live with the angels, and Cookie, who, two weeks later, followed his Miss Molly home.

# Prologue

## *Cumberland, Maine*
## *Early Spring, 1942*

T he snowshoe hare twitched his nose at the pleasant smell. He'd just squeezed between the broken slats in the front door of the barn, drawn in by the sweet aroma. Yes, it was fresh clover the old man had plucked for the goat, who was now quietly munching at the pile. Cautiously, the hare approached. He was familiar with the interior of the barn, having a home in a blackberry bush nearby. This saved him the trouble of foraging supper in the outside gloom with night creatures wandering about. He was also familiar with the old man's habit of picking treats for the goat, and he often visited to check out the latest offering.

His nose twitched in appreciation as he approached the goat, who ignored her night visitor. The hare was nibbling at the clover when a sound alerted him. His long ears swiveled around as he stood frozen, watching the barn door slowly creak open.

A human dressed in black and carrying a long, skinny roll under his arm walked in. With a silent bound, the hare moved into the shadows as the man approached.

The dark-brown horse in a nearby stall had been dozing, but now he looked over curiously, wondering why someone was entering the barn at this time of night. He, along with the hare, watched the figure bend down and pull an old, moldy bale of hay away from the barn's wall.

The goat, in the meantime, chose to ignore it all and stood nonchalantly munching on her treat, much to the hare's dismay as the last of the pile disappeared into the bigger animal's mouth.

In the swath of moonlight from the barn's only window, the hare saw the man tuck the long roll in next to the wall and then push the moldy hay bale back to its original position. He did not notice the roll's metal cap fall away, exposing the paper within. But the hare noticed.

Wordlessly, the figure departed, slowly closing the huge door, and once again the barn belonged to the animals within.

The disgruntled hare twitched his long ears at the soft clucks of the chickens as they slept, completely unaware of the barn's human night visitor. His snack now gone, the dissatisfied hare slipped through the broken slats in the door and hopped off to find his supper.

# Chapter 1

*Momauguin, Connecticut*
*Friday, March 6, 1942*

J osh laid the newspaper he was reading on his lap and once again inspected the bottom of his foot, much to Cookie's annoyance. "Four-F! Can you believe it?" he complained. The gray tomcat sat next to him on the couch, idly reading the newspaper headlines while picking halfheartedly at an old nail sheaf. Cookie was a cat of many talents that were seldom given to an ordinary feline.

"I'm only twenty-three," Josh complained. "I'm young, physically fit, and yet the army won't take me! Flat feet! Who ever heard of not getting into the army because of that?"

He held out his foot for Maura, his wife, to look at. She was busy baking in the kitchen, something she loved to do. She smiled at her husband of three years and continued stirring her cookie dough. She had not noticed that Josh's feet were flat until the classification letter arrived, and though he was frustrated and angry about the local enlistment board's decision, she was secretly glad that the army would not take him or his identical twin, Jim, for the same reason. She felt guilty, but she definitely was grateful for their flat arches. "Flat feet must run in the family," she said.

The marmalade, a dark-orange-striped cat who had been dozing on the rose-colored, oval braided rug, opened a sleepy green eye at the comment. Holding a paw up in the air to peer closely at it, he asked his brother, "People's feet usually round?"

Cookie looked up from the nail he was gnawing on and sighed deeply. "No, Tiggy. Most people have an arch under their feet to hold them up. Josh and Jim don't." He went back to his ablutions, much to the other cat's consternation.

"Feet fall off?" Tiggy began to howl at the picture.

Leaning over, Cookie whacked his brother with his paw.

Josh looked up. "Maura, they're at it again."

Maura paused in stirring the wet dough. "Shhhhhh! Stop that!" She pounded her large wooden spoon on the counter, causing dough to splatter all over.

Startled, both cats jumped and raced behind the couch, much to the humans' amusement.

Maura found a wet cloth and wiped the counter and her apron while Josh grabbed a dishtowel and mopped the floor. Both humans were laughing, much to the cats' annoyance.

Josh had married Maura right after she graduated from high school, a year later than he did. His twin brother, Jim, newly married to Gina, lived in the cottage behind them along with her large Italian family. Homes stood close together in the small village of Momauguin on the Connecticut shore of Long Island Sound.

Josh picked up the newspaper's front section again, and Cookie jumped up next to him again to peek at the headlines.

"Someone stole a Monet painting from the Metropolitan Museum of Art in New York City," Josh remarked to Maura.

"Isn't he the famous watercolor painter?" she asked.

"Yes." He read on. "They don't know how the theft was accomplished."

"What do you suppose they want with it? Is it worth much?" she asked, still mixing batter.

"Thousands of dollars."

Maura raised her eyebrows. "But other museums won't buy it now that everyone knows it's stolen, will they?"

"Anyone can sell anything on the black market for the right price," Josh said. "If these thieves are anything like the guys who were smuggling stolen rifles off our dock last summer, they'll probably sell it to buy arms."

Maura sighed. It made her anxious to think about their frightening brush with those smugglers. "Well, I hope the picture doesn't get ruined."

"Pictures snitchers!" thought the gray tomcat. Art didn't interest him. He continued to read the front page.

"Hmm. The US Boy Scouts collected thirty million pounds of rubber in two weeks," Josh said. "Because of the rubber shortage, they won't make any new tires."

Cookie sniffed disdainfully. What did he care? He didn't drive anywhere.

Reading the story along with Josh, he learned that arms manufacturers were making hand grenades out of shovels and similar tools. "For heaven's sake!" Cookie thought, snorting. "What do they expect farmers to plow their fields with? Whisk brooms?" Annoyed, he flicked his ear. Sometimes humans could be so shortsighted!

"They're melting statues to make bullets," Josh said. "Well, there go history's heroes!"

"Shouldn't the war be over by now?" Cookie wondered. "It's been going for four months!" Then he had another thought. If the war kept going, maybe there would be more spies to hunt as the cats had done last summer, solving a local murder in the process. Perhaps he should advertise their sleuthing services in the newspaper.

He started to clean himself as he mulled what to say in a newspaper ad. "How about," he thought, *"Cat's Incorporated. No job too small. Catching German spies our specialty."*

He smiled, liking the sound of that, as he gave his tail a vigorous wash. Cookie wondered how much an ad like that would cost, ignoring the fact he didn't have money. He was a cat!

He picked a foot up to wash the brown pads underneath. Since they'd solved the case last summer, life had gotten decidedly boring. What they needed was some excitement.

3

Unfortunately, at precisely that moment, Cookie happened to glance over at Lucky, the tuxedo lounging on the easy chair. Lucky lived in the third cottage, across the narrow lane called Hogan's Alley, with her human housemate, Debbie, but spent her days at Maura and Josh's cottage with the two tomcats. She had just opened one large, yellow eye and was staring intently at him.

A small shiver raced across Cookie's silky, gray fur. "Now what exactly did that look mean?" he wondered. Lucky's talent for *seeing stuff* before it happened unnerved him.

Right now, Cookie chose to ignore her and stood up, rubbing his jaw against the sewn rip in the bolster of the couch, where a bullet had lodged last summer. Maura and Josh, with whom he stayed most of the time, had gotten a new front window to replace the one shattered by gunfire.

Cookie glanced down at his brother, contentedly sprawled upside down in a patch of weak winter sun on the rug, his favorite resting place. Tipping his head, Cookie studied his brother's large, double paws, which were lying atop the white expanse of his stomach. Tiggy's sea-green eyes, so like his brother's, were closed in sleep. He was happily dreaming of chasing hermit crabs back into their muddy homes—something he loved to do.

Shaking his head at the comical picture Tiggy made, Cookie had to admit that without Tiggy's help last summer, the police might never have solved the case of the rifle thefts or the murder of one of their favorite people. Too bad they'd been too late to arrest Max and his fellow spy. But by now the spies had probably returned to Germany. "No more excitement," Cookie thought. "No more Max." The war seemed far away.

He sighed and began to wash another paw, just for something to do.

Winter had been a series of light snowstorms, leaving blankets that melted quickly in the salty, shore air. Still, the cats preferred the warmth of indoors. They did their business outside, only to rush back in through the cat doors that Josh had fashioned in all three cottages. At night, safely ensconced in Gina's family cottage in the rear, they had a litter box.

The winter also made it difficult for the tomcats to visit their feral relatives living down a ways, behind the Beachhead, the restaurant that locals affectionately called "the Bucket of Blood" for a reason no one could remember.

The frequent snows kept the four humans in, too. They cancelled their usual Sunday excursions. Instead, they saved the money they usually spent on movies and ice cream floats or pizza in an old cigar box. They'd decided not to spend it until something special came up, and their savings increased each week.

"What's for supper, tonight, hon?" Josh asked.

"*Merrrrr*," Cookie meowed, looking up at Josh. He wanted to know too, being a regular recipient of supper scraps.

Josh chuckled, mistakenly thinking the cat was demanding his share of attention. "I still say he sounds like a rusty old door hinge when he does that," he said, scratching the cat's chin.

Maura smiled in agreement. The cookies were in the oven, and she had turned to preparations for dinner. Jim and Gina would soon show up. They came over several nights a week for supper and company. Josh swore it was because Jim wanted to get away from all the noise of Gina's big family, which included two dogs that provided a chorus of barking. Friday usually saw the foursome laughing and talking over cards or a board game.

Gina worked at the diner as a waitress, and both twins worked at the town garage. Jim was a mechanic, while Josh, the older of the two by five minutes, was a welder. That they worked together was handy, as the only car between the four of them was the station wagon given to Maura by her uncle Jack, who was a local police officer.

Money was somewhat scarce for both couples, but they knew they were fortunate. Many people in Momauguin and beyond were earning a decent wage for the first time in their lives after struggling through the Depression years. They were working for the war effort.

Gina loved to reminisce about standing in bread or soup lines with her grandfather Pop-Pop and her dad to get food for the family. Work was difficult to find after the stock market crash. And the Great Depression that followed caused more hardship. Many people lost their jobs in those years, and some lost their homes and were forced to live in garages or abandoned chicken coops.

5

Gina's dad, Gino, finally found work driving a semitrailer loaded with goods across the country. He still did long-distance hauling.

Because Gina was only ten at the time, she didn't remember much about having to eat bread soaked in gravy for supper. "But when I complain about not having enough money," Gina said, "Dad reminds me how much luckier we are now."

"Well?" Josh asked Maura, still wondering what she was stirring with the rotary mixer.

Cookie paused in his washing to flick an ear in her direction. As he'd had the ability to understand "people talk" since kittenhood, he was interested.

Maura tucked a lock of brown hair back into the elastic band that secured her bun and kept hair from falling in her face when she baked.

"Shepherd's pie. It's easy to make, and everyone likes it." She put the mixer down to stir the hamburger frying in the pan. "I'll put the hamburger in the loaf pan, top it with mashed potatoes, and add a couple cans of corn."

"Ah. Good," Josh said, still reading.

Having added butter and milk to the cooked potatoes, Maura started the mixer again.

Drool dripped from the side of Cookie's mouth. He was definitely a meat man, but he'd acquired a hankering for mashed potatoes. As for the corn, he could always spit it out.

The back door opened, ushering in cold air along with Jim and Gina.

Jim quickly slammed the door, waking Tiggy, who leisurely stretched his long body.

As Jim stomped the snow off his boots, the marmalade jumped up and hustled toward the couch. He liked to be close enough to see what was going on, while staying a safe distance from Jim's feet. They were always moving, almost as if they had minds of their own.

Gina carefully removed her boots, placing them on the old towel that Maura had put on the floor by the back door. She'd also propped a big pillow next to Lucky, who always reclined on the easy chair next to the door. The pillow kept the cold draft from reaching her.

"Smells good. What's for supper?" Jim asked, leaning over the counter that separated the kitchen from the living room.

Maura had just finished putting the supper together in a large loaf pan and was dicing some cheese to sprinkle on top. As the newlyweds were often there for supper, Jim always set aside money to give Maura for groceries.

Maura smiled at her brother-in-law. Leaning over, she opened the oven door and slid the casserole inside. "You'll find out. It'll be ready as soon as you set up the card table and the folding chairs in the living room." The kitchen was too small for any size table, so they made do as best they could.

Maura smiled at the thought that even the cats would like the casserole. Everyone who knew Maura was aware of her partiality to cats.

"Uh-oh!" Josh put down the newspaper to look over at his wife.

"What's the matter, dear?" Maura was handing the silverware to Gina.

"You won't like this, hon. They're thinking of rationing sugar along with gas."

"Why on earth would they do that?" Maura stopped what she was doing, put her hands on her hips, and glared at him. Baking was her passion. And it all needed sugar!

"Seems it's no longer safe to bring it from the islands," Josh said. What wasn't in the news story—but locals knew—was that German U-boats often patrolled the waters off the East Coast.

Maura shook her head, wondering what would be rationed next.

After supper, the two couples played a stirring game of Parcheesi, and the night passed quickly. Later, as was their habit, Jim and Gina picked up the two tomcats and took them home for the night, while Lucky walked back to Debbie's cottage. Her human, a nurse who worked the night shift at the local hospital, would be home soon. In deference to Josh, who had allergies, none of the cats spent the night at Josh and Maura's cottage. Both couples quickly fell asleep, unaware of the life-changing news to come.

# Chapter 2

## *Saturday, May 9, 1942*

Josh and Jim sat at Elmer's kitchen table, drinking his strongly brewed coffee. Elmer, a coworker, was quite a bit older than the twins, but he liked the young fellows, just starting out in life. And they liked his stories, particularly about Maine, where he used to live and where fishing was said to be good.

Elmer had invited them to stop by without saying why. Now, he picked up his cup and tilted his head. "How 'bout some coffee cake, fellows? My neighbor just brought it over this mornin'."

"Whatcha got, Elmer? A new girlfriend?" Jim loved to joke with Elmer, whom he considered "the old man," although no one really knew Elmer's age. The old Mainer could be thirty or sixty.

Elmer chuckled as he got out napkins to put pieces of coffee cake on. "Nah! She's no girl! Gotta be eighty, if she's a day." After serving the cake, he dropped down on his kitchen chair and took out his false teeth so he could gum his food—something that tickled the twins to no end.

"She does bake me a lot of desserts, though." Elmer smiled, breaking a large chunk of coffee cake off and shoving it into his mouth. The kitchen, warmed by the potbellied stove in the corner, was quite comfortable. The house had only two rooms and seemed small to the twins, but it was all Elmer needed. That and an old, scratched-up radio he'd rescued from the dump. The radio now stood silent, making it easier to talk.

"Glad ya fellows came over this morning," Elmer said, wiping his mouth with his gnarled land and putting his teeth back in. He took a sip of the dark, rich, fragrant coffee, silently studying the twins.

"Had a note from my daughter yesterday," he said finally, referring to his only daughter, who lived just outside of Portland, Maine, with her husband, a surgeon. "Said her husband got his notice. He got drafted into the army, and they have to move to a base in California. He'll eventually be sent overseas on a hospital ship." He put down his cup and leaned toward them. "Seems she wants me to move back up there when they leave at the end of the month. Said someone should stay in the old house to keep it livable."

Josh looked at Jim and nodded. Nature did have a way of repossessing any building that wasn't cared for.

"But no way I'm goin' back up there," Elmer said, shaking his head. "I've been here so long people say I've even lost my accent. Cumberland was nice when I was growing up, but it's been years since I was back there. Black flies that bite are ferocious in the summer. Plus, winters are too damn cold." He took another sip of coffee. Realizing it was now cold, he put the cup down on the table and rubbed his weather-worn hands together. "I'd like to sell the old homestead ta ya. It's mine, ya know. Dad left it to me in his will."

The twins' jaws dropped open. Why in the world did Elmer think they had that kind of money?

"Sell it to us?" Jim asked incredulously. "You don't want it?"

"Hell, Jim, at my age, what would I do with a large, old farmhouse? No, thank ya. I'd just as soon stay right here." He smiled a toothless smile, as he had removed his teeth again to readjust them. "The house is rundown and in need of some repairs, because they'd just recently moved in. Although they did put in running water. Up to that time, we rented it out."

Elmer wiped his false teeth off with a napkin. "Needs an upgrade to electricity, something you're good at, Jim." Then he looked at Josh. "And you'd be good to repair stairs and the like." The old man thought for a moment. "Might need a new roof, though."

Elmer looked steadily at the pair sitting opposite him, noting their interest but knowing they weren't in any position to buy a house for the going price.

"It's yours if ya want it." The old man took a last sip of cold coffee. He motioned to the coffee pot, smiling as both fellows nodded their heads. He rose to get it. He wasn't finished with what he wanted to say.

Filling all the cups, he sat down at the table. He held up his hand to stop them from turning down the offer as he took a leisurely sip of coffee. "I like ya fellows," he said. "Like to give ya a hand up, like Dad gave me when he deeded the house to me long ago."

Then he looked at Jim and said something that astounded both twins. "Give me a dollar to make it legal, and it's a done deal."

Elmer remembered his false teeth and slipped them back in, clacking them together to make sure they were positioned correctly. Then he looked expectantly at Jim, who had been about to decline the offer. Meanwhile, Josh sat back in his chair, a shocked look on his face.

The old Mainer reached for the shelf behind him and grabbed a small bottle of whiskey, adding some to his black coffee. He offered the bottle to the fellows, who shook their heads. Elmer took a sip, grinning at them over the top of his cup.

"Seriously, Elmer?" Jim asked. Then he used a term he'd heard from the old Mainer. "You aren't funnin' us, are you?"

"Nope. I'm dead serious." The old man smiled broadly at the twins' stunned expressions.

"But Elmer," Josh finally said, "what about your daughter? Perhaps she'll eventually want the house."

"Nah! She's got plenty of money with that doctor husband of hers. Plus, she really wants to move someplace where it's warm all the time. Can't wait to go to California, with all that sunshine. She'll buy a house there, once her husband's outta the army."

He motioned to the coffee pot again and got another nod from both fellows, who now intended to stay a bit longer than they had planned.

"My daughter said she doesn't want to pay any more taxes on the house, little as they are," Elmer said as he refilled their cups. "That's why she gave it back to me. Ya fellows are more than capable of fixin' the house up. And it would be a perfect place for ya all to live together, somethin' you've been talkin' about forever."

The boys looked at one another. Elmer was right. They'd often talked at work about their desire to own houses. And living together was a perfect solution! Didn't they just about do that now? Gina and Jim spent more time in the front cottage than in their own.

Elmer took another sip of coffee and looked directly at Jim and then at Josh. "So, give me that dollar and take it off my hands. But ya gotta do the paperwork!"

Jim looked at Josh, who nodded his assent. A slow smile washed over Jim's face. "Deal!" he said simply. He stood up, drawing some folded bills from his back pocket. Removing the rubber band, he leaned over the table and handed a dollar to Elmer, who also stood up. Then the two men gravely shook hands, settling it as simply as that.

They thanked Elmer for his generosity and walked out of the small house, eager to go home and tell their wives the news. Jim had some last-minute regrets, as he knew how much Gina loved the give-and-take of conversation at the diner, where she worked. But he would deal with that later.

He and Josh were opening their car doors when Elmer called to them. The fellows both turned around.

"Forgot to tell ya somethin'," Elmer said. "The deal comes with a slight hitch. Luanne will leave her horse there, at least till she gets settled in California. She'll pay for food and vet care, but ya'll have to care for Star—including riding him occasionally." The old man leaned against the doorjamb, the coffee cup still in his hand. "She made me promise to sell the house to someone who would take care of the horse in case she decides to leave him there permanently."

Josh and Jim looked at one another, considering what Elmer had just said. Neither brother had ever been near a horse. Then they both nodded in agreement. "After all," Jim would later remark to the women, "how hard could it be to take care of a horse?"

What they didn't know then was that Jim would later accept a cow in payment for fixing an old tractor so the horse would have company. And after Josh learned how to milk her, they'd start drinking the milk. What they never realized was that the cow had indeed been lonely, and she found the horse to be good company, although she never did learn to understand his language.

~

ARRIVING HOME, Jim ran next door to get Gina so the twins could tell both women the good news at the same time. Gina was helping her mom, Adele, hang the wash outside on the clothesline.

"Come on!" Jim grabbed her hand as she put a clothespin on a pair of pants that belonged to her six-year-old brother, Mark. "You can do that later!" He pushed a protesting Gina up the front cottage's steps and into the house, slamming the door behind him.

That woke the cats, whom Maura had just fed a snack. Sleepily, they looked up, wondering about all the noise.

"Sit down." Jim guided his young wife to a seat on the flowered couch next to Cookie, who sat up in alarm and jumped off, just in case Jim sat down next to her and unintentionally squashed him.

Maura was likewise surprised when Josh took her by the hand and seated her next to Gina, now that the gray tomcat had vacated the couch. The two brothers stood in front of their wives, excitement on their faces.

"What? What is it?" demanded Gina, still mad at Jim for dragging her away from helping her mom.

Josh took hold of Maura's hand and smiled at her. "A dream come true, hon. Our dream came true!"

Gina stopped looking upset and blinked when Jim said quietly, "A house, Gi! We just bought a house!"

She shook her red hair and rose to sniff his breath. "Did Elmer put whiskey in your coffee this morning?"

Jim grabbed her by the waist and swung her around while she screamed delightedly.

"No, Gi! We did! We bought a house! A house big enough for us all to live together!"

Josh pulled Maura up too and hugged her tightly.

"For real, Josh?" she whispered, afraid that if she asked aloud, she would wake up and find she'd been dreaming.

Josh gently kissed her cheek and held her away from him. "For real, hon. For real."

Irritated by all the noise, Tiggy walked over to his brother and bopped him. "What say? What say?"

Cookie shook his head. Sometimes Tiggy tuned in on what the humans said, and sometimes he didn't. Lucky called it "selective hearing." But now that Cookie knew his brother could understand people talk—apparently, thanks to his profusion of black inner-ear hairs—he wished the marmalade would pay attention to all people conversations.

It was Cookie's theory that only cats with black whiskers had special talents. He himself had shiny black whiskers, and Lucky and extra-long black whiskers among her white ones. Most cats' whiskers were simply white.

Cookie quickly filled Tiggy in on the astounding news. He couldn't help but notice Lucky's interest in the conversation. But suddenly, she looked toward the door and perked up. Cookie was instantly alert, straining his ears. Usually, he could hear a sound before the others could, due to his exceptional hearing. Now, all he heard was silence.

A few seconds later, there was a rapid knocking at the back door. Maura walked over and opened it for her friend, Debbie, Lucky's housemate. "Come in. Come in, Deb. Wait till you hear the news!"

Debbie walked in and hugged Maura before going over to the easy chair. She picked Lucky up and sat down, placing the tuxedo cat on her lap. "Unsettled a little, huh?" Debbie asked the cat softly. "Wait a bit. Wait a bit." And with that vague assurance, Debbie asked Maura to tell her the news.

"A house, Deb! We've just bought a house in Maine. We're moving!"

Debbie smiled, gently stroking Lucky's back to settle her. She was aware of how this news would affect the cat. Every day for two years now, Lucky had been an almost constant companion of the tomcats. She knew the tuxedo cat was attached to Cookie and Tiggy. She also knew Lucky understood what was now taking place in this cottage, thanks to her many special talents. "Wait, little one. Wait," she whispered to her cat.

"When?" Debbie asked Maura.

Maura looked at Josh. They hadn't discussed that yet.

"Middle or end of the month, probably." Josh looked at Jim, who shrugged his shoulders. There was still much to be discussed.

"Perfect." Debbie smiled, still stroking Lucky, who looked inquiringly up at her.

Maura blinked. Perfect for what? She looked at Debbie, who smiled back at her. "I have news myself. Fred's been drafted! He leaves for the army in two weeks."

Lucky looked up at Debbie and waited.

"I've decided to move to Arizona to live with my aunt until he's home again. I'll be leaving at the end of the month, just when you leave." She stopped stroking Lucky, who still looked pointedly up at her. "Just like Josh, Aunt Sue is allergic to cats, and she lives in a tiny house. Plus, it's terribly hot in Arizona. Too hot for Lucky to go outside and roam like she's used to."

Debbie stood up, putting the tuxedo back on the cushion. Then she walked over to Maura and took her hand. "That's why I came over to ask a favor of you. And it's perfect timing, now that you're moving to a large, old farmhouse with lots of land to roam on."

Cookie cocked his head at that pronouncement. "Maura hasn't told Debbie anything about the house. How did she know it's an old farmhouse?" he wondered.

Debbie smiled and turned back to the easy chair, where Lucky sat in rapt attention.

"Somehow, she knows what Debbie is going to say," Cookie thought.

"I came to ask you to take Lucky. It would be a favor to me *and* to her." Debbie sighed deeply. "I love her, and I'll miss her dearly. But I know she won't be a bother. Plus, she would miss these two." She gestured at the tomcats.

Cookie was astounded.

Tiggy was in ecstasy—or would be, if Maura said yes.

"Say yes, Maura. Please say yes!" Debbie implored, still holding Maura's hand. "I'll send money to the local feed store and make sure the cats have a goodly supply of the dried food she likes."

Lucky jumped down from the easy chair to join the others beneath the card table as Maura looked over at Josh, whose allergies were the reason Jim and Gina took the tomcats to their house at night and Lucky went home to Debbie. But Josh made a quick decision. He knew how much his wife cared about the cats and how easily Lucky had become part of the family. He just couldn't split them up.

He smiled and nodded his consent. Perhaps, he thought, living in a large house would tamp down his allergies. At least they'd have a room or maybe a whole floor that could be kept free of fur and dander.

"EEEOW!" Tiggy implored. "Say yes, Mom! Say yes!" He wound around Maura's legs, purring as loud as he could. Lucky came over to join him in the figure eights he was making and purred as loudly as he did.

Maura smiled, looking down at the cats. "Well, it looks as though we're all in agreement." She looked over at Josh to make sure she'd understood him correctly.

He smiled and nodded once more.

Smiling broadly, Maura hugged her friend. "Oh, Deb, of course we'll take Lucky."

Cookie was astounded. He was glad they'd all stay together, although he would never admit it aloud. He'd suddenly remembered the wish he'd made under the meteorite shower a year ago. He'd wished that he and Tiggy and Lucky could stay with Maura and Josh and not have to leave at night. That wish just came true! Someone up there really listened to little cat wishes! "Maybe," he thought, "there really is a cat godmother!"

Tiggy was beside himself with happiness. To have his ladylove with him forever! He was so happy he began howling and purring at the same time.

Maura laughed. "Welcome to the family, Lucky." She smiled at the tuxedo cat, who had always seemed part of the family anyway. "Now, we just have to get organized to move into our new home."

"Do you have any job leads?" Debbie asked Josh.

"Well," he said, glancing at Jim, "Elmer says the Portsmouth Naval Yard is close to Cumberland. Maybe we can work there."

"Naval yard?" thought Cookie. "Hmm. The way the war is going, I wonder if there are any spies up there." Then he shook his head, chuckling at the ridiculous thought. But a sharp look from Lucky made the laugh catch in his throat, and he coughed violently. The tuxedo seemed to know things ahead of time. What did that look mean?

Debbie scooped Lucky up and sat down in the easy chair again as the humans discussed what they needed to do before they moved. Debbie would be sad to part ways with her housemate, and Lucky patted her cheek with a gentle paw.

Maura, seeing this, assured Debbie that she would write often about Lucky and send pictures she'd take with the Brownie camera she'd gotten for Christmas. "And," she promised, "I'll put some money aside so I can call you at Christmas and let Lucky hear your voice." This brought huge smiles from both Debbie and the tuxedo. Debbie left shortly, promising—over Maura's objection—to bring over fifteen cents to buy a new roll of film.

# Chapter 3

## *Sunday, May 10, 1942*

The next morning, as the twins and the cats made their way toward the beach, the twins discussed the latest result of the war: the advent of gas rationing. The cats walked in front of them, all in a line as usual, with their tails waving in the breeze. They were unconcerned about rationing.

The three cats and the two brothers were all headed for the Beachhead. Cookie and his brother intended to tell relatives who lived behind the restaurant that they would be moving away. Tiggy especially dreaded telling Theresa, whom he dearly loved, that he would no longer be able to see her. She was his and Cookie's mother.

The twins planned to give the same message to Lou, the owner of the restaurant, who let them use his fishing boat in return for a fresh catch for his menu.

"Maura's really upset about sugar rationing, what with her passion for baking," Josh said, looking overhead as a seagull flew toward the shore. "But I can't believe they rationed gas. They're even thinking of limiting us to three gallons a week!" He shook his head in disbelief. "That could be a problem when we move up to Maine."

"Gino is borrowing a semi to put all our stuff in, and he said he already scrounged some coupons from fellows he's done favors for," Jim said. "We should have more than enough gas to get there." Jim's father-in-law was even planning to take time off from the trucking company to help them move.

"Yeah, I'm sure anybody who works at the town garage will get more coupons after we leave. Especially now that the vehicles coming in for repair are used for the war effort, like police cars and fire engines," Josh said.

"Gas rationing, sugar rationing…What next?" Jim sputtered. "Gi said what with all the rationing they're talking about, the war is fast becoming a pain in the neck." He kicked a pebble into the weeds, causing all three cats to look in that direction. "Actually, I've got to agree with her."

They walked on, enjoying the warmth of the day. They passed the white picket fence as Miss Toomey let her dog out. "Hi, Miss Toomey," called Josh. "Lovely day, isn't it?" He and Jim waved, and she waved back.

Cookie flicked his tail at the dog's belated barks but kept going without a backward glance. Josh and Jim soon passed the line of cats, skirting it cautiously.

The caravan arrived at the restaurant and made its way down the driveway. The brothers walked by the thirty-five-foot boat they fished from in the summer. *Big Blue*, as they had christened her, reclined atop a sturdy trailer. Last fall after fishing season, Gina's dad had hooked a heavy chain to the boat and dragged it from the ocean with his old, black truck. Now it rested next to an old boat behind the Beachhead, under which was a snug, wooden complex that Josh had built at Maura's urging.

The shelter kept the stray cats safer—thanks to open doors on each end—and warmer during winter. In warm weather, the colony resided in wooden crates tucked among the tall weeds lining the shallow channel to the ocean.

Joe, son of the restaurant owner, was just coming out to feed the stray cats when the twins approached. He carried a bucket of dry cat food donated to the colony by a grateful dog owner whose precious pooch the cats had rescued the previous summer.

"Hi, Joe. Where's Lou?" Josh asked.

Joe pointed inside. Sure enough, the owner was busily filling a huge coffee pot in anticipation of the lunch crowd.

"Hi, fellas," Lou said, turning from the spigot. "How are things?"

"Well, we won't be able to fish this year, Lou," Josh said.

"Yeah!" Jim jumped in. "We're moving. We just bought a house!"

"A house?" Lou said. "You bought a *house*?"

"In Cumberland, Maine, right on the coast," Jim said.

Lou was well aware of the fellows' money problems, and he stood there staring at them until he noticed the coffee pot was brimming over and water was spilling to the floor. He quickly turned the faucet off. Then Jim told him the cost of the house, and he smiled and made a quick decision.

"Well, fellows, tell you what." He grabbed the mop and soaked up the puddle, as his son was still outside feeding the stray cats. "Seeing as you're moving to a place noted for its fishing, and you'll be close by to the water, you're going to need a boat."

The brothers looked at one another. A boat would be nice, but—

"Buy my darn boat! What am I going to do with it?"

"Buy it?" Josh loved *Big Blue*, but they couldn't afford a boat.

"Sure. And if you register it up there, taxes will be almost nonexistent."

To Josh's questioning look, he added, "Those Mainers are prideful people. They like to pay for what they get by hard work or in trade."

"How much?" Jim asked anxiously. Could this be another lucky day? He'd been wondering how they were going to be able to fish once they moved. Here, they made extra money selling the fish left over after they supplied the Beachhead and took some for their suppers. He held his breath as Lou started ticking something off on his fingers.

"One, two, three, four…"

The twins hung on his words, only looking up briefly when Joe entered, slamming the door behind him. Joe looked curiously at his dad as he held his hand up.

"Five!" Lou said triumphantly.

Josh took a deep breath. There was no way they could come up with five hundred dollars. He looked at his brother, who appeared stricken as the same thought washed over him. *Big Blue* was lost! Lost to them forever. Jim sighed and started for the door.

"Well, thanks, Lou, but—"

"Five what, Dad?" Joe interrupted.

A chuckle stopped the twins in their tracks. "Five dollars."

"Five dollars?" Jim stopped on a dime and turned around. "All you want is five dollars?"

Lou smiled. "For all the times that I've used the boat, it's really been yours all along."

Jim jumped up in the air and then grabbed Joe's hands and swung him around shouting, "Yippee! Yippee!"

This noise drifted outside, startling the cats, who'd been quietly discussing the move.

Lucky looked once toward the door and then nonchalantly continued her morning wash.

"She looks like the cat who ate the canary," Cookie thought, trying to spot the pesky sand flea that periodically nipped him. Didn't it know that fleas don't dare bite *him*?

In the kitchen, Josh asked a sensible question. "But Lou. How will we get it up there?"

Lou motioned to the coffee pot, and both twins nodded. Pouring cups of the freshly made coffee, they added sugar and milk and stood, stirring the liquid.

"I'll throw in the trailer," Lou said. "What would I need it for now?" He put his cup down on a cabinet and rifled through a drawer . "You can even have my gas coupons. I won't need them. Where do I go? Everything I need is delivered. Plus, I live here." He shoved the three books he'd been given as a restaurant owner into Josh's hand.

"Gosh, Lou. You made our day!"

"Yeah, Lou," Jim said, "anytime you want to visit, you'll be more than welcome." Both twins tried to shake his hand and, to Lou's embarrassment, ended up giving him a tight hug.

~

MEANWHILE, SIX STRAY CATS had emerged from the tall, green reeds surrounding the parking lot when Joe brought out a bucket of kitchen scraps and three cracked soup bowls. They greeted their tomcat relatives and Lucky as Joe began to fill the bowls.

The scruffy, motley-colored leader of the pack hobbled toward Cookie and Tiggy on three legs. "Hi, boys," Theresa said to her sons. "Miss," she added, ever respectful of Lucky, especially after she had helped solve a local murder mystery the summer before, thanks to the very special talent she possessed.

"Oh, Mom," Tiggy cried, ducking his head down for a loving lick. "*EEEOW!*" he squeaked in his high-pitched voice. "We're leaving!"

While Tiggy babbled what he knew of their impending departure, Cookie hung back, sitting down on the gravel to listen to his brother's rush of words. Lucky began to wash, all the while keeping an ear on the conversation. Grandma and the other four cats sat nearby, ears twitching as they listened, too.

"Son!" Theresa motioned Cookie forward. "Tell me quick exactly what he means."

Cookie quickly told his mom about the farmhouse and said Maura and Josh planned to leave at the end of the month.

Theresa looked over at Lucky, who wasn't a relative but was a respected friend, as though for confirmation.

Sighing deeply, the tuxedo looked up at her and smiled. Theresa nodded.

"We'll sure miss you guys," said Smokey D, a handsome gray cousin with pointed, furry ears.

His brother, Smokey, who was a mirror image of him, agreed. "That's wonderful, guys. But we'll all miss you."

He sneaked a quick look at Lucky, who stopped washing a long, white glove with her rough pink tongue and smiled slightly. A sharp look from Cookie made her go back to washing.

"Tell us about Maine," urged their uncle, Honey Boy, while their aunt Stripey pushed forward, the better to hear, along with Grandma, whom everyone knew was almost deaf at her advanced age of twelve.

The rest of the colony formed a tight circle around the tomcats, eager to hear about the north country.

"I wonder what cats eat up there," Smokey D said.

"Lots of wood rats," Lucky answered.

"Great!" Smokey said. "Wonder how they taste?"

"Ratty," Tiggy remarked sagely, causing everyone to laugh.

When the twins came out of the restaurant, Josh called to the cats, "Hurry home, now." He and Jim were heading home to get the money for *Big Blue*. Both were thankful they had pooled the cash they would have spent on Sunday excursions through the winter. Something special had just come up!

As the humans disappeared down the road, the strays came up one by one and rubbed their chins against the tomcats' chins to send a familiar family scent to Maine, even though the toms wouldn't be leaving for several weeks.

Cookie was touched, but later that night, he would wonder a bit why the colony cats had been so eager to hear about a place they would never see...

~

"WE'VE BOUGHT *BIG BLUE*!" Josh rushed in, grabbing Maura up and swinging her around. He quickly filled her on their new good fortune and then ran upstairs for the cigar box filled with dollar bills. He took out five.

"And look, hon," he said, pointing to the rest. "We've still got some leftover money to work with."

"But how will you get the boat up there?" Maura asked.

"Lou tossed in the trailer for free!" Josh smiled. "We'll simply tow it behind the station wagon." It occurred to him, as he thought about the tires on the car and the trailer, that they should buy patching material in case they had a flat. How he and Jim hated those inner tubes!

The weeks flew by in a flurry of planning and packing. Maura had just finished wrapping dishes and breakables in newspaper and filling the empty boxes Josh had brought from the corner store when she heard a truck braking on Cosey Beach Avenue to turn onto Hogan's Alley. It was Gino in the large truck he'd borrowed from his employer to help them move to Maine. The truck filled the whole road when he parked near both houses.

"I'm going to the restaurant to give the veterinarian's telephone number to Joe," she told Josh and Jim. "I'll also give him our new address so he can keep in touch and tell me how the colony is doing." She looked at the cats lying around and called to them before she opened the kitchen door. "I'm going to take the cats for a last visit. They'll want to say good-bye."

"Why, Maura? They're only cats," Jim remarked. "Cats go their own ways all the time."

"Not these cats." She smiled down on them as they trotted past her and waited on the sand. "They seem almost human. There's something special about them." She walked down the steps and started for the restaurant with all three cats walking in a line behind her, their tails drooping instead of waving merrily in the breeze.

When they arrived at the Beachhead and walked to the rear parking lot, for some reason, the colony was waiting for them. They all gathered round while Maura walked to the back door, looking for Joe.

Tiggy sobbed as he bowed his head for a last loving lick from Theresa. "Good-bye, Mom. I love you. I'll never see you again!" His sorrowful meowing made Maura turn and look from the kitchen door. Seeing he was all right, she went in, intent on the business at hand.

Theresa sighed and started to say something but decided against it. Instead, she murmured, "When you see a bird flying overhead, think of me, son. That will be me." Theresa knew he would definitely miss her.

In the restaurant, Maura gave Joe the telephone number of the vet, Dr. K, who said he would continue to care for the colony cats.

To help transport the house cats, he had loaned Maura a large cage, saying the felines would be more comfortable in it than riding loose in the car. When she objected, saying she wouldn't be able to return it anytime soon, he said retrieving the crate would give him a reason to check out the prospect of opening a practice in Maine. He had mentioned before that he was thinking of moving.

Maura made sure to give Joe the slip of paper with their new address on it and promised to call as soon as they hooked up the telephone. She said she'd write now and then to see how the cats were faring.

Then she gathered her cats, and they made their way home—Maura, eagerly, and the tomcats, morosely. However, Lucky held her head high and marched smartly behind Maura.

# Chapter 4

## *Saturday, May 30, 1942*

The day the Indianapolis 500 race was cancelled for the first time in its history due to the war, the two couples moved to Maine. Gino and Jim rode in the big rig with the furniture and boxes filled with their belongings. Maura, Josh, and Gina—along with the cats, in a large cage nestled in the rear of the car—rode in the station wagon, pulling *Big Blue* behind them.

At seven o'clock in the morning as they turned the corner from Hogan's Alley onto Cosey Beach Avenue, Maura looked back at the corner cottage where she and Josh had spent the first three years of their marriage. She smiled.

She hoped the new people moving in would be as happy as she and Josh had been. "Good-bye, Momauguin. Good-bye, Adele and family. Good-bye, colony cats. I'll miss you, but I know Joe will take good care of you."

Then she turned forward, smiling at the thought of the new adventure unfolding before them.

From the rear of the station wagon, Tiggy's howls accompanied them almost all the way to Maine's state line. Exhausted, the marmalade finally fell asleep, dreaming of the loving mom he left behind. Little did he know that behind the Beachhead Restaurant, Theresa had begun making a mark in the dirt each day. Eventually, there would be a series of long lines of marks under the boat, where they wouldn't wash away, creating a puzzle for Joe. It was, he'd think, almost as though she was counting the days...

The house cats were content in the large cage that Dr. K had loaned to Maura. After lowering the back seat, there was plenty of room for the cage. Before putting the three cats in, Maura placed a litter box in one corner and attached bowls of water and food to the bars. With fluffy towels to sit on, the cats were quite comfortable.

Now and then, the felines stood up, hooking front claws over a wire to look out at the passing countryside. The appearance of tall pine trees especially fascinated Tiggy, when he finally woke up. He'd never seen or smelled a tree like them. He tipped his nose to sniff the pine aroma drifting through the slightly lowered window. Eventually, the car's minor sway coaxed all three cats into a deep slumber.

Eight hours after they left Connecticut, pushing their speed up to forty miles per hour, the caravan slowed when they crossed the town line into Cumberland, Maine, where their newly acquired house waited.

Josh elbowed Maura as the landscape spilled over with farmhouses, red barns, and rolling fields. Winter wheat blew in the wind, soon to be cut for hay and stored in the barns.

"Look, Maura. See how far it is between houses?" He waved his hand in a big arc. "We won't be able to lean out our window and shake our neighbor's hand anymore!"

Maura smiled and leaned forward to see better as they began driving down the main street, cluttered with small storefronts.

"Look, Gina. A theater! We can go to the movies!" Maura peered at the marquee as they drove slowly by. "Didn't that Andy Hardy, Judy Garland movie play last September?"

"Yep. We had a great hot fudge sundae afterward. Hard to forget." Gina gazed out the window at the other side of the street. A hardware store was nestled between the post office and feed store. On the front porch, they could see pitchforks, shovels, barrels, and rakes resting against weathered shingles. An old, beat-up pickup truck pulled up in front of the store, and a man got out and stomped angrily up the wooden steps. Josh spotted a large plow in the back of the truck.

"Looks like we can get just about everything we might need right here in town," he noted, wondering if the man needed someone to repair the plow—perhaps someone with a hookup for a torch. "He could take it to the town garage and have someone fix it, like we did back at home. If I worked there, I could weld it really easily."

Then, looking in the rearview mirror, he checked the boat. Looking out at the side mirror, he made sure Gino was right behind him. Seeing the large rig rumbling closely behind, he smiled. "Now we need to see how far it is from town to the farmhouse."

They drove slowly past a few more stores on the short street, a village grocery store, much to Maura's relief, and a family drugstore, along with others she would love to investigate later on, like the Woolworth 5 and 10 store. Suddenly, Gina cried, "Oh, look, Maura! A sewing shop with fabric to make all kinds of clothes!"

Maura looked and then shook her head. "You need to get a job along with the fellows, because we're going to need lots of stuff, especially food, before we can think of other things. Hopefully, I can sell some desserts to add money to the pot."

As she noticed a meat market, two older women exited the door and stopped to stare at the procession before them.

Seeing them, Josh waved, and the two started chattering to each other as the boat he was pulling came into view. Maybe their husbands fished to supplement their food supply as the twins planned to do. After all, the ocean was only a short distance away.

Some of the small stores had second floors, and a few had colorful awnings. With the naval yard nearby, the workers and their families must frequent the Cumberland shops, Maura thought. The few people milling about, intent on their business, looked idly up as the caravan, including Gino, driving the large semi, passed on the almost empty street.

Right now, the town seemed sleepy, as most men worked either on farms or at the navy yard. When they passed a recruiting office, Josh shook his head, still smarting from the 4-F deferment he and Jim had received when they tried to enlist in the service, any service.

"Oh, well. Maybe we can get jobs easier, now that some men have already left. They'll need somebody to fill their positions."

Maura smiled as they passed an old man walking a boxer. The dog drew a big hiss from Tiggy, who was standing in the cage, with his long claws hooked on a bar, allowing him a view of the town. He frowned, thinking of his nemesis, Princess, the bulldog who would charge the white picket fence as the cats strolled by on the way to the shore to visit their relatives. Remembering this, his ears drooped at the thought of the mom he'd left behind and would never see again. He sat down.

Seeing Tiggy's sadness, his ladylove, Lucky, leaned over and gave him a long lick on the ear. Tiggy brightened immensely and was able to drift back to sleep, leaving his brother, Cookie, to give an exasperated sigh.

The gray tomcat was glad they had left Princess back in Momauguin. But there'd be no more spies to catch, either. The lack of excitement left him a bit deflated.

Then he happened to catch Lucky's sharp glance. "Hmm," he thought. "What, if anything, does that mean?" Then he promptly forgot about it when, a short distance from the business district, the road forked. They took the fork leading to the left, clearly a less-traveled road, judging from the ruts and potholes. It led into the country, with rolling acres of corn and wheat bending over at the gentle wind's soft touch.

A couple of minutes later, they passed a right fork that led to the shore and the sprawling naval yard, a few minutes from town. The facility was situated on a long spit of land jutting into the wide Piscataqua River.

The familiar, soothing smell of salt air faded as the caged cats looked out the windows at the white-bark trunks of the aspen trees. Their ears swiveled this way and that at the crackle of the trees' flat leaves in the breeze.

The town gave way to rolling hillsides dotted with farmhouses and red barns. Fir trees grew in abundance. Nestled in a grove of tall pine trees, they saw a squat, silver, trailerlike building.

"Look, Maura!" Gina squealed, waking Tiggy up. "A diner! I bet I can get a job there if it's not too far from our new home!"

Maura peered out the window as Tiggy opened his mouth in a giant yawn, just now realizing he was hungry. "*EEEOW!*" he howled, drawing quick looks from the women. Seeing he was all right, Maura commented, "But they probably already have waitresses."

"Sure, they do. But once they give me a try and see how many more people I bring in, they'll hire me permanently." Gina was sure of that. She just needed the chance to try.

A few minutes more found them driving down a long, dirt driveway and passing an old, ramshackle farmhouse in desperate need of repair. A wizened old woman stood on the rickety porch, shaking out a small rug. She looked curiously at the caravan as it headed for a farmhouse in the rear.

As they moved down the driveway, passing an old barn, Cookie heard an unusual sound drifting out of it. "What is that strange noise?" he wondered.

Tiggy, hearing the sound, shut up as they passed. He'd never heard that noise before either. "What strange creatures do they have here?" he wondered. Lucky, washing a long white boot, raised her head to stare at the barn's open door.

They crept down the driveway, the boat bouncing along behind them, followed by Gino and Jim in the truck, driving very slowly so as not to break anything in the boxes.

Then the farmhouse came into view, along with a large red barn standing off to the side, much newer than the one near the front house. Josh brought the station wagon to a stop in front of the farmhouse.

Opening the door, Gina got out and walked back to greet her dad, who had stopped the truck a ways back so Josh could back the car up and deposit the boat trailer behind the house. Then Josh and Maura opened the cage and let the cats out to do their much overdue business, all three having mostly ignored the litter box.

Standing there in the warm, summer air, Maura drew in a big breath and looked happily at the building before her. It was built in the 1800s by a sea captain, Elmer had told them, and its gray shingles were accented by windows trimmed in white. The wide, white porch beckoned to her. She smiled to see a porch swing suspended from the ceiling to the right and a rocking chair to the left of a pair of big double doors. The rocker she'd brought from Connecticut would go in the living room, she decided.

"Look at those doors, Josh," Maura said. "What a grand entrance!"

Josh nodded. "Elmer told me about those doors. He said he only ever used one of them. But back in the old days, when people died at home, you needed an entrance wide enough to fit a casket through."

Maura was surprised. That thought never would have crossed her mind. "Well, I'm sure we'll only use one of them, just like Elmer."

The rambling farmhouse looked in fair shape, thanks to Elmer's daughter and son-in-law. A grape arbor, vines drooping with clusters of immature fruit, stood to the right of the porch, while a huge maple tree grew on the left side of the house.

Maura looked up at the second floor and smiled. The abundant windows would allow bright sunshine to stream inside. "Oh look, Josh, a skylight." She pointed to the thick-paned window atop the roof.

"Yes. But I wonder what those two metal rods are up there for. Guess I have to ask someone." He adjusted the box he was carrying and started to climb the porch steps.

Peering up to the top floor, Maura spied a single, small, arched window on the top floor of the house. "Must be the attic," she surmised. Something she'd explore later.

Cookie followed her glance, seeing the translucent blue curtain blowing in the breeze. Then, he glanced around, startled. There wasn't a breath of air stirring…

"Come on, cats," Maura called, distracting him, as she eagerly climbed the porch steps. She didn't want them to wander too far away until they were familiar with the territory.

Cookie hurried after her, hoping Maura was on her way to give them a snack. He was hungry! Maura had put dry food in the bowl in the cage, but that was something he had vowed never to eat again after a near disaster the summer before.

The others followed closely behind, thinking the same thought.

Josh was looking for the key to the house. Thanks to Elmer's instructions, he bent to pick up the scruffy mat below the front door. "Ta da!" He held it up triumphantly.

"Well," Maura urged, "don't just stand there. Let us into our new home!" She wondered about the key so casually left beneath the mat. Perhaps, she thought, people here are more trustworthy than back home. She smiled, realizing that *here* was now her home. Maura would later discover how easily old Mainers trusted each other. Neighbors were almost like an extended family. She would come to love this new way of living.

Josh smiled at his wife's eagerness to see their new home. Actually, he felt pretty much the same. Quickly unlocking the door, he held it open for her and the cats.

They rushed into the house and found themselves in a small anteroom with a bench and a series of pegs on the wall. A sign hanging over the bench read, LEAVE YOUR MUD HERE!

To the right was a huge living room with large windows overlooking the front yard. It contained a fairly new couch along with a couple of end tables. To the left was a small, empty room. Walking toward the rear of the house, they entered a large, sunny kitchen with a huge mahogany table. The kitchen was connected to the living room by an archway, making the layout somewhat open.

Maura motioned for Josh and Gina to deposit their boxes on the table, noting a stairway leading upstairs to the left of the kitchen.

While the two couples were busy bringing in the boxes, the cats were otherwise occupied, sniffing the old, wide floorboards that reeked of mouse.

"Mousies!" Cookie grinned. "What great hunting this old house holds. That is, until Maura gets out her broom, mop, and mousetraps," he thought. However, they'd still have the surrounding land, along with the barn, which was probably teaming with tiny creatures.

The three felines had their noses to the floor, investigating all the delightful smells in the rooms. Their whiskers quivered in expectation. Even Lucky was looking forward to good hunting. She dearly loved to bat tiny things around, be they mouse or mole. "An occasional bird would be fun to play with, too," the tuxedo mused.

Unaware of the drama going on about her, Maura walked into the kitchen and was delighted to see how large it was. Gina followed with a small box labeled "food" and placed it on the mahogany table that dominated the center of the room.

She looked around in awe. "Oh, look," she said, twirling in delight at the high ceiling. "We can get a twenty-foot Christmas tree this year."

Maura smiled at her young sister-in-law. "Gina, for heaven's sake! It's not even June! Don't rush the seasons. Let's move in first and enjoy the summer."

At nineteen, Gina still had a childlike quality about her at times. Actually, twenty-three-year-old Maura enjoyed Gina's way of looking joyfully at things.

Maura smiled when she noticed the large window directly over the kitchen sink, providing an ample view of the big maple tree. "I'll be able to watch the birds when I'm working in the kitchen." As she was an avid baker, this was where she would spend most of her time.

Maura ran her hand over the smooth surface of the mahogany table, thinking that it probably had been there for decades. She smiled again. "Look, Gina. We won't need to eat on the card table anymore." She turned to open the tall, skinny door to the pantry, giving thought to what groceries she could put there.

She also discovered large bins in the pantry, which pulled open with knobs. They were made of oak and lined with aluminum to repel mealworms, so she would be able to buy large bags of flour for baking, worry free. One of the bins held a plethora of tea bags, something Maura would appreciate later on when they became scarce, and she needed coupons to buy them.

~

IN THE MEANTIME, Josh, under Jim's hand direction, backed the station wagon into the backyard and unhitched *Big Blue's* trailer behind the maple tree. Then Jim's father-in-law pulled the truck to the front of the house, parked, and the men all began lugging boxes into the house, under Maura's direction. Some went to the kitchen, while others were stacked against a wall in the living room to be unpacked later. Maura, being a good housekeeper, had labeled all the boxes.

Looking around, Josh noted, "Well, now we have more furniture." He was helping Gino lower their couch against the wall next to the couch already there. Jim was right behind him, carrying Lucky's favorite easy chair, much to her delight.

"I forgot that Elmer said his daughter left everything except their bed here," Josh said.

Gina wandered into the next room. It apparently had been a dining room, since it was right off the kitchen, but it was bereft of a dining table and stood empty. "Oh," she said, motioning to Gino and Jim when they hauled in the pedal sewing machine. "Put it here." She danced around the room. "I claim a room of my own! Finally, a sewing room!" She grinned as the men deposited the heavy machine against a wall. "That's fine. I can move it later, if I want to," Gina said.

When Josh carried parts of a bed upstairs, Gina made a note to look for the bedding later and went back to the kitchen to help Maura unpack.

"Oh, look what I found!" Maura cried, pointing to a gadget attached to the kitchen wall.

"What is it?" Gina raised an eyebrow.

"An old coffee grinder!" Maura cried in delight. "Now we can buy coffee beans and grind them here, fresh every day, instead of having to wait for the store to grind them." She smiled happily, while pushing aside the food in the box they had brought, looking for something to make sandwiches with, as she knew everyone would be hungry.

Gina, for one, was always eating, but her constant motion kept the pounds off her slight frame. She burned calories with nervous energy, just like her tall, lanky husband did. The young woman was tall and thin, while her sister-in-law, Maura, was shorter and slightly plump.

Gina went over to the grinder, which was nailed to the wall. She swung the large ball on the end of the handle in an arc. Then she moved to the refrigerator, opening the door to peer inside it.

"Ugh!" She crinkled her nose. "It stinks." She quickly slammed the door. "Been closed up too long." She rummaged in a box, looking for a small pan to fill with soapy water so she could clean it out. "What box did we pack that small pan in?" she asked.

Ever the homemaker, Maura opened a door of the cabinet below the sink and drew one out. "Looks like we got left some things." While she filled it with water, she drew a bottle of liquid soap from the cabinet as well, and Gina was soon cleaning the inside of the refrigerator. The thought of filling it with food kept her scrubbing away.

Though they left the majority of boxes unpacked that day, Maura and Gina opened all the large windows fitted with screens, letting stale air out. Fresh air filled the house, pleasing even the cats. The furnace wasn't necessary, since it was summer, and they were pleasantly surprised to find the house cool despite the heat of the day.

However, they would later discover the house cooled down a bit too much with the sun's setting, and they would need to stoke the small potbellied stove first thing in the morning, even in June.

Soon, they all had fully explored the interior, except for the attic, which would be looked into at some future time.

The cats were busy scurrying this way and that, intent on finding the small critters that had left their distinctive smells and tiny turds on the wide floorboards.

Maura finally unearthed some bologna and made sandwiches, and she poured the lemonade she'd made earlier and stored in a couple of jugs. The cats, smelling the tantalizing aroma of sandwich meat, clustered around and had their fair share of bologna too, along with some dry cat food that Tiggy and Lucky partook of, while Cookie sat nearby, carefully washing the dust from his paws and looking banefully in their direction. The bologna would have to do for now.

Later, Maura and Gina opened the door next to the huge, solidly built, wooden icebox and went down the rickety old stairs to the cellar, ruefully noting the wobbly railing. Seeing the dirt floor, Maura remarked that they'd have to close the cellar door to the cats. "I'll have to ask Jim to fill a box with dirt for the cats to use at night," she said.

Carrot tops indicated the basement had been used as a root cellar for preserving vegetables through the winter. Then, she spotted shelves lining the rocky walls of the old foundation. "Oh look!" Maura exclaimed. "A few jelly and jam jars!"

"I'm thrilled." Gina wrinkled her nose at the dusty jars, as Maura grabbed a glass and excitedly mounted the rickety steps, making a mental note to ask Josh to reinforce the treads to make them safer and install a more stable handrail.

"Look what I found!" Maura excitedly waved the jar under her husband's nose.

He raised an eyebrow, and the hammer he was wielding to fix the cellar door paused in midair. "Looks like a jar to me." He put the hammer down and put his arm around Maura's shoulder.

"It looks like a jar to me, too," Cookie remarked.

"It is, Josh. A jar for jam and jelly!" Maura excitedly waved the jar around. "I can't wait to explore and see what berry bushes we have nearby. I know we have grapes, at least. The arbor is so loaded with them, it looks like it's about to collapse."

"What she say?" demanded Tiggy, his long, striped tail swishing back and forth, showing his irritation at missing the conversation.

"Jam. She wants to make jam." Cookie pulled his head out from under a small table in the living room and snorted dust from his nose. Such great new places to investigate!

Tiggy yawned and rolled over on his back on the rag rug Maura had brought with them and spread out on the living room floor. Jam held no interest for him. But just to make sure, he checked with his brother.

"Can't eat it! Don't like it...do I?"

"'Course not!" Cookie swatted the marmalade's ear, resulting in an "*EEEOW*" that startled Maura, who looked over at them through the open archway between the kitchen and living room.

As she unpacked the dishes, she threw the old sheets of newspaper on the floor, and the sound attracted the cats, who all rushed into the kitchen, the tomcats diving into the pile of paper.

Josh entered then, bringing an armload of wood for the potbellied stove in the corner. He paused to watch the cats, and then smiling, sidestepped them and stacked the wood next to the stove. Luckily, the kitchen stove burned gas, something they needed to look into having turned on. This would be their priority the next day.

Josh was glad Elmer had told him to bring a box of matches. "Have to make sure to have the newspaper delivered," he commented, stepping in to help unpack the rest of the dishes, along with the pots and pans, while Maura washed the ones she would need to cook breakfast on the potbellied stove.

Meanwhile, Jim had gone down into the cellar to investigate the coal furnace they'd use in the fall, when they would need some heat. He discovered the coal chute that let the coal-delivery man fill their bin from outside the house. He'd noticed the telephone numbers Elmer's daughter had left on the refrigerator. They would need to notify the iceman, the bread man, the milkman, the gas man, and the coal man that they wanted to open accounts.

"We need to find a working phone," Jim said. "Maybe we can use one in town. I'll copy down the phone numbers and do that tomorrow. And I'll make sure to have our phones here connected—this one and the rotary phone for the living room." He looked at the phone hanging on the wall. Life would be a bit different here in Maine.

He sighed, wondering what they would all have for supper. But Maura had that covered. She made liverwurst sandwiches for the humans and cut some up for the cats, who all sat around afterward, licking the flavorful stuff from their whiskers.

Later, as they sat in the living room, drinking lemonade, Maura pointed to the felines all lying about on the faded-rose braided rug from the cottage. "Look at the cats," she said. "They're exhausted from all their activity."

"Hmm," Josh said, stretching his legs out in front of him. "Maybe we should take a hint from them and go to bed early ourselves. I didn't realize how tired I was until I looked at them."

"Did you remember to fill the litter boxes and put them in the space below the stairs and leave the door to that space open?" Maura asked Jim. She already had a "to do" list for Josh to tackle, and making cat doors topped the list.

Jim nodded with a tired smile and bid the others good night as he and Gina headed up stairs to one of the beds he and Gino had assembled.

Gino was a short man. He would bunk down on the living room couch and then leave early the next day to travel back to Connecticut.

"Bedtime?" Josh stood and turned to hold out a hand to his wife. She took his hand and rose, glancing over at the easy chair, where Gino was sprawled, snoring heavily.

"He'll be OK," Josh said. "If he wakes up later, he can stretch out on the couch—provided it's not full of cats!" He smiled, carefully skirting the cat-covered rug.

"We're home, Maura." He lightly kissed her cheek. "We're finally home. You got your wish, hon. You got your farm." Then, arm in arm, they climbed the wide stairs to their bedroom to spend their first night in their new house.

The three cats slumbered on, dreaming of hunting. Little did they know there was more to hunt here than the tiny creatures whose presence they'd already sensed. There was a bad creature who moved about on two feet, wreaked havoc, and killed...

# Chapter 5

*Cumberland, Maine*
*Sunday, June 1, 1942*

The next morning found Maura in the kitchen, sipping a cup of newly made coffee, the aroma of which eventually drew Gina downstairs, still wearing her pajamas and a light robe. When the cats wandered into the kitchen, Maura opened the back door to let them out to do their business and lured them back in when they finished with the scrambled eggs she had scooped into their dishes. Later, when she had a moment, she would go outside with the cats and walk around the house with them. She knew that they wouldn't get lost as long as they could find her scent on the ground. And she knew she could trust Lucky to lead a lost cat safely back.

The twins soon came down and foursome sat at the kitchen table for breakfast.

"Josh, as soon as you eat, you need to cut a cat door in the front door," Maura said.

Josh looked up with a mouthful of scrambled eggs and nodded. Swallowing, he smiled, reached for his steaming, fragrant cup of coffee, and said, "Anything for the love of my life."

That caused Jim to spit the coffee he had just drunk.

"Oh, please!" Gina reached over and gave him a cuff on the ear. "Some people need some lessons from their brother!" This comment made Maura chuckle. Getting up from the old table, she reached for the sun hat she'd hung on a hook on the wall.

"Come on, cats! Time to explore!" she said.

She walked toward the front door, followed by Cookie, with Tiggy loping behind. Lucky just looked up from her cushioned kitchen chair and turned around in a circle before curling up in a ball for a much-needed nap after devouring her breakfast. She'd explore later, when all she had to do was to follow Maura's scent back to the farmhouse. This moving was tiring!

Maura held the screen door open, letting the cats out again. Seeing Lucky snoozing, she went over, picked her up, and shoved her gently out the door. "*Everyone* out!" she admonished.

Maura paused on the porch for a moment, looking out at their new land. She smiled, seeing a couple of apple trees and a pear tree, all heavy with tiny green fruit. Leaning over the railing to the right, she spotted a vegetable garden with some early June vegetables, probably peas. A garden! Something she always wanted! Plus, a grape arbor! Already, she was picturing herself busy making jam—something she needed to find out how to do.

Her mind was already crammed with ideas for new suppers and delicious, fresh desserts. Remembering her Uncle Jack's comment about her skill as a baker, she thought perhaps she could sell some desserts to the diner for much-needed money until the boys got jobs. She couldn't wait to get started exploring their land.

But first things first. She began to walk around the house, making sure the cats stayed close. They followed her, pausing to smell the unfamiliar smells, while she waited for them. They paused for a long time under the huge maple tree on the left side of the house and then made their way past *Big Blue* on its trailer.

Maura delighted in finding an old fashioned, copper hand pump behind the house, to the right of the back steps. Trying it, she discovered it produced cold, fresh water from a well in addition to the new one Elmer said they'd dug to run water into the house. Next to it was a prickly bush full of unfamiliar white berries. Maura made a mental note to find out if people could eat them or they were a treat for birds only. Coming around to the right side of the house, Maura and the cats walked underneath the grape arbor, which was heavy with fruit that was not quite ripe yet.

The cats, having familiarized themselves with the smells around the house, meandered to the front porch steps and waited for Maura. "Now, don't go too far until you know the lay of the land," she cautioned, wondering once more why she treated them as though they could understand her.

"Makes sense," Cookie murmured, winding his way around her legs to thank her.

Maura smiled and reached down to scratch him behind his good ear, causing a rumbling purr. "*Merrrrr,*" he said, tilting his head to look up at her. Then, he followed the others as they meandered across the grass, stopping to sniff new smells as they went.

Satisfied that they would stay around the house, Maura climbed the porch steps and entered the house. She walked into the kitchen and began to fill the empty cabinets and food pantry with the supplies she had brought from the cottage. She'd baked some sugar buns a couple of days ago, before they left Connecticut. She knew Adele, Gina's mom, would miss having them, and she would definitely miss spending her mornings Adele, chatting over a cup of coffee and a pastry after doing the wash. But surely she'd make some friends here, too.

She grinned, thinking how happy she had been to discover a wringer washer in the cellar. Thankfully, Elmer's daughter had left it behind.

Well, Maura thought. First things first. She peered out the kitchen window as she filled the sink to wash the dishes that lay unwrapped on the table, happy that Elmer's daughter, Luanne, had installed running water. She smiled when she saw the cats wandering tentatively across the wide expanse of vivid-green grass dotted with sunny, yellow flowers.

~

"WHAT'S THAT?" Tiggy demanded, hesitant to step any way near the bright petals.

Lucky bent down to smell the flowers and grinned. "Dandelions," she said serenely.

"Dandelions?" Cookie and Tiggy bent down to smell the flowers. "A bit different from the shore weeds," Cookie said. "But just as interesting. Perhaps more so."

He eyed the slope beyond the nearby meadow. It was crowded with fir trees and seemed like a mountain to the gray tomcat, as he'd never seen anything higher than the small hill by the roller rink. What he couldn't see was the lake beyond, but he would discover it later.

Tiggy, the sun worshipper, had stretched out to his full length on the sweet grass, luxuriating in its softness. "No no-see-ums to bite us," he said to the others.

Lucky joined him on the blanket of green. "And no horseflies to bother us." A bird flew overhead and alighted on a branch. Tiggy looked up and smiled, remembering what his mom had told him. "Hi, Ma," he whispered, drawing a smile from the tuxedo.

Ever alert, Cookie remained sitting on his haunches, ears twitching at each new bird song. His nose was active too, with all the mysterious smells.

"Yes," he murmured, "I am definitely going to like it here, even though there won't be any more spies to catch."

This comment caused the tuxedo to open both bright-yellow eyes to stare at him.

Cookie began to scratch his ear, which he always did when he didn't understand or like something Lucky did. He stopped suddenly, as his ear, ever sensitive, began to bleed. So, instead, the gray tomcat yanked at an old nail sheaf. How Cookie wished Lucky wouldn't do that! Why did she have to look at him that way when he talked about spies? What did she know that he didn't?

Suddenly, the tuxedo got up and trotted over to the stout maple tree spreading its leafy branches across the side yard. Cookie quickly followed her, and Tiggy wandered over too. The marmalade wanted to be wherever the action was, and in this case, the action was a small hole in the ground at the base of the tree.

Maura idly watched the cats through the kitchen window as she stood there, drinking a cup of coffee. They were probably searching for moles or mice, she decided. The dishes were soaking in the sink filled with soapy water when Gina, now dressed, descended the stairs.

"Any coffee left?" she asked.

Maura motioned to the potbellied stove on which perked a new pot of coffee, thanks to Josh, who'd stoked the fire before he and Jim headed into town.

Gina poured a cup and set it on the table. Then she yawned, stretching her arms. "Haven't slept this long since I don't know when. Must be the clean, Maine air." She yawned again as she walked to the refrigerator and drew out the ice cube tray.

"What in the world are you doing?" Maura asked, turning to stare at her sister-in-law, a soapy plate in her hand.

"I'm putting ice cubes in my coffee. It's too hot to drink it regular like," Gina said matter-of-factly as she dumped four ice cubes into her cup.

Maura knew Gina hated hot coffee, but she still shook her head at her sister-in-law's foolishness. "No one but you drinks coffee that way. You'll cool it down too much!"

"Yep." Gina smiled as she stirred the cubes, making them clink against the side of the cup.

"Well, make sure no one sees you," Maura scolded. "People will think you're daft, for sure!"

With the windows now open, their conversation drifted to the gray tomcat outside. "Well," Cookie thought. "Humans show some promise, after all. Who wants to drink something hot when it's too hot to move?"

He stretched out on the dewy grass, all the better to feel cool, and half-heartedly licked a paw. "People call the hottest stretch of summer the *dog days*," he thought with a sniff. "Not *cat* days. Sometimes humans do get things right!"

Gina motioned to the pot on the stove before she sat down. "Want a refill?"

Maura, washing a dish, shook her head.

Gina sat down, running her hand through her curls. "When the fellows come back, I'll have Jim drive us into town. I want to go to the diner, and you can go to the store for some supplies. We need to get something for supper."

When she had finished her coffee and felt more awake, Gina rose to go back upstairs, calling over her shoulder, "I'll help you unpack more and clean up when we get back."

Maura nodded, washing the last of the dishes and laying them on a clean dishtowel. They'd be dry by the time they got home.

She went outside and stood on the porch while Gina got ready. Wondering what the cats were still so interested in, she started down the steps to investigate. But she changed her mind when Gina came out the front door just as the fellows drove up in the station wagon. Josh got out, but Gina put her hand on the open driver's-side window frame, stopping her husband.

"Take us to town," Gina said. Looking at Maura, she added, "You really need to learn how to drive, Maura."

Maura tilted her head. If Gina indeed got a job at the diner, she could walk to work. But maybe she was right anyway. There weren't any buses in Cumberland, and Maura herself would need to get around if she intended to sell desserts.

"How hard could it be?" she wondered aloud. "The town's nearby, and there are hardly any cars on the road until the shifts change at the naval yard."

She smiled at Josh, who was headed behind the grape arbor to chop some wood that lay there.

"Talk to you later, hon," she called, rushing to catch up to Gina, who had just climbed into the station wagon. With a backward look at the cats, still sitting motionless beneath the tree, Maura rode the short distance into town.

~

LATER, AFTER SHE HAD SHOPPED for food and Jim had carried it out to the station wagon, they drove over to the diner to pick up Gina.

Maura held a borrowed box filled with eggs on her lap. She'd have to go to the hardware store and see if it sold baskets. Seems people brought their own baskets for the grocer to load with eggs from a large box on the counter, and the grocery store didn't have any.

Maybe Maura would find a farmer who sold fresh eggs. Someone in Cumberland should have chickens!

Gina was standing outside the diner, her red curls blowing in the breeze. She waved when she saw them. Jim pulled over, and she slid into the front seat.

"How did you do, Gi?" Jim smiled her way as he pulled onto the road again. He liked the way his new bride bubbled with excitement. "Did you get a job?" He slowed down as a farmer crossed in front of him, driving a couple of renegade cows back to his pasture.

"You'll never believe it! I lucked out!" she said excitedly. "Seems the waitress, Ginny, is very pregnant, and she's ready to leave to have her baby. The owner, Charlie, said he'd let me have the job until she comes back!"

Gina giggled as she recounted the other conversation she'd had while Charlie was busy in the kitchen, cooking. "Ginny took me aside to whisper, 'I ain't comin' back. My Dan has a good job at the naval yard. Says he wants me to stay home to raise the baby. Don't want someone else raising it!'"

Gina smiled widely, relishing the thought of being a waitress again. She loved the give-and-take with customers. She knew she'd fit in perfectly here, in this small Maine town. She couldn't wait to get back to work.

"I told him how you make fantastic desserts," she told Maura. "He wants to see you to talk about it."

"Gina!" Maura protested. "We just got here! I don't have time to bake."

"Told him that," her sister-in-law said, nodding. "He said to drop in any time you're ready." Gina grinned. "Once that happens, and he tries some of your desserts, he'll be beating down our door for more!"

This set Maura thinking. Perhaps she could make some chocolate-chip cookies. Everyone seemed to like them. She sat back, silently wondering if she had packed the makings for cookies or would have to return to the store. She definitely needed to talk to Josh about teaching her how to drive.

Later that afternoon, after Maura washed the last of the dishes, she glanced out the window. She tilted her head, seeing the three cats still lying under the tree, napping in the tangle of grass and wildflowers.

Gina came over and looked out too. "Jim," she said to her husband, who was sitting at the table, reading the sports news. "Look at how tall the grass is! You need to use that old push lawnmower I saw in back of the grape arbor."

"Oh, Gi. Let the cats enjoy the grass," he said, peering over the newspaper at her. "At the beach house, all they had was scrub brush and sand." He reached for a glass of iced tea and sipped some. "Besides, it's really tough to push it through that tall grass. What they really need to do is put a motor on lawn mowers to make it easier."

Gina reached over and yanked the newspaper down, causing Jim to jump up and run after her as she raced off to the porch swing—just wide enough for two—laughing.

Maura looked out the window after they left. The cats still lay under the tree, partially hidden from view in the tall grass. "Perhaps," she mused aloud, "they're still tuckered out from the move." Then she promptly forgot them as she rummaged in the box marked *food,* thinking of the ingredients she needed to make cookies.

It *would* require another trip into town.

~

THE SUN WAS BEGINNING to drift beyond the tall hill when Lucky suddenly sat up from her nap and retreated behind the tree to hide under a bush. As she sat motionless, watching the hole, a small, orange-gold rodent with dark-brown stripes running down his back poked his head out. He studied the area and saw the tomcats lying asleep. Suddenly, he darted across the lawn, his little tail sticking straight up in the air like a flag.

Lucky burst out of her leafy hiding place in quick pursuit. Squeaking, the chipmunk turned around and headed back for his hole.

His loud squeaks woke Tiggy up, who opened his eyes to see his ladylove's mad dash. "I never knew she could run that fast!" he thought.

Cookie had awakened to watch the chase, too. "Well! What do you know! The old girl has some spirit in her, after all!" he commented admiringly. And then he frowned because he was missing out on the chase.

Lucky caught up with the hapless critter, pouncing on his tail and pinning him to the ground. The excitement brought the tomcats running, and they hunkered around Lucky, who held the frightened chipmunk securely by the tail.

"Orange mouse?" Tiggy asked. He had never seen a chipmunk.

Neither, for that matter, had Cookie. He looked at Lucky.

"Chipmunk," she answered. Suddenly, another head poked out of the hole, chattering away. This one was larger.

Lucky looked over as the tomcats prepared to pounce.

"Stop!" she said sternly. "Let me hear what the lady has to say."

Tiggy looked up, surprised. "Just hear squeaks."

"Shhh," she hissed, tilting her head. "I want to listen."

Both tomcats blinked, and then they glanced at one another. Did she understand chipmunk talk?

"Why not?" Cookie muttered, plunking down in the grass and motioning for the marmalade to do the same. "If she can understand bird talk and people talk, why not chippy talk?" They had learned back at the shore about this talent of hers for languages.

They looked at the lady chipmunk who had wiggled out of the tight hole. She was a very, very pregnant animal—about to have a baby any day. She was chatting excitedly with the tuxedo.

"What say!" demanded Tiggy. "What say?"

"Quiet so I can hear her!" came Lucky's disappointing reply.

As Lucky would tell the tomcats later, the chipmunk was begging Lucky to let her husband go.

Meanwhile, the husband was struggling to wiggle out from under Lucky's steely paw. He suddenly yanked so hard that the end of his tail broke off, and both chipmunks scooted into the hole.

Lucky looked down at the short piece of tail under her paw. Now that poor chipmunk's pride and joy—his beautiful bushy tail—was only half of what it had been!

All three cats peered down into the hole. "What say? What say?" Tiggy again demanded to know. He was well aware of the tuxedo's unusual talent for bird talk, and unlike his brother, was never surprised by Lucky's talents.

"Shh!" Lucky put her head down against the hole. The chipmunks were still chattering away. "I'll tell you later."

This satisfied the marmalade, who sat down next to a disgruntled Cookie. "After all," the gray tomcat thought, staring banefully at Lucky,

"I can understand people talk as well as she does. How come I can't understand critter talk too?"

Later, after the cats ate supper and the humans had gone to bed, Lucky relayed what the chipmunk with the newly shortened tail, whose name was Mickey, had told her. One thing he said was that most of the human Mainers were descended from Irish immigrants and spoke the language quite easily. Mickey was proud to point out that with his reddish-orange coat, his ancestors must have come from the old country too.

Mickey had begged Lucky to let him live, saying he had information the new homeowners should know. He kept an eye on the property, he said. "Let me hunt," he'd told Lucky, "and I'll find out what the mysterious man does when he visits Gus's barn in the middle of the night."

"Mysterious man?" Cookie was instantly alert. Perhaps they had spies here too! The cat patrol should be reinstated! "What was a stranger doing in the barn?" he wondered aloud, getting excited.

"What was he doing visiting the barn *late at night* when no one can see him?" Lucky said. "That's even more important."

She went on to say the chipmunk had seen that she wondered about that, so he had filled her in on how he'd heard about the Night Visitor, as they had begun to refer to him.

Mickey told her he has a distant relative, Harry Hare, who lives next to Gus's barn, under a blackberry bush. Harry sneaks in to eat the food that people leave for the goat. The hare also visits the chipmunks now and then to share the latest news about animals prowling about at night.

Lucky looked at the tomcats. "Mickey promised he would find out more about this night-visiting man."

So, when the chipmunk poked his head tentatively out of the hole, eyeing Lucky cautiously, and asked if they had a deal, the tuxedo had simply nodded her head yes.

Tiggy asked, "Like Sammy?" Sammy, a seagull, had been their snoop at the shore in Connecticut.

"Yes. Like Sammy. So, don't hurt him."

Sammy had helped them solve the mystery of who killed their friend, Bob. Remembering this, the tomcats agreed to leave the chipmunk alone. However, the whole incident left Cookie unsettled. Like Lucky, he wondered why on earth someone would visit the old barn in the middle of the night. Humans were creatures of habit, and they were active mainly in daylight.

Cookie wished his mom and uncles and aunts were there so he could bounce ideas off them. But he'd left them far behind at the restaurant in Connecticut. "Oh, well," he thought, sighing. "This will take some investigating.".

# Chapter 6

## *Saturday June 6, 1942*

Maura cut an orange in half and squeezed the juice out by grinding each half over the upended bump in a special glass juicer. "Fred, the storekeeper, says this might be the last shipment of oranges for a while." She sighed. "Then he heard bananas, pineapples, and other fruit will also be scarce. First, sugar is rationed, and we need to buy it with a coupon book. Now fruit. Who knows what's next?"

She had met their neighbor, Maude, in the checkout line at the grocery store, and they had commiserated over the effects of war. "Maude was complaining about the shortages, and I said, 'It's war, Maude. They need the boats to do other stuff. We have to make sacrifices too, some more than others.'"

She cut another orange in half and pressed it onto the juicer. "Then I said, 'Each day, more gold stars appear in people's windows. Too many soldiers lost!' That stopped her complaining."

Gina grabbed a glass of orange juice, delighted. "Yum!" She went to the refrigerator to get some butter for the bread she was about to toast. Instead, she drew out a bag of squishy, white stuff with a little yellow ball inside. "What's this, Maura?" she asked, holding it up to peer at it.

"Oh, that's something new. They're thinking of rationing butter, so now they sell that. It's called oleo margarine."

"But what's this ball for?" Gina asked.

"Squeeze it," Maura said. "It turns the white stuff yellow to make it look like butter."

Gina squeezed, and it did turn the stuff yellow, but she put the bag back in the refrigerator, drawing the butter out instead. "This will never replace butter!"

Maura glanced at Josh. She could tell he was wondering how she managed to buy the expensive oranges. "I traded an apple pie that I made from some of the apples Luanne left in the root cellar." She grinned, having seen promise in the Mainers' way of trading, especially since the apple and pear trees on their new land would soon have an abundance of ripe fruit. She was already picturing the applesauce, apple-butter, and canned fruit she could use for dessert all winter.

"Well," Jim said, putting his coffee cup in the sink and starting out the door, "since we're pretty much finished settling in, it's time to get to know the horse."

Josh put his cup in the sink too and followed him out. They walked the short distance to the front house on their lane, where an old, wrinkled woman sat in the rocking chair on her front porch, slowly rocking back and forth.

She got up when she noticed them, taking up an old, gnarled wooden cane, and hobbled slowly down the steps toward them. She was eighty-two years old, they would learn, and she wobbled a bit on the uneven pathway. Bone thin, she looked as if the slightest breeze would blow her away.

Both twins shook her hand and introduced themselves.

"Well, about time ya showed up." Her voice sounded like old, crinkling tissue paper. She smiled at them, displaying her few remaining teeth. "Name's Alice. Alice Nester. My old man calls me Allie. But I prefer Alice, please." She motioned to the nearby barn with its door wide open. "My Gus is in the barn now, feedin' Marilyn and the chickens."

The twins didn't have time to ask who Marilyn was before she continued. "He's pretty old; too old ta take care o' Star, the horse." Waving her cane toward the building, she sniffed. "So, Rubin, from the

49

neighboring farm," she pointed with her cane, and they saw another barn in the distance, "he volunteered ta feed and clean up afta Star."

Clean up after the horse? What did that mean? Jim wondered. He recalled the conversation the foursome had had about who would take care of Star. "Not me," Josh had said. "Not me either," Maura added. "And certainly not me!" Gina said.

"Oh, for gosh sakes!" Jim had said. "What could be so hard?"

He and Josh had decided that Josh would work on repairing the house, while he'd be responsible for tending to Star, including exercising the animal. Now, Jim made his way to the barn, where he would soon find out what could be so hard about taking care of a horse.

Josh watched him walk away and then pointed to a small building between the house and the barn. It was down a dirt path, over which somebody had placed long, wooden planks. "What's that small building set off a bit?" he asked Alice

"That's the outhouse," Alice cackled, leaning on her cane. "Ya don't want it too close ta the house! No, siree! Too stinky!" She paused, thinking. "But on a cold winter night, ya wish it was a bit closer ta the house!" She cackled again. "Better ta use a chamber pot, then. Although that does wake ya up! The porcelain feels pretty cold ta sit on! Heavy ta pick up and dump outside, too. Makes me feel like a lumberjack!" She was silent for a moment, looking thoughtfully at the small, rickety building. "But ya might want ta get up anyway and go outside ta do 'pip emma' so's the house won't smell."

She whacked herself on the arm as a large fly bit into her tender skin. "Damn black flies. Have ta get more flypaper and another flyswatter next trip ta town. Won't help ya that much, though, walking outside at night. Misqitahs just as big. Just as bad!" Alice sniffed. "Ya need ta learn ta make some bug dope if ya plan ta stay outside fur long. Lucky fur ya, ya missed most of the hatching. That's when they arrive in droves!"

Josh just blinked as she continued to ramble. "The 1938 hurricane tipped the outhouse over. Rubin had ta come with his tractor ta right it again." She grinned at the memory, shaking her head. "Stunk the whole place up fur a piece. Now, my Gus ignores it all. Middle of the night, no matter how cold, he throws a jacket over his long johns and practices whizzin' over the porch railin'." She laughed. "Says it keeps his aim accurate."

Josh stared at her with an open mouth. These Mainers certainly had their ways, along with their peculiar accent. He wondered if he would ever get used to it. They seemed a friendly sort—maybe too friendly!

Then old lady smiled, showing a mouthful of missing teeth. "Ya don't have ta worry, though, 'cause Elmer's daughter insisted on indoor plumbin'—and her husband had enough money ta do it. Yar lucky."

She gazed off, leaning on her cane. "Most old houses here in Maine, like mine, have a cistern to catch rainwater for washin' and an outdoor pump for drinkin' water. Once a week, we heat water on the stove and pour it in the tub for a bath.

"Some Sundays, we chop off an old hen's head and clean and cook the bird. But boy! What a stink when ya dip the carcass in a pot o' hot water and pluck the leftover feathers!"

Josh was glad that they had running water and an indoor toilet, which they normally took for granted. His attention turned, once more, to the old barn, where his twin had met the farmer who'd been taking care of the horse and was talking to him.

Rubin was about to let the horse out into the fenced-in field so he could clean the stall. A dirty old shovel leaned against the wall next to a forked hay rake that he would use to spread new hay on the floor of the stall.

The farmer smiled as Jim introduced himself, glad that he wouldn't have to take care of Star anymore. "Nice ta meet ya, son." The handshake he gave Jim was firm and strong from his farm chores.

In a corner, Alice's husband, Gus, was busy milking his goat. He merely acknowledged Jim's greeting with a nod.

Soon, the farmer, Rubin, would be knee deep in haying. "Perhaps," he wondered aloud, "ya fellas would help me in return." The twins were soon to experience Mainers' way of trading for services as well as food.

"Sure," Jim said.

Rubin took hold of Star's halter and then gave the reins to Jim, standing by nervously. He'd never been so close to such a large animal.

"Hang onta him, and I'll get ya the saddle and horse blanket that goes under it from the other room," Rubin said as Jim tentatively led the horse outside.

Alice stood silently by, leaning on her cane, as Rubin introduced himself to Josh and then placed the saddle on Star. Jim jumped back as the horse, who had been munching on grass, jerked his head up and snorted.

Rubin shook his head at Jim's reaction and chuckled as he headed home to tend to his own animals. "Don't forget ta buy some galoshes as soon as ya can," Rubin said over his shoulder. "Ya'll need 'em."

Galoshes? Jim wondered, frowning. Could he mean boots? He shook his head. It would take a while before he got used to the Mainers' way of saying things.

Maura had walked down to see what was going on and had a bag of cookies for Alice as way of greeting.

Rubin saw her and went over to introduce himself.

Maura decided to give the cookies to him instead as a thank-you for taking care of Star. She'd give some to Alice later, as she'd baked up a storm before they moved, thinking they might need some desserts. However, she'd still need to bake some to take to the diner when she introduced herself to Charlie.

Meanwhile, Josh and Jim were getting acquainted with Star, who was snorting and dancing as they tried to stroke his side.

"Tighten the girth!" the old lady said.

"What's the girth?" Jim asked.

Alice pointed to the buckle under the horse's belly, and Jim leaned down, giving the girth a yank and buckling it more tightly.

Star immediately lay down on the grass, panting loudly. "Oh, my God!" Jim said. "I killed him!"

Cookie, along with the other cats who had followed the fellows to see what they were up to, approached the horse's head and cautiously sniffed at him. "Still breathing," Cookie observed as he backed away.

"Whip 'im!" the old lady said with a cackle. Jim hesitated. But at the old woman's encouragement, he picked up the whip and did as she commanded, lightly striking Star on his rump. The horse snorted and turned his head to look at Jim.

"Ayuh! Again!" commanded the old woman.

This time, the horse snorted and rose suddenly, causing all to back away from him.

"What happened?" Josh wanted to know.

"Oh, he's a wimp!" Alice smiled. "Faints at the slightest provocation. Typical male."

As she hobbled away, Jim shrugged and then tried to mount the horse to ride him. But Star whinnied and did a quick side step to get away from him, looking wild-eyed over his right flank.

"Uh-oh!" Jim said, while Josh kept a hard hold on the reins.

"Oh, I forgot ta tell ya. Always get up on the horse's left side, or he won't let ya ride 'im," Alice called as she bent over her rocker to pick up her babushka. She placed the scarf on her head, tying it under her chin.

Jim rolled his eyes at the late direction and moved out of range of the horse's tail, as Star kept swishing it at the tenacious black flies. The biting insects had everyone slapping at them.

Jim then walked around the back of the horse. Luckily, he could move fast and evaded the horse's quick kick in his direction.

"Oh," yelled the old woman, pausing on the rickety steps of the farmhouse, "anotha thing. Never go 'round the back o' the horse. They can't see back there and get a mite nervous!" She snorted under her breath, shaking her head at the stupidity of people not from "down east."

"*Now* she tells me!" grumbled Jim. He finally jumped up into the saddle, causing a surprised Star to set off at a fast trot with the twin hanging onto the reins for dear life and bouncing in the saddle.

They headed to the fenced-in field, now sporting lush, green grass, with Jim vowing to find someone who could teach him to ride as he bounced up and down on the hard, leather saddle. He was sure he'd have to sit on a *very soft* pillow at the supper table that night.

Josh, in the meantime, had gone into the barn to clean out the stall according to the directions Rubin had given them.

Soon they would need to move Star into their newer barn, taking all the horse's supplies with them. They would have to talk to Rubin before they did that. After Jim's ride that day, Star could stay outside in the fenced-in field for the afternoon.

Much later on, Jim hobbled off to bed, rubbing his backside, vowing to find someone to teach him how to ride properly so he wouldn't be so sore.

~

WHILE THE TWINS WERE BUSY with the horse, Maura walked home to finish the dishes. The cats followed her but stayed outdoors, and now she could see them from the kitchen window. The tomcats lay in the lush grass beneath the spreading maple tree, snoozing in the morning sunshine.

Though there was no breeze at all, one branch of the maple tree was swaying slightly. Maura looked closer, a soapy cup poised in midair. Was something hidden there?

Lucky sat motionless underneath the tree, head raised, as she too had seen the movement. The leaves rustled once more, revealing a small cat sitting on the low branch.

Maura's eyebrows rose in surprise. A kitten! High up in the tree! Just sitting there! What on earth was it doing there? Maura hurriedly wiped her hands on the flowered dishtowel she had made from a burlap flour sack and rushed outside.

Walking cautiously toward the maple tree to avoid startling the kitten, she positioned herself beneath the branch and looked up. Lucky moved away.

The dark, multicolored, tortoiseshell kitten, who reminded Maura of a tiny owl, sat perfectly still on the branch. Only her ears flicked back and forth as she watched a momma bird feed her nest of fledglings. The torti seemed perfectly content to watch the antics of the young birds as they opened their mouths wide, demanding food from their momma until she dropped some in.

Where was the kitten's momma? Maura looked all around to no avail. She didn't see any mother cat. She made her way quietly inside to fetch a kitchen chair. Lucky watched curiously as Maura placed it under the tree and slowly stepped up on it.

Cookie came to immediate attention, though he he'd been napping in the sun. This woke Tiggy, who sat up to watch the goings on.

Maura held onto the back of the chair as its feet sank into the soil, but it held steady, making her tall enough to reach the kitten, who was looking curiously down at her.

Talking soothingly to the little scrap of torti, Maura picked her up and gently cuddled her against her chest. The kitten immediately began softly purring and washing Maura's hand with her tiny, rough, pink tongue. Maura had turned away from the adult cats, so they couldn't see the little kitten, leaving them wondering what was going on.

She carefully stepped down off the chair, and with the small bundle nestled in her arms, went inside, where she poured some milk into a bowl and watched as the kitten immediately began to lap it up. Next, Maura rummaged through the refrigerator, finding a bowl of macaroni and cheese. She dumped the pasta into a pot, added some milk, then warmed it on the stove.

The kitten gobbled it up, slurping hungrily, as though she hadn't eaten in quite a while. Finished, she sat contentedly on the linoleum floor, her pink tongue making a scraping noise as she cleaned herself.

Suddenly, the flap on the cat door exploded, as Cookie, Tiggy, and Lucky bolted inside, startled by a red-tailed hawk screeching his battle cry as he swept low over the field, looking for wayward field mice.

The gray cat skidded across the newly waxed floor and came to an abrupt halt upon spying the tortoiseshell kitten. Tiggy fluffed out his long, orange tail as the startled kitten fluffed hers out like a small puffball.

"Well, well." Lucky trotted over and stood looking down at the kitten. "What do we have here?"

"Yes!" Cookie blinked, walking cautiously around the little cat. "Who do we have here you?"

"I'm just me!" The kitten stood up with her back humped in fighting mode. Then she hissed, spitting at the gray tomcat's startled face.

Cookie had to hand it to her: she had gumption! The tomcat diligently began washing her head, while she sat down and purred ever so softly.

Maura watched the drama unfold as she made a bed for the kitten, whom she believed was only about three weeks old. In her mind, the torti was already part of the family. After all, how could she turn such a tiny slip of a thing—perhaps only weighing a pound—outside by herself? Apparently, her momma had either been frightened off or…she shuddered to think of the other option.

Who knew what lay on that high hill beyond the meadow. Her cats had enough street smarts to take care of themselves. But this little one?

There was no way she'd turn her out. Now that Maura had decided that, she wondered what name the little torti would like. She'd have to try some names out and see what went well with the other cats' names.

How about Polly? No. That sounds like she's a parrot. Although it might be fitting, since the kitten did like being high in the tree.

Perhaps she should speak the names to see how the kitten and the others reacted.

Maura said some names out loud. However, none of them caused the cats to look up at her.

Maura was sitting down on a kitchen chair, thinking, when Josh came in and stopped in his tracks, seeing the little kitten sitting on the kitchen floor looking curiously up at him. "Well, what do we have here?"

He bent down to pick up the kitten and rubbed her ear. "She's a wisp of a thing, isn't she?" He looked at her colorful fur, black with flecks of sunshine. "Looks like an owl," he remarked. Then the kitten washed a back paw that had golden fur. "Oh look, Maura. She has one yellow paw." He studied it for a moment, then smiled. "She has a honey-pot paw!" he declared.

Maura laughed, reaching over to scratch the kitten all over. A surprised look came over her countenance. "Listen, Josh! She's purring! But it's so soft you need to put your ear right next to her."

Josh leaned over to listen. "Wow! What a soft purr! Just like her fur is soft."

"Yes." Maura smiled at the two, looking at each other. "She's going to be a new addition to the family, if that's all right with you."

He smiled and nodded. After all, they now lived in a huge house. His allergy hadn't bothered him one bit, to Maura's delight. She had always wished the cats could live with them and not have to go somewhere else at night.

"I tried out various names, including Polly, which I like the sound of, but got no reaction from anybody, especially the kitten."

Josh thought for a moment. "I like the sound of Polly, but not for a cat." He cocked his head, thinking for a moment. "How about Molly?" he suggested.

At that, the kitten immediately began to wash Josh's face with her small, pink, tongue.

Tiggy chose that precise moment to let out a high, pitched "*EEEOW!*" that caused them to laugh. Cookie looked up from where he had just yanked off an old nail sheath, and Lucky let out a large sigh.

"See!" Maura pronounced, "they all like it, especially the kitten!" She gave the torti a quick rub. "Molly, it is." And so, Molly became the fourth tail to join the group, causing Cookie to remember that one afternoon the summer before, Lucky had mentioned there would be a fourth tail.

Cookie decided that he would take care of Molly. When Josh set her on the floor, he began to wash her. She tolerated it for a while, but then she popped him one. "Don't wash me!" she snapped. "I'm a big girl! I can clean myself!" And just to prove her point, she hissed at him, causing Cookie to sit back on his haunches and stare at her in amazement.

Later that day, after the rotary phone on the wall was connected, Maura tried to call Joe at the Beachhead Restaurant in Connecticut to let him know the telephone number and the new address so he could keep her informed about the colony cats.

However, when she picked up the receiver, she heard a conversation on the other end. "Oh, I'm sorry," she said. "I didn't know that someone else could use the phone."

There was a pause on the other end, and a woman said, "Yes, my dear, and we're going to talk for a piece. It's a party line, ya know. We all have to share our time."

The other women burst in with, "Say, are ya that new family that just moved up in Elmer's old house? We heard his daughter and husband moved out. We heard that she had given it ta her father."

"Yes. I'm Maura. We bought the house from Elmer, who didn't want to move back to Maine. I might be baking desserts for the diner."

"Oh, ya're the one my Rubin's been talking about. He raves 'bout yur chocolate-chip cookies. Ya gave him some fur taking care of Star. Says they're delicious." There was a slight pause, and then she introduced herself and her friend. "Oh, by the way, I'm Gertie and my friend's Emma. We're close neighbors ta ya."

"Also best friends," Emma put in. Maura would later learn that while Gertie had retained her Maine accent, her friend Emma, the more elegant of the two, had worked diligently to drop hers.

"Oh, by the way..." Gertie hesitated and then said, "My Sadie is gonna have a birthday soon. Is there a chance ya could bake a fancy birthday cake? I'd pay ya."

Maura sighed, not wanting to disappoint this woman, but her rations had already been doled out. "Well, sugar is rationed, and I only have enough coupons to take care of my family, with a little extra for the diner."

She waited for Gertie to respond. But instead of addressing her, Emma said, "Gertie. How 'bout asking Bessie if she'll give Maura her unused coupons? She just throws them out now that it's only she and Ted. Little Jamie grew up, married, and moved away. But Bessie still gets enough coupons for the three of them. She can't be bothered calling the office and telling them."

"That's a good idea!" Gertie was getting excited. "How about calling Ethel and Bertha too? Oh, I have a great idea! We can ask sewin'-bee ladies when they all gather ta work on the quilt fur the church Christmas fair. Most of them toss their unused coupons away too!"

"Fine! Do that, and I'll discuss it with the women at church Sunday. Why waste good coupons when someone can definitely use them?"

"Ladies, I thank you. But I think...I'm not sure I can bake for everybody!"

Maura heard a delighted laugh on the other end of the phone line. "Oh, my dear, don't worry about that! We're doing this mostly because we don't like anyone telling us what to do! These coupons have done just that since last May! Although, once those ladies learn about your cookies, you're sure to get offers to pay or trade for some. They'll be knocking at your door nonstop!"

"She's right," Gertie said. "The government means good. But we Mainers like ta do things our way. We don't like anyone poking their nose in our business." Delighted laughter spilled from both women.

"Well, we must get off the phone now and let you do your business. However, we do plan to be busy calling people later. Isn't that right, Gertie?"

"Yep."

"Well, thanks, ladies. Nice to meet you."

And just like that, Maura started her dessert business in Maine. She made a note to drop Uncle Jack a line and tell him that he had been right when he commented that she could easily sell the delicious desserts she baked.

# Chapter 7

"Let's move Star into the barn today," Jim said, standing up from the kitchen table and putting his empty coffee cup in the sink. Josh agreed, and they walked over to Gus's barn to move the horse and his belongings into their barn.

The goat looked curiously up when Jim led Star away and Josh came in to collect the saddle and other gear. Later, they returned with the station wagon and loaded the remaining hay bales, glancing over at an old, moldy one and dismissing it as unusable.

They had to step around the chickens meandering underfoot, clucking angrily at them. They'd been disturbed from laying their eggs, an important task that they took very seriously.

Maura stood on the porch, watching the twins transfer the horse's gear. Then she walked over to the fenced corral to put a tentative hand on Star's nose. She smiled as the horse lowered his head to look at the crew of cats who had wandered over from their favorite place under the maple tree, where, unknown to Maura, each morning they heard the chipmunk's latest news of the Night Visitor.

The tomcats stood back. But Lucky inched her way forward toward Star. He threw back his head and whinnied at her, and she calmly meowed back.

At this exchange, Maura laughed, completely unaware that the cat had just introduced herself, even though the horse didn't understand "cat language."

She went into the barn to help the fellows put the horse's paraphernalia away while the cats all huddled near the fence, getting familiar with the barn's new occupant.

The tomcats didn't understand Star's language, of course, but Lucky turned her head to look up at him each time he made a noise.

~

AFTER THE HORSE WAS SETTLED, Jim said, "Let's visit the diner and see how Gi is doing." He loved to shorten words. Josh sometimes kidded him, saying Jim thought so fast he couldn't be bothered to pronounce all the letters.

They climbed into the station wagon as Maura rounded up all the cats, who loved to go for a ride. She knew that after eating and washing up, they all took short naps. But they could nap in the car. She would crack the windows open, and they'd be all right.

They drove the short distance, parking in the lot in front of the diner, and the twins and Maura entered the smoke-filled building. Unknown to them, Cookie was following them and managed to slip in when an old man opened the door very slowly to leave the diner. Cookie hated to miss out on any action or news.

Gina saw the group and waved as she stopped by a booth to take an older couple's order. "Two Adam and Eves on a raft," she called to the cook. Then she leaned down toward the man to hear what he was saying. "Add a sinker to that, while I pour some suds."

Jim smiled at the puzzled look on the customer's face. He was well versed in diner jargon, thanks to Gina. It was Mainers who sometimes seemed to be speaking a foreign language.

Gina tore the top sheet off her pad and leaned through the kitchen window to drop the ticket where Charlie, who was cooking, could refer to it. Then she hurried over to her relatives with a fresh pot of coffee, completely missing the gray tomcat, who had slunk under an empty table and was peering out at her.

"Hi, gang! Come to see me work, did you? Well, starting today, I only work during the week and have weekends off."

She set coffee mugs in front of them and poured the steaming liquid. "That'll be fifteen cents. Charlie ran to town and bought an apple pie. Do you want some?" She knew they all had eaten the honey buns Maura had made that morning for breakfast, but she asked anyway.

Then, in a loud whisper intended for Charlie's ears, she said, "Your pies are so much better, Maura."

At this comment, Charlie looked up from the eggs he was cooking. "You're the one who bakes?"

"Yes, I bake a bit," Maura said shyly.

To which Jim burst out laughing. "You could say that! She makes the best desserts ever!"

Josh smiled at his brother's declaration. "Stay a bit," Charlie called while sliding a slotted spoon under two eggs simmering in a pot of water and reaching for two pieces of toast to place them on. Then he added a doughnut to the plate and put it in the window for Gina to pick up. "We'll talk after this group finishes breakfast," he said, cracking an egg on the grill for a customer who ordered the same thing at the same time every morning.

Josh had declined Gina's offer of pie, but Jim decided to try it, as he loved to eat. Gina sighed and shook her head, but she brought him a piece anyway. "How about you, Maura?"

"No thanks. I'm full. Just coffee for now. Maybe I'll try a piece after I talk to Charlie."

Gina grinned, having accomplished what she had set out to do. Once the customers, especially the men, got a taste of Maura's desserts, the word would get around, and she'd be able to add to the group's finances. "Eve with a lid on," she called to Charlie.

"How about a nickel for the jukebox?" Maura asked Josh, who promptly handed her a couple of nickels and went back to reading the morning paper, available for all the diners to read.

He frowned after reading the blaring headline. Monet's "Water Lilies" Missing. Second Painting Stolen. Police Baffled.

Showing the headline to his brother, he muttered, "Someone could sell that on the black market for a lot of money."

"But who could be stealing the paintings?" Jim said.

"Somebody who wants to raise money. Maybe Germans who want to buy guns and ammo."

"Is it worth much?" Jim asked, looking up as Gina purposely plunked the piece of apple pie down in front of him to show how she felt, then turned to help another customer who'd just walked in.

Josh read on. "Estimated to be worth $3,800!"

"Wow!" Jim paused with his fork in the air. "Maybe we should take up painting!"

Josh laughed and went on reading. "Too bad they only gave the artist seventy dollars for it when they bought it from him in 1898. Wonder how much it'll be worth in another forty or fifty years."

Gina went back to the counter, brushing crumbs off one of the stools topped with round, red, vinyl seats, before grabbing the two plates of eggs, the doughnut, and the coffee pot and approaching the older couple's table. She poured some more coffee in the man's cup before he could stop her, saying, "Unlimited coffee's on the house. That's why the workers like to stop here."

She grabbed a couple of heavy porcelain mugs and poured coffee for a pair of men who'd just come in.

In the meantime, Maura was flipping through the musical selections when a man sat down in the booth next to the jukebox and drew out his pipe. "Do ya mind?"

She smiled and noted everyone else was smoking, although she and her group didn't. "No. Of course not," she said. "My grandpa smoked a pipe, and I still love the smell."

"Yada, yada, yada," Cookie thought, under the table. His nose was twitching at all the delicious aromas wafting in the air. Finally, he could not help himself. He followed the smell of bacon frying into the tiny kitchen, keeping a careful eye out to dodge Gina's quick footsteps as she retrieved steaming plates heaped with lunch goodies.

Charlie, about to turn some bacon on the griddle, paused with the spatula in midair. He smiled down at Cookie, who had sat down next to him and was staring pointedly up at him.

"Cookie!" a horrified Gina cried, having spied him too. "How did you get in here?"

"That's a strange question from her," Cookie thought. "She should know by now that I can get in anywhere I want to."

"He yours?" Charlie asked, laughing at the sight of the cat sitting so quietly, his black whiskers quivering at the smell of bacon. How Cookie dearly loved meat, and there hadn't been much at home lately, due to rationing as well as a lack of money.

"Sort of." Gina reached down to grab him and carry him out to the station wagon, but he evaded her by scooting further into the kitchen. "He lives with us. He's Maura's."

Maura had gone out to the car for the sample of cookies she'd packed for Charlie and returned to the diner, unaware of the drama now going on. She looked curiously at Gina as she approached the counter with the cookies.

"Let him stay a bit," Charlie said, smoothing the stained white apron over his abundant stomach. He liked a cat who enjoyed eating as much as he did!

He picked up a couple of strips of bacon, broke them into little pieces, and then placed them on a napkin in front of the now-drooling cat.

Cookie quickly gobbled the bacon up before an abashed Maura, who could now see him in the kitchen. She put the cookies on the counter and then strode over, picked him up, and took him back to the car, where she found the back door open.

Maura saw Lucky and Molly in the car, but not Tiggy. "Oh, for heaven's sake," she said, depositing Cookie in the car and closing the door firmly.

Tiggy was wandering outside. He had waited until Maura and the twins went into the diner and then he'd pushed down on the handle of one of the rear doors with his big double paws, opening it, so he and Cookie could explore. While Cookie had gone into the diner, Tiggy stayed outside, wandering close to the building. He was busy smelling the food aromas coming from the diner's windows, which were open and had screens in them, plus all the animal smells he'd not encountered before.

Maura looked sternly at the marmalade when she spotted him. She put her hands on her hips. "Tiggy! It had to be you and your huge, double paws!" She bent down and picked him up when he moseyed over, winding round her legs.

"Try that again, and you'll find yourself left behind the next time we go out." She walked back to the car with the purring marmalade.

"Bad cats!" she scolded, opening the back door and depositing him inside. She slid into the driver's seat. "But not you ladies." She smiled into the rearview mirror at Lucky, who smiled back at her. Maura always talked to the cats as though they understood her, thinking they only really responded to her tone.

Molly tilted her head, knowing Maura had just said something about them, but she couldn't fathom what the words meant.

Seeing her confusion, Lucky leaned over and gave the kitten a quick lick on the cheek. The torti purred softly as she lay down next to the tuxedo. Molly had unshakeable faith that whatever the problem, Lucky would take care of it.

In the rear cargo area, Cookie, now contented, lay down on the towel and promptly went to sleep, as Tiggy sniffed his brother's whiskers curiously.

Drifting off to dreamland, Cookie muttered, "I'll explain later." And he promptly started snoring, much to Tiggy's consternation.

~

AND SO, SUMMER FOUND THEM all busy. Maura took care of the victory garden and baked desserts to sell. Gina loved her job at the diner, and the men helped the neighboring farmer, Rubin, who had taken care of the horse.

They found out he had used dynamite to blast away a stump in his field, which left him with a deaf ear. That had made him ineligible for military service, just as they were. However, there was now a shortage of farmhands, so Josh and Jim pitched in when Rubin needed help haying, and they repaired his barn roof one weekend. He, in turn, rewarded them with vegetables from his farm and a chicken, already killed and plucked, for Sunday dinner.

They also worked on their farmhouse repairs, deciding not to fence in the porch so the cats could stay out at night after Rubin told them about the large forest creatures that roamed about. Jim tended to Star and had gotten quite good at the Mainers' way of trading. He repaired Rubin's tractor in exchange for riding lessons.

Turned out, Rubin was the farmer they had seen storming up the hardware store steps when they first drove through town. Once he found out Josh could weld, Rubin introduced him to the foreman at the town garage, who allowed him to work on Rubin's plow there, using the town's equipment.

When the foreman saw Josh's welding expertise, he hired him on the spot and later hired his twin brother when another employee signed up with the army. The town's equipment was old. Trucks were always breaking down and needing repair, and the town didn't have money to replace them. The fellows had applied for work at the naval shipyard, where there was more money to be made, but these jobs were welcome.

The cats took to exploring the meadow behind the farmhouse, a tangle of weeds, briars, bushes, and tons of rocks. Most of all, the adult cats loved to sit under the shade of the maple tree in the side yard, watching in amusement as Molly ran through the dandelions that had gone to seed, scattering white seeds to the four winds. The torti also loved hiding behind bushes and batting at butterflies and moths with that lightning-fast paw of hers.

Life went on...

# Chapter 8

## *Monday, June 15, 1942*

Maura had planted a larger victory garden in late spring, and she was out one morning, hoeing the weeds around the cucumbers, when an engine noise alerted her to visitors. A 1935 Model T Ford was slowly chugging up the driveway. Leaning on the hoe for a moment, she saw that the visitors were her neighbors, Gertie and Emma. They got out, excitedly calling to Maura to come and see what they had.

She smiled and let the hoe drop to the ground to greet her new friends. She'd joined the sewing circle to help sew the quilt for the Christmas raffle in return for all the sugar coupons the women had garnered for her.

Walking toward the car, she welcomed them warmly, while wondering about this early morning visit.

Emma, whose steel-gray hair was tied neatly in a bun, opened the driver's door and got out, smiling. She smoothed down her long, flowing, gray dress, ever the elegant lady. Thick-wedge platform shoes with perky bows at the open toes completed her outfit.

Seeing Emma, always impeccably dressed, made Maura feel unkempt, and she automatically tucked a stray strand of brown hair back into her bun and smoothed her ever-present burlap apron.

Gertie, her short, dirty-blond hair all askew from enjoying the breeze through an open window, got out on the passenger side and left the door open so she could lean in and pick up a box from the back seat. She was the bubblier of the two women, who had been best friends since their school days in the one-room schoolhouse down the lane.

"Here ya go," Gertie said, shoving the box she was holding into Maura's hands. Inside the box, a great clacking noise arose as various jars in which to make jam or preserves or can vegetables jostled against each other.

"Where? How?" Maura sputtered as her neighbor reached again into the back seat to pick up another box.

Emma, the more sedate of the pair, smiled and walked around the back of the dusty car and toward the front porch.

Chortling at their gift, Gertie walked quickly behind her. "Asked all the ladies fur the jars they no longer needed or used," she said.

"Oh," Maura said, "that was nice of them."

"Well, they probably expect to get some jam or preserves for Christmas gifts in return," Emma wisely predicted.

As they walked up the steps, Emma admonished her friend, whose blouse was half tucked into her skirt and half out. "Gertie, how is it you always look like you've thrown your clothes on?" She looked down at her friend's feet. "And for heaven's sakes! Look at your stockings!"

Gertie paused look down at her stockings as Maura went ahead to hold the screen door open. Gertie grinned and put down the box she was carrying to pull a crumpled stocking up. As always, she wore saddle shoes, one of which was dotted with a clump of mud. Spotting this, she hastily rubbed it off against the other shoe. To her chagrin, she also noticed one of her stockings was black and the other was brown.

"Mayhaps I'll start a new trend, Emma. Who says both stockings have ta be the same color?"

Emma just shook her head at her friend's foolishness. "Gertie, you need to take better care of your appearance."

Gertie smiled. "I leave all that in yur capable hands, Emma."

As they walked into the house Emma demanded, "Doesn't Rubin care how you look?"

"Rubin?" Gertie turned around, surprised, and bumped into Maura with the box. "Sorry. No, Rubin only cares whether his meals are on the table, the house is clean, and I've taken care of Sadie." Sadie was their child, or "yow'un," as Gertie would say. "And fur sure, the cows don't care what I look like!"

She laughed, following Maura into the kitchen and putting the box of canning jars on the sink. "Know ya'll want ta wash them, even though most are already clean."

"Oh, by the way, Gertie," Emma said as they went back to the car for the remaining boxes. "How's that new boy helping Rubin milk the cows?"

"Oh, Kenny. He wants ta be a bull rider." She snorted. "Says he's off when he gets ta be eighteen. Rubin just shakes his head when he mentions that. Says kids nowadays certainly have imagination."

"Is Kenny from up here?" Maura asked, following them and already visualizing filling the jars and jugs with all kinds of food.

"Nah." Gertie shook her head. "Kenny comes from Massachusetts but lives up here in the summer. Stays with his grandpa, who insists he bring home money fur food and living expenses. Told Kenny it builds character."

She leaned into the back seat of the car and grabbed another large box, leaving the smaller one for her friend, something Emma appreciated because she had trouble with her back. That was the reason she always stood so straight and walked so slowly.

"Kenny's grandpa says kids shouldn't be handed things," Gertie went on, climbing the porch steps while Maura held the screen door open. "Makes life too easy. Then, when the bumps come along, they're lost. He says life isn't fur free. Ya have ta pull yar own weight in this world. His grandpa doesn't want marshmallows governin' us, ya know." Gertie chuckled, thinking about it. "Then, Kenny said, after each lecture, his grandpa reaches in his pocket, takes out a wooden match, and relights his corncob pipe, which always goes out soon as he lights it. Says his grandpa chews on the end of the pipe the rest of the day."

Maura found the tale fascinating and said so.

"Kenny thinks it's because his grandpa doesn't want ta spend the money fur new tobacco!" The two friends laughed all the way into the kitchen, leaving Maura to wonder what was so funny.

69

They visited for a while, sitting at the kitchen table. Maura served them iced tea, lemons for lemonade now being scarce because of the new shipping problems. When the women left, both waving good-bye to Maura standing on the front porch, they drove slowly back down the lane, stopping to talk to Alice, who was busy spraying a tall weed with fluffy, white seeds in the garden.

"Hello, Alice," Emma said. "Whatcha ya doin'?"

"Damn weeds grow everywhere! Using the last of ma white vinegar ta kill them." She stood up and rubbed her aching back. "Next time Maura shops, I'll ask her ta pick some up."

Emma nodded, as she knew Maura had taken over shopping for the older woman, adding some groceries for Alice to her own order and paying for them herself in return for the eggs Alice gave to her. It was the old Mainers' trading practice, but with a different flair.

Emma and Gertie waved to the older woman and chugged off down the road, Gertie making a mental note to bring a jug of vinegar for Alice on their next visit to Maura. That's what neighbors were for, at least in Maine.

# Chapter 9

## *July and August 1942*

J uly Fourth passed quietly with everyone so busy. With Rubin's help, the twins at last put their boat, *Big Blue,* in the Piscataqua River, where it merged with the Atlantic Ocean.

Rubin had told them about a small boatyard whose owner, Tom, was a friend of his. Tom was considering opening a restaurant because his boatyard was so close to the naval yard, and he visualized the workers becoming a steady customer base. So, the twins made an agreement with Tom to trade a portion of their catch for dockage.

When Charlie, the diner owner, heard of the brothers' penchant for fishing, he saw an opportunity to expand his menu to include fried fish, something that would go over well with the townspeople, and he offered to buy part of their catch too. Soon, they had fish for their suppers and cash in the kitty.

The fellows ate their breakfast quickly one morning, after stoking the fire in the potbellied stove. The fire would last for a couple of hours—until the sun rose high enough to warm all it touched.

"You get the can of worms, while I get our poles," Josh told Jim as he drank the rest of his coffee. Maura sat at the table, still drinking hers as Jim started down the cellar stairs. It had rained the day before, and they'd harvested worms that evening and put them in the cellar overnight. It wasn't until later they discovered that local fish preferred sandworms, much to Tiggy's horror.

Josh took the fishing rods from the small closet in the mud room by the front door. He always made sure to fasten the hooks on the line to protect the cats from injury. Cookie and Tiggy loved to go fishing with them as long as it wasn't too cold. They'd ride in the cabin of the boat when the twins fished. Sure enough, when he pulled out the rods, the two tomcats strolled to the front door and sat down to wait.

"Me too! Me too!" An excited Molly ran back and forth, rubbing against Josh's legs. She knew they were about to go somewhere and didn't want to be left behind. For Cookie, her inability to understand what people were saying was a bit trying at times.

Cookie had investigated the kitten's whiskers and fine ear hairs to see if she, too, had black hairs, which he theorized were the reason Tiggy, Lucky, and he each had special abilities that other cats lacked. But alas, the kitten had white whiskers and ear hairs, Cookie discovered, his inspection drawing a quick swat and a low growl from her.

"Where are we going?" she demanded of Cookie, who simply replied, "Fishing."

Josh picked her up and laughed as she licked his cheek. "You want to come too?"

Of course, she didn't understand any of the words, yet she figured out pretty much what he was asking, so she reached out with her little pink tongue and kissed him squarely on the nose.

He laughed again as he put her on the floor. "Best to check out our safety code to see if she understands it, huh, boys?"

The two cats looked solemnly at him. "He wants to know that you'll come when he's ready to go home," Cookie told her. "When he whistles, go running to him."

Molly watched as Josh went into the bathroom, a room Molly rarely entered. He pursed his lips and let out a shrill whistle. Molly tensed and started to run the other way, but Cookie stomped on her tail, making her growl and puff it out to three times its normal size.

"If you want to come with us to the boat, you better run to him when he whistles. He's testing you," Cookie reminded her.

A startled Molly immediately stopped tugging. She looked solemnly at Cookie and hesitated only a moment before racing into the bathroom and jumping lightly into Josh's waiting arms.

He scooped her up, laughing and getting a rough, wet kiss on his cheek. "So, you do want to come, do you?" He set her down, giving her a quick pat. "Well, Miss Molly, you got yourself a deal. A-fishing we will go."

Molly was so excited when Cookie told her what Josh had said that she smiled and hopped around. "I'm all grown up now!"

At that comment, Cookie sighed deeply.

"She's your responsibility," Josh said, looking sternly at Cookie, who somehow knew what was coming. "Boys, it will be up to you to make sure she doesn't get herself in any trouble while we're at the shore. And when we're ready to leave, she best be at your side."

For some reason, Tiggy suddenly felt like standing up and saluting. Maybe Josh's tone made him feel like that. However, seeing Cookie's warning look, he quickly leaned back to give his extra-long tail a vigorous wash, much to Lucky's amusement.

~

MAURA WAS OFF DELIVERING a coconut-cream pie to the diner, and Gina, who wasn't working that day, had offered to cook a spaghetti supper. Standing at the stove, stirring the sauce, she was doing a little jig as she sang along with the Andrews Sisters on the radio. She had no idea what the real lyrics were, but she made up her own. "Hutza Ralston on the Rivera and a brawla, brawla Susan!" she sang.

"What mean?" Tiggy demanded.

Wakened from his midafternoon nap, Cookie yawned and stretched out on the flowered couch cushion just as Maura walked into the kitchen, voicing her own question about the lyrics.

"I don't know. But it sure is a catchy tune." Gina laughed, grabbing a dust cloth midway through the song and waving it about, leaving the sauce to bubble away in the pot. "And it's great to do dusting to." She twirled around as she flicked the cloth over the kitchen chairs and then moved into the sewing room.

Dropping the dust cloth, she picked up the iron instead. She pulled a blouse from a basket of clean laundry and moved over to the ironing board, still open nearby.

Jim came in from the backyard, wiping his dirty hands on his pants. Spotting Gina, he went over and put his arms around her. She immediately shoved him away, grimacing, and brushed off her shorts.

He laughed and walked over to slump on a kitchen chair, wiping the sweat that trickled down his cheek. "You care more about your clothes than you do me!" he said to Gina, who immediately retorted, "Do not!"

"Do so!" Jim winked at Maura who smiled and shook her head as she handed him a cool glass of iced tea. How he loved to tease his new wife.

Staring at the bottom of the iron, Gina frowned and returned to the kitchen to wet a tangle of steel wool, which she used to scrub the bottom of the iron. Turning it on, she ironed a piece of wax paper to make the iron's surface smooth and shiny again. She sang merrily with the radio as she worked.

The battles in Europe seemed far away. But the clouds of war were much closer than the humans of the house thought. Much closer.

~

AIR RAID SIRENS periodically sounded at night, testing people's reactions and shaking up the cats, until they got used to them.

The federal government had issued gray, wool blankets to the residents of Cumberland, instructing them to throw the blankets over the curtain rods at night when the sirens sounded, to block any light coming from their houses.

"Just in case an enemy plane flies overhead," Jim commented as he painted the top halves of the cars' lights black. The cats watched them from their favorite spot under the large, spreading maple tree, but they did not understand.

Gina was very happy to work at the diner. Her paycheck and her tips, which added up because she was cute and sassy with the workers and sailors who flocked to the restaurant, helped to cover the household expenses.

74

Maura, being the homebody, cooked most of the meals. But some weekends, Gina made a huge pot of tomato sauce. Maura, being a thrifty person, promptly canned most of it for the winter months, leaving enough for a couple of days of spaghetti and meatballs.

Everyone, even Molly, loved it. "Perhaps," thought Cookie, "we are all Italians!" Still, the bits of bacon that Maura often crumbled for the cats' scrambled-egg breakfast remained Cookie's favorite food.

Maura spent the summer weeding the victory garden and picking the vegetables when they were ripe. Thanks to the local ladies, especially under the instruction of her new friend, Gertie, she had canned an abundance of vegetables. The shelves in the cellar now held rows of sparkling jars filled with the fruits of her labors. There were jars of stewed tomatoes, pickles, green beans, and corn, along with various fruits, especially apples. Their trees had produced a bumper crop this year, to everyone's delight.

Soon, when the frost came, she would harvest the last tomatoes, still green, and slice them and pack them in jars of oil and savory herbs to add to the enjoyment of a sandwich. She would harvest the potatoes and onions, which she'd hang in burlap bags tied to a sturdy clothesline. Carrots, Hubbard squash, beets, and turnips would be buried beneath the loose dirt of the cellar floor.

One morning, Maura saw Tiggy rolling in a field nearby. When she went to investigate, she discovered wild catnip. Gathering the plants, she tied bunches together and hung them with clothespins on a line in the cellar, along with onions, potatoes, and some garlic. She would ask Gina to sew some small bags from scraps of cloth that could be stuffed with catnip, once it dried, and then sewn closed. They'd make fragrant Christmas toys for the cats.

The cellar had always been off limits to the cats, who might be tempted to use the loose dirt floor as a litter box. Now there were two reasons to keep that door closed.

The catnip bunches hung over the washing machine, which had a roller for squeezing the water out of clothes and into the old sink. Every time Maura did laundry, she thanked Elmer's daughter for leaving the machine behind, as she didn't fancy scrubbing the clothes on a washboard.

Each weekend, Gina and Maura explored the countryside, discovering bushes of blackberries and blueberries. This pleased them immensely, as they'd have gifts of jam to give to their neighbors and other new friends during the Christmas season.

Thanks to Jim's impatience to taste her first gooseberry pie, Maura had discovered how bitter the white gooseberries on the bush by the back steps were. They needed extra sweetening to be edible in jam and pies. Luckily, she had adopted the Mainers' practice of using local maple syrup and molasses in baked goods in place of sugar, whenever she could.

The copper pump sat by the outside steps, a reminder of how the house had gotten its drinking water before Elmer's daughter and son-in-law had hired a well driller to run a line underground into the house—something they were all thankful for, especially when Alice described the variety of spiders she'd seen in the outhouse.

The fellows ordered the newspaper delivered every day, and they arranged to have the coal bin in the cellar filled before the weather turned. The furnace provided most of the heat to warm the house in the winter, augmented by the potbellied stove in the corner of the kitchen. That was a cheery addition to the cat's sleeping quarters.

Both men had also been busy chopping fallen trees on the nearby hillside and toting the wood home. Soon the stack was as tall at Jim and very wide. The arbor, picked clean, thanks to everyone pitching in, had produced many glistening jars of grape jam.

One of the sewing-circle women had even shown Maura how to make grape wine. Although they had yet to taste it, several jars of it were nestled among the jam. She'd give the wine—something local farmers prized—as gifts too. Emma told her that after a long day in the searing sun, harvesting corn for the cows and bales of hay for their winter feed, they'd appreciate a nice glass of wine.

~

ONCE THE FOURSOME had settled into a routine, they revived their Friday-night card games, sitting around the large mahogany table in the kitchen, which gave them plenty of room to play on. Their old card table was consigned to the spare room. Gina had set it up beside the treadle sewing machine and stacked her sewing paraphernalia on it.

Tiggy particularly liked the new setup, as it allowed him plenty of room to stretch out on the braided rug in the living room, safe from Jim's twitchy toes. Cookie couldn't have cared less. The kitchen table was near enough for him to hear the humans' conversation from the comfort of the living room couch. Lucky sat on her favorite easy chair, which they had brought with them from the Connecticut cottage. She was only slightly unnerved that she now had to share it with Molly, who had attached herself to the tuxedo cat.

The hot, August breeze wafted in through the front windows. As all were fitted with screens to keep out the tenacious black flies, they were open all day. The windows were shut at night—it still amazed everyone how cold the nights were here! The Piscataqua River cooled the town off after the sun went down, and they lived fairly close to it.

Josh was sitting at the table, leafing through the front section of the newspaper, while Jim sat across from him, reading the sports news. "Hot tonight," he said, wiping a bead of sweat from his forehead, although he wasn't rushing around, making supper as Maura was.

Jim looked up, grimacing. "Can you believe Ben Hogan is paid to win a golf match?"

Gina put a dinner plate in front of him. "Don't put the newspaper down on it," she cautioned.

"Told you we should have dug for oil in the old cottage's backyard," Jim said, peering out the window at the darkness now descending. "Maybe we should try digging here!"

Gina rolled her eyes as she filled his glass with iced tea—a staple now that the price of lemons had gone sky high.

His brother ignored him; his attention was on an article on the front page. Jim noticed his interest and asked, as usual, "What's the news, Bro?"

Josh didn't like being called "Bro," but by now he was so familiar with it that he ignored it. "We're in the Solomons now," he said.

"You mean the islands?" Gina asked, pouring iced tea into another glass.

"Yes. Guadalcanal is there." Josh kept reading, but Tiggy, a bit groggy from his nap, caught the tail end of that conversation, and always the questioner, asked, "What's an island?"

He looked over at Lucky for an answer.

"A piece of land surrounded by water." She looked down at little Molly, curled up with her, and gave her a quick wash.

Tiggy, ever the sensitive soul, began to howl. "*EEEOW!*" he said, causing startled looks around the kitchen table.

"People fall off! People drown! EEEOW!" Tiggy howled again.

Cookie snorted. "No, silly. Remember how we passed Faulkner's Island on the way to fish? We could get there by boat."

Tiggy hung his head, feeling foolish, now that he remembered. But seeing Maura coming over to check on him, he rolled over on his back so she could rub his tummy.

Realizing that he was all right—his yowl must have been the result of a bad dream—she gave him a quick rub, then returned to the kitchen to fry the meatballs.

Gina sprinkled salt and pepper into sauce in the pot and checked the water to see if it was bubbling before dumping a box of spaghetti into it. She smiled to herself, thinking of her mom making the pasta from scratch and hanging it to dry on the clothesline strung up in her kitchen. She missed the fresh taste of homemade pasta, but not the work!

Maura was cooking alongside her sister-in-law, and Cookie's nose twitched at the aroma of the meatballs she was frying, even though he had drifted back to sleep. How he loved meat! Tiggy could have his share of spaghetti any day! Pasta wasn't his cup of tea.

Gina stopped stirring the sauce to look over at Jim, who was sitting back in his chair, resting a foot on the table, while he picked at his teeth with a toothpick. She leaned over and whacked his foot. "We don't need to eat whatever your shoe picks up!"

Startled, Jim sat up, pulling his foot down. "Sorry, Babe."

"And don't call me *Babe*! I am definitely not a baby!"

This comment caused Josh to look up from the newspaper and chuckle.

"Why don't you go out and bring in a load of wood and stop bothering me!" Gina added.

Jim rose and started out the door, grinning at his brother as he passed him. Each morning, one of them started a fire in the potbellied stove to take the chill out of the kitchen, something any early riser would appreciate.

When Jim came back and dropped the wood by the stove, Maura was putting the finished meatballs into the sauce pot. She came to the table to sit down for a few minutes. "Oh, by the way," she said suddenly. "Bessie told me about her son in the Seabees when we were standing in line for the butcher."

Jim and Josh looked up to listen; they had never heard of Seabees.

"They're a construction battalion. She says the Seabees go in first, before the marines, to cut away the jungle and prepare an airfield so the troops can land on the islands." She sighed deeply, murmuring, "I'll say a prayer for him."

"Oh, that reminds me," Gina said. "Dora, the waitress that I work with at the diner, has a cousin who's a WASP."

"A bee?" Tiggy wanted to know.

"What are WASPS?" Josh asked.

"They're women pilots who test Flying Fortresses and train men to fly them."

Tiggy anxiously looked skyward. "Big castles flying?"

"Don't know." Cookie shrugged.

"Flying what?" Jim frowned.

Gina sighed at his lack of knowledge. "You know! The B-52s that fly soldiers, supplies, and trucks to the front lines overseas for the Seabees, who, like Maura said, go ahead of the marines and eke out landing fields in the jungles."

Tiggy sat up in alarm. "Did she say EEEK?" he asked his brother, tilting his head.

Cookie sighed. It was rare that his brother paid attention to people talk. Though Tiggy's ears were full of fine black hairs, which Cookie had deduced were the source of their unusual talents, he only tuned in occasionally. Unfortunately, Cookie didn't know what that word meant either. He made a mental note to ask Lucky later.

The gray tomcat had been washing his own black whiskers, and now he paused to look over at Lucky. Her head was tilted as she listened to Gina's explanation. "Ha!" he thought, triumphantly. "So, she doesn't know *everything* after all!" Next to her, Molly slept on, unconcerned with what was being said around her.

"Maybe I should fly," Gina mused aloud.

Tiggy blinked at the picture of Gina flying a huge castle overhead. "Would duck!" he said, causing a snort to slip from Lucky.

"Oh dear." Maura looked worriedly at the tuxedo as she rose to serve supper. "I hope Lucky's not coming down with a cold."

This caused Cookie to chuckle, which sounded like he was about to upchuck. Now everyone was looking the cats' way. Seeing nothing amiss, Maura and Gina served supper, then cleared the table. Later, after the dishes were washed and dried, the usual spirited Friday card game began.

At the sound of a rumble in the sky, Gina looked up. "Sounds like rain. Maybe we should close the windows." She rose, but Jim stopped her.

"Leave the windows open, sweetcakes. It's too hot to close them." He noted that the wind had picked up, blowing the kitchen curtains. "Besides," he said, reaching over and pulling her down on the chair again, "we need the cool breath of air that usually comes before a storm."

Reluctantly, Gina stayed put. Maura glanced into the living room to make sure the cats were still lying about, although she knew they would be.

Cookie was dozing when he remembered that he intended to investigate the footprints he'd seen in the dust in Gus's barn. Were they somehow connected to the Night Visitor the chipmunk talked about?

Suddenly, the tuxedo stood up and jumped off the easy chair, dragging a befuddled Molly to the floor by the scruff of her neck. "*MERROWW!*" Lucky yowled, causing the foursome to stop the game and stare their way.

"Run! Under the couch! NOW!" Lucky shouted in a loud meow.

The tomcats reacted quickly, following her directions without question, though she'd never before commanded them to do anything.

Lucky pushed the protesting kitten underneath the couch and quickly crawled in after her.

Suddenly, a loud crack echoed throughout the house, followed by *KABOOM!*

"*MRROW!*" Cookie hollered after the assault on his sensitive ears.

"*EEEOW!*" echoed his frightened brother, who slunk further down under the couch and covered his ears.

The four people at the kitchen table turned just in time to see a bolt of lightning streak in through an open front window, crackle as it circled the living room, and then exit through the same window. It was over in seconds.

"Oh, my God!" Maura screamed. Like the others, she was frozen in place for a moment.

Then they stood up and rushed to close windows, Josh slamming the living room windows while Jim shut the one behind the kitchen sink.

"Thought you said Rubin said we were safe with the lightning rods on the roof, Bro!" Jim shouted, completely unnerved.

"It came in the open window!" Josh said, as his twin raised his eyebrows. "Next time, we'll know better."

Amid the wash of rain now sounding on the roof, they heard a scraping noise.

Jim raced up the stairs to the attic to investigate. "Skylight blew off," he said when he returned for a bucket to put under the hole. "We'll have to wait till tomorrow to find it and put it back on."

Josh nodded in agreement, sighing deeply. He hoped the attic wouldn't get too wet. Maura and Gina had closed the bedroom windows and now they were coming down the stairs. Hearing Maura's gasp, he followed them into them living room and saw the black line the lightning had etched on the walls all the way around the room.

"We'll need to touch up the walls, too," he called after Jim's retreating figure.

Both women got down on hands and knees to peer under the couch. Cats with wide eyes greeted them. Lucky crawled slowly out, her electrified fur standing up in all directions. Molly scooted out on her stomach and lay there on the braided rug, panting. The tomcats remained where they were.

"Oh, my God!" Maura repeated, scooping the befuddled Cookie out from under the couch. He looked stunned when he saw the burn line across the walls.

He'd almost been a fried cat! he realized, struggling to get down. Maura put him down on the floor after seeing that he was OK. She watched in amazement as he walked over to the tuxedo, who had just given herself a violent shake to get her fur to lie down again, and licked her cheek in gratitude for saving them.

Thanks to the lightning, he had completely forgotten about the footprints in the barn. Tiggy stayed where he was, peering fearfully from beneath the couch, until Maura pulled him out. She picked him up gently and cradled him in her arms, smiling as he purred and purred and didn't struggle to get down as he usually did.

Gina scooped up little Molly and held her until she stopped shivering. Only when both couples sat down at the table again, with the windows closed, did the four cats slink warily into the kitchen.

There they stayed the rest of the night, huddled in the corner, where Maura, seeing they were still fearful, placed fluffy pillows for them to lie on. However, each time they heard the slightest sound, their ears flicked back and forth.

Later that night, when all had finally drifted to sleep, Molly awoke. She slipped out from under the safety of Lucky's arm and climbed up the back of the living room couch. From her vantage point, she could see through the front window and watch for any creatures moseying around.

Suddenly, a movement caught her eye. A black car pulled slowly up the driveway from the road. Quietly, it parked next to Alice and Gus's farmhouse and the driver, a tall figure, got out and crept to the old barn, carrying a long, skinny roll. The person's dark clothing merged with the inky blackness as he opened the door and went inside. Moments later, he exited without the object.

Molly saw the figure slide into the car and drive back toward town. Then she caught the movement of a hare squeezing out between the broken slats in the barn door, and she watched him hop silently away, melting into night's blanket.

A moment later, Molly was jumping up and down next to Cookie, who was still trying to sleep in the kitchen.

"I saw him!" she said. "I saw him!"

Cookie opened a sleepy eye to stare into Molly's bright green ones. "Wha...saw who?"

"The Night Visitor! I saw the Night Visitor!" she said, expecting him to congratulate her.

Instead, Cookie closed his eyes. "That's nice," he mumbled. "That's nice." And he drifted back to sleep. Whatever it was could wait until morning...

Molly tilted her head. Then, being a kitten, she curled up next to Cookie and went to sleep too.

# Chapter 10

## *September 1942*

Maura was in the living room, sprinkling water from a bottle topped by a cork poked with holes. She shook it all over the braided rug, then proceeded to sweep it with the corn broom she had recently purchased from the local hardware store. The water kept the dust down when she cleaned the rugs. It also caused all the cats to scatter.

Josh, who was sitting on the old couch, reading the newspaper, put it down to watch her. He smiled at her diligence.

"Can you believe some women pay fifty-five dollars for a Hoover vacuum?" Maura tsked and gave the rug another few swipes before stopping to lean on the broom handle. "Think of it! I only paid one dollar for this broom. Does just as good a job!"

Josh nodded, going back to the newspaper. "Wow! They just built an aircraft carrier called the *Lexington*," he said. "Guess how much it cost to build."

Maura looked at him and shrugged. "How much?"

Josh let out a deep breath. "Sixty million dollars! Where in the world did we find so much money? The country will go broke before long, spending money like that!"

Maura began sweeping again. "Well, that's mostly from people buying war bonds. The kids at school even have war-stamp drives.

Every little bit helps. Besides, all the women say the war will be over soon." She thought of the gold stars that continued to appear on neighbors' windows when a family member died fighting, and she fervently hoped they were right.

During one of her visits to the ladies' sewing circle in the church basement, where appliqués were being sewn on the finished quilt, Emma showed Maura how to knit. Soon, she'd be making Christmas gifts for everyone. But first she had to finish her canning chores. The sewing ladies had asked her to join them when they wrapped bandages for the troops and the gray ladies—volunteers at the Portland Hospital. But Maura had opted out, saying she was too busy.

Now Cookie wandered in from outside, looking to see if she had a snack for him. Maura chose to ignore him, instead telling Josh to move his feet so she could sweep in front of the couch. "Lift your leg, Josh. I want to sweep there. Lift your leg!"

To their surprise, Cookie leaned against the end of the couch, lifted his leg, and stretched it out behind him.

"What?" Josh stared at the cat, hesitant to believe what he'd just seen.

Seeing this, Maura commanded, "Lift your leg, Cookie! Lift your leg!"

To the delight of both humans, the cat turned around, leaned against the couch again, and lifted his other rear leg and stretched it. Laughing, Maura scooped him up and gave him a squeeze.

While Josh chuckled, she walked into the kitchen, opened the refrigerator, and snagged a piece of fried chicken for Cookie. Putting him down on the linoleum, she watched as he gobbled the treat up, meowing his "thank you."

Then he marched smartly out the cat door, past Tiggy, who was snoozing on a kitchen chair. "Darn," Cookie thought, "if I had known it was that easy to get a snack, I would have done it long ago!"

Molly was already outside, nosing around and exploring as usual. Being a kitten, she had almost forgotten what she had seen during the night. And when a fire truck pulled into the yard, she forgot it completely. She watched from the safety of the maple tree while men set a very tall ladder against the house.

Gus had called the firefighters and asked them to bring a long ladder and put the skylight back on Jim and Josh's roof. Sometimes it paid to know people you could ask for a favor.

~

JIM HURRIED FROM THE BARN, having just cleaned Star's stall. Josh was still inside, feeding the horse, after which he'd milk the cow.

Maura had come out on the porch to slap a small rug against the railing to dislodge the dirt collected in it. They kept it just inside the front door, where it got the heaviest foot traffic.

"Where are you rushing off to?" she asked Jim in between whacks.

"Off to spray the trees," Jim said, pointing to the spray device he held in his hand. It had a bowl filled with liquid on one end and a trigger connected to a simple pump to release the spray.

"What do you have?" Maura leaned over the railing as he held it up to show her.

"DDT. Rubin just brought it over. He said to spray it directly on the apples and pears. It kills bugs. Says it's a boon to farmers and anyone with fruit trees, like us."

Maura looked skeptically at the yellow liquid in the bowl. "But if it kills the bugs," she asked, "won't it kill us?"

Jim grinned as he walked off toward the apple trees. "Nah. Rubin says it's perfectly safe!"

Maura wasn't sure about that logic. She resumed banging the rug against the railing, looking skeptically at Jim's retreating figure.

~

THE CATS WOKE UP one crisp morning to see little Molly enclosed in the cat carrier. Maura was busy frying eggs and sausages in a large, cast-iron frying pan.

Cookie licked his lips, and Tiggy sat by Maura's feet, looking intently up at her. She smiled down at him and looked over at Molly, who had settled down in the carrier.

Tiggy was puzzled as to why Molly was in there.

"She's off to the vet," Lucky said, sitting down on the floor.

"Why?" Tiggy asked. She had gotten her shots at the same time as the others had. "Don't see why she has to go again." He scratched his ear, completely befuddled. His long sentence, given in an extended meow, caused Maura to look down at him, worried.

"No more kittens," Lucky said.

Tiggy looked all around for kittens. "Where?"

"No, you boob," Cookie groaned. "That's *why* Molly is going."

Maura stopped cooking when she saw Molly moving around in the carrier. She picked up the carrier and held it at eye level. "Not to worry, Miss Poopy," she said, using a favorite name for her. "You'll be fine." In response, she heard a very faint purr from the kitten, who promptly went to sleep.

After breakfast, Maura—a newly licensed driver, thanks to lessons from Josh—drove off in the station wagon with Molly and eventually returned without her, causing Tiggy to be disturbed all day.

The next day, Molly came home. As she slowly walked out of the carrier, Tiggy wrinkled his nose at the antiseptic smell.

"Molly doesn't feel well," Maura said, waving a finger at the other cats, as she made a little bed in a basket lined with a fluffy blanket. "I want you to leave her alone until she feels better." Which the cats all did, although Lucky periodically went over and reached down to give the kitten a lick on her nose, causing Molly to smile weakly and offer a soft, wobbling purr.

It took the better part of a week before the torti began to move about freely. Maura kept an eye on her and had a litter box nearby, so she could stay in the house. On Saturday, she checked the incision to make sure it was healing all right. Satisfied, she let the kitten outside to rest on the porch. It wasn't until the next week that the torti felt well enough to go exploring again.

~

"I HEARD THAT BING CROSBY is coming out with a new song around Christmas called 'White Christmas,'" Josh said, looking up from the newspaper one Saturday afternoon in October. "He does have a few hits, but guaranteed, this one will never last."

"Why not?" Maura wanted to know.

"'Cause how many people want a white Christmas? That means you have to get out the snow shovels and put chains on your tires so you can get around. Not an easy task." He returned to his newspaper, not wanting to think about the coming winter weather yet.

Maura smiled, hoping to hear the song on the radio soon, as she loved to hear Bing Crosby sing.

Gina shuddered. "I don't want a white Christmas. Maura, if you can't drive me to the diner for work, I might have to walk."

Her sister-in-law looked up from making dinner rolls to say, "No, you could just go in with the boys—and take the desserts so I don't have to drive until they clear the roads." They were a two-car household now. The twins had repaired Rubin's tractor, and he had given them an old truck in return. It had been sitting in his barn and wasn't running when they got it, but thanks to Jim, it purred like a kitten now. "I'm glad they finally taught me how to drive," Maura said with wry smile, "but I hate having to roll the window down in the cold weather and stick out my hand to make a turn signal."

Their road was at the top of the list for plowing, since Jim and Josh worked at the town garage. Only the roads to the naval yards were plowed before theirs. The leaves were already brilliant shades of red and orange, as winter came sooner in Maine than it did in Connecticut.

The turn of seasons fascinated all the cats, even Lucky. Molly sat under the maple for the longest time watching leaves twirl to the ground. The torti was into everything, chasing everything and anything that moved—especially leaves that had already fallen. She was utterly confused every time a bird flew overhead and Tiggy looked up and called, "Hi, Ma!"

Cookie, Molly's self-appointed guardian, watched out for her and often prevented disaster by stepping on her fluffy, ever-moving tail. The tomcat also took on the job of washing her, something her absent mom would have done. However, now that she was older, the torti occasionally popped him in the ear when he tried to bathe her. Much to Lucky's amusement, the kitten often told him, "I'm a big girl now! I don't need your help being clean."

Molly often cuddled up to Lucky, her heroine, much to the tuxedo's consternation. Lucky definitely wasn't ready to be a mom! But Cookie was always quick to remind her of the wish she'd made during the meteor shower the summer before: Lucky had wished for another girl kitty to cozy up to. Now she had one.

Maura retrieved the icebox cake from the refrigerator, checking to make sure it had set so she could deliver it to Charlie at the diner. It was ready.

The fellows were sitting around the kitchen table, listening to the last innings of the World Series between the Yankees and Cardinals.

"Charlie needs this for the supper crowd," she said, covering the pan. She took off her apron and picked up her purse and the cake. As she went out the door, she called back to Josh, "Supper's in the oven. I won't be long. I just want to check on something there." Josh nodded and waved. He knew what she was referring to.

A movement by her feet caught her attention. Lucky had rushed outside too.

"Got a hurry call, Lucky?" she asked, smiling as she opened the car door.

To her surprise, the tuxedo jumped inside on the front seat and quickly crawled over into the back.

Maura stood there looking. "Lucky? Since when do you want to come along by yourself?"

The cat calmly washed a long white glove and did not look at her.

Maura shrugged, placed the cake on the floor, shut the door, and rounded the hood to the driver's side. As she got into the car, she murmured, "OK. But you have to stay in the car. I don't want you to tell the others about my surprise."

Lucky licked doggedly at something between two of her toes.

Maura parked, got out, and rounded the hood to the passenger side. As soon as she opened the door, Lucky leapt out and trotted quickly toward the building. Maura frowned, watching her disappear around the corner. She'd retrieve Lucky later, after she had delivered the cake and talked to Charlie about the next weekend's desserts.

When she got back to the car, she was surprised to see the tuxedo sitting there, waiting for her. Maura opened the car door, looking quizzically at Lucky. As was her wont, she addressed the cat as though she were another human. "Now, don't you ruin my surprise. I'll let things settle a while before bringing everyone over to see what you just saw." And then she repeated the latest war slogan. "Remember," she whispered, "Loose lips sink ships."

That drew a delighted chuckle from the tuxedo, which Maura mistook for gagging. All the way home, she kept glancing in the rearview mirror at the black-and-white cat in the backseat to make sure she wasn't upchucking.

# Chapter 11

## *Early Autumn 1942*

O ne morning, a couple of days after she dropped off the icebox cake, Maura needed to go to the diner again. Two lemon cakes sat cooling on the counter. She'd tried two new recipes, replacing the oil with applesauce in one cake and with mayonnaise in the other. She couldn't wait to find out which worked better. Dusting her hands on her newest apron, sewn from one of Star's colorful burlap feed bags, she was ready to deliver them.

Glancing out the kitchen window, she saw all the cats lounging on the grass under the maple tree, washing themselves. Since her ride with Lucky, she had found ways to deliver desserts without the felines tagging along. But that day, she decided she'd invite them to take a ride. "Yes," she said. "Today's a good day for all of us to go."

She was unaware of Lucky's conversation with Mickey, the Irish chipmunk. He had just told them the Night Visitor had entered Gus's barn again the previous night. This was indeed a puzzle, and it made the felines uneasy. They lived with humans who were still unaware of the visits, immersed as they were in the unsettling news of war.

"Let's go investigate Gus's barn now," Cookie said, getting up and heading that way. The others followed, with Lucky eventually taking the lead, as usual.

Arriving at the open door of the barn, they saw Gus, who had just finished milking Marilyn, the goat. He put the milking stool away and glanced at the cats quizzically as he let the goat out into the fenced-in yard. Then he headed to the house with his small bucket of milk, which he looked forward to drinking each morning. He remembered to leave the barn door ajar so the chickens could get out.

This allowed easy access for the cats, who looked around the inside. They spotted large human footprints among the variety of animal prints in the dust. "Probably the old man's and Rubin's footprints," thought Cookie.

However, the footprints in a less-traveled area around a moldy hay bale caught his attention. They were narrower and the tip was more pointed than the others were. Cookie knew that like cats' feet, people feet came in different sizes. But who wore shoes that didn't have ridges on the bottoms, like Gus's and Josh's and Jim's work boots?

He had not seen prints like these. And why would that person be drawn to that particular bale of moldy hay? He was about to investigate when he heard Maura calling.

Lucky immediately headed outside to see what she wanted, but Molly was engrossed in batting around an old goat poop.

Cookie nosed the kitten outside, minus the poop.

"When Maura calls, it's either to take us for a ride when she has an errand in town, or…" He paused to lick his lips. "She has a snack for us."

They hurried up the driveway, all in a line, their tails waving in the breeze—even little Molly's. Completely forgetting about the odd trail of footprints, Cookie hoped there would be a snack.

Maura stood on the bottom porch step, looking for them. "Come on, cats." She opened the station wagon door, and they all scrambled in. Everyone loved to go for a ride, even little Molly.

Maura placed the two yellow cakes with buttercream frosting on the floor of passenger's side, so they wouldn't move around.

Lucky meowed all the way to the diner, almost as though she was decidedly happy to go there. As she sang, Cookie kept a wary eye on her. He felt something was up. He just didn't know what…

Tiggy was happy. He loved to sit in the car while Maura dropped off desserts, sniffing all the delightful smells drifting from the diner, as she always cracked open the window while she was inside. The marmalade certainly loved his food! Molly just loved adventure, whatever it was!

"Stay here for a moment," Maura told the cats when she picked up a cake. "I have a surprise for you! I'll be right out." She smiled at the reaction she knew would be coming from everyone but Lucky when she led them to the rear of the diner.

Molly put her paws on the window and stretched up to watch Maura make her way across the parking lot to the front door with the cake.

"What she mean?" Tiggy asked. Then he yawned and rolled over on his back. He'd find out later. Riding made him sleepy.

"She must have something special for us to eat," Cookie surmised, anxious to see what it was. This seemed logical, since they were at the diner. He decided to stay in the car so he wouldn't miss out on any unusual snack she might be bringing out for them.

"No," Lucky said with a veiled smile. "Better than food!" She closed her eyes for a moment. Then opening them, the tuxedo licked a paw with her long, rough, pink tongue.

Cookie was instantly on alert. He started to pace, waiting for Maura to return. "Now what could Lucky mean by that comment?" he muttered under his breath, casting the black-and-white cat a questioning glance. However, he knew better than to ask. She'd just say, "Wait!" as she had done many times before.

His question was answered a short while later, after Maura had delivered the second cake and opened the door to let the cats out. "Follow me!" she commanded, somehow knowing they would.

The tomcats followed her. However, for some reason, Lucky held back, letting the others go ahead. When Tiggy looked questioningly back at her, not used to being in front of her, she just smiled knowingly and ordered him to go with a swat on his backside. Which he promptly did. Little Molly pranced this way and that, unconcerned about the new order in which they walked in a line and batting at anything in her path.

Cookie led the way. A first for him. This made him uneasy; he wasn't used to being first! What did Maura want to show them? Did she expect them to catch one of the forest rats behind the diner?

As Maura peeked around the corner of the diner, Cookie hesitated. Tiggy plowed right on.

Molly, being the kitten she was, danced this way and that, staying out of everyone's way. But she stopped short and sat down on her rump upon seeing a smiling, three-legged cat standing there. Other cats were clustered behind her—cats she would soon know as Smokey, Smokey D, Grandma, Aunt Stripey, and Uncle Honey Bun.

Smokey D edged forward, grinning broadly, but waited to greet them until their leader spoke.

"Ma!" Tiggy cried joyously, running toward the scruffy, muddy-colored leader of the colony. Theresa stood proudly erect on her three legs, beaming at him. The marmalade put his head down under her chin and purred loudly as she began to give him love licks.

A flabbergasted Cookie barreled toward her. "Ma! You're here!" he cried, grinding to a halt and curving his tail in a snakelike wave with the base of his tail in a backward *C* and the top in a regular *C*, which denoted his absolute love for her. "But...how?" he sputtered. "Why?"

Theresa knew she could tell him simply that Lou had sold the restaurant and Doc had brought them up to Maine because Charlie wanted the colony cats to get rid of the rats around the diner. But that wouldn't satisfy this inquisitive son of hers.

She knew he'd want all the nitty-gritty details of the story before he'd be satisfied. "Relax, son. Let me tell it in my own way."

In the meantime, Molly stared wide-eyed at the older cat. "Where's her other leg?" she asked no one in particular.

Lucky trudged over and jumped up onto a wooden crate, which had served as the cat colony's abode behind the Beachhead Restaurant back in Connecticut. Now it was nestled in the woodpile behind the diner. "A fox ate it," she said, hoping that would have a cautionary effect on the youngster.

Maura stood off to the side, silently smiling as she watched the scene for a few minutes before going into the diner to have a cup of coffee.

"Isn't this great?" Theresa stopped washing Tiggy, who lay down beside her, purring a deep, rolling purr while she greeted her other son.

"Lou sold the restaurant!" She smiled, looking down at the purring marmalade, utterly content by her side. "He decided ta move ta New Haven, where he and Joe could help his cousin Pepe run his pizza parlor. But the Beachhead's new owner didn't want any cats hanging around, and he said ta get rid of us."

"But Ma. You're *here!* How? Why?" sputtered Cookie. He was about to burst. He still didn't understand how the colony had come to be behind the diner.

Theresa smiled again. "Wait, son. Let me tell ya in my own way."

She paused to recollect. Lucky had told her what happened, thanks to her many talents.

"First off, Maura got a call from Joe, telling her what happened. She'd sent him her new phone number, saying ta call her an' let her know the news of the colony." She scratched her head, thinking for a moment.

"When she heard the news, Maura called Dr. K right quick. Asked him ta bring us up, pretty please. Then she casually mentioned the vet here was retiring an' suggested maybe he might want ta look 'round. Sort of check out the lay of the land, ya know. Just in case he might ever decide he needed a change of scenery." She bent down to give Tiggy a lick, sending him into another torrent of rolling purrs.

"Doc saw right through the suggestion." She chuckled. "He could tell she was hopin' he'd move up here, 'cause she knew she'd need someone ta take care of us! So he agreed ta catch us an' bring us up here. Simple as that!"

Cookie frowned. He knew all this could never be as simple as that! He waited impatiently for the rest of the story to unravel.

Theresa smiled broadly. She knew her son wouldn't be satisfied until he heard the whole story. "What Maura didn't know, but Lucky sensed, was that Doc was already thinkin' of movin' his practice somewhere else. Bringin' us up here gave him a chance ta check things out. So he said yes." She sat down, throwing her arms wide open. "An' here we are! Ain't ya pleased?"

What even Lucky didn't know was that Dr. K. needed a new challenge—perhaps even learning how to treat other animals in addition to the cats and dogs he usually treated. In the back of his mind, he saw a vision of having a building where animals would stay until he found good homes for them. Of course, he knew this dream of his might never come true...

When Theresa finished her tale of how the colony got to Maine, the gray cat still wasn't satisfied. There had to be more to the tale than what she'd said. Cookie still had questions.

"Well? Ain't ya pleased?" Theresa asked again.

"Ye-s. Yes." Cookie came forward like a dutiful son and lowered his head for a wash.

"Ya'd better be!" His mom gave him a quick swat on his backside after she deigned to give him a wash.

The rest of the colony waited, watching for their leader to give them permission to greet their relatives.

"But Ma, what's going to happen when Charlie finds out?" Cookie questioned, as he still didn't have the whole picture.

Theresa knew she'd have to tell him the whole story, from the very beginning, before he'd be satisfied. He hated not knowing the whole story. "Wait, son. Lots ta tell. Let me start at the beginnin'."

So, Theresa began unraveling the entire tale to the waiting cats, starting with Lucky's visit.

"It was a warm day in the winter, before ya came an' told us ya were movin'," she said. "Lucky came an' visited us. Told us flatly not ta worry. Said ya'd tell us, come summer, that ya all were movin'. Then she said we'd follow, she wasn't exactly sure when. Only that she knew we'd be movin' up here too."

She scratched at a vicious black fly determined to get a last meal before the cold season descended upon this northland.

"Told us ta let Doc catch us real easy like. Said he, himself, would bring us up here, as he wanted ta look 'round. Said he was thinking of selling his practice and movin', ta see new stuff. But she added that we needed ta let him give us our shots before we came up here." She wrinkled her nose, remembering. "If I'd have had hands instead of paws, I would have held my nose!" The others agreed, mumbling among themselves.

"So we practically jumped into the traps an' didn't give him no guff when he gave us rabies shots." Theresa smiled, remembering Dr. K's startled reaction.

"Doc put us in two cages; three each in a cage. Drove us up here in the back of his van." She paused, remembering. "Not too bad a ride. Only made me a bit woozy, with all that swaying around. We even had a litter box an' some dry food an' water."

That made Theresa remember something else. "Lucky told me she saw a vision of the man who dropped off food for us at the Beachhead asking for our new address. He wants ta continue ta buy us food for saving his little dog, Gigantiga!"

The mention of this past episode caused a delighted chuckle to ripple through the group. The cats had saved the silly little dog from a wild, rogue fox intent on gobbling him up. Theresa laughed when she remembered how tiny he was.

"Lucky assured us that Doc would call him, once we were settled, an' let him know where ta send the food."

Theresa smiled at the tuxedo sitting on the crate, listening intensely to the proceedings.

"But Ma," Cookie persisted. "What about Charlie?"

Turning back to her gray tomcat son, Theresa continued her tale. "When Gina found out that Maura knew she needed ta move us somewhere, Gina mentioned how Charlie was complainin' 'bout the wood rats makin' holes in the back wall of the diner, where they were tryin' ta get in for the food." She paused, turning her attention to the determined fly now attacking her tail.

"So the day Joe called Maura with the news, she went right ta Charlie. Told 'im we needed a new home. Said if we could live here, he'd never have any problem with rats again. Told him how we almost ran those *big* wharf rats outta town."

She frowned, looking down again at her tail. "He still wasn't too sure. Said he was afraid some hunter would shoot us when he saw us. But Maura insisted, we'd never be seen! Told him we'd be long gone into the forest  before anyone saw us! " She jerked her head around, as the fly had just nipped her in the butt.

Theresa sat down abruptly.  The biting stopped.  She didn't know if the fly had flown away or was still underneath her. She didn't care!

She went on with her tale.  "But he still wasn't sure he wanted us here, even though Maura said we'd make short work of the rats!  He finally gave in, sensing how much Maura cared 'bout us and not wantin' her ta stop makin' desserts!"

"But Ma," Cookie demanded, "how is it you know all this?"

"Lucky told us."  Theresa smiled at the tuxedo again.  "She heard Maura tell Josh 'bout the plan. That's how she knew what was going ta happen, and that's how *we* know!"

She looked sternly at her son. "Knows things, she does.  Should listen ta her!  Great lady, she is!"

Theresa bowed her head in deference to the tuxedo, who acknowledged the compliment and bowed her head in return.

Theresa rose, pausing to look down at the dark, crumpled form of the tiny insect below her on the dirt.

"So," she continued, "these wood rats are smaller than the wharf rats in Momauguin and were gnawing on the back wall of the diner, making tiny holes. When Charlie saw we made fast work of them, he was happy.  Said we could live here as long as we wanted ta.  Maura assured him we wouldn't have any kittens and said she'd tend ta our needs and make sure we'd  keep up with our rabies shots."

She glanced around before continuing. "Charlie said he'd allow us ta live in the woodpile back here as long as no one sees us." She was glad for Lucky's abilities to overhear and understand what humans said. It made things so much clearer.

The stray cats did make sure to melt into the background whenever people they didn't know approached.  Charlie eventually relaxed when no one attempted to shoot them.

"Doc even brought up all of our crates," Theresa went on.  "We know Maura will stuff straw or old sweaters in them, come winter."

She thought for a moment and then added, "Plus, we were getting a bit tired of all that fish. Maura told us we'd eat different food here, like deer and moose."

"Big mouse?" Tiggy whispered.

"Don't know. Shh. I want to hear Ma," murmured Cookie. What he missed was the smirk that had washed over Lucky's face as a picture of a large, gray moose suddenly appeared before her.

The three-legged cat tilted her head. "Don't know what moose is, though. Something delicious, I hope." The others nodded their heads. "A new place ta live and new foods ta try."

Gina had already noticed that Charlie got various meats from the hunters who frequented the diner, and there were sometimes chunks of that meat in with the patrons' leftovers, which she always gave to the strays.

Theresa sat down and looked around her. "No rats around here now!" she said proudly, finally motioning to the others of the colony, who all came forward to greet their relatives, rubbing against them to familiarize them with their particular odors again.

Gina appeared around the corner of the restaurant then, smiling at the cluster of cats, who, by now, knew her as "the feeder." She dumped some scraps out of a small bucket onto a large platter and then went back inside to talk to Maura.

While the rest of the colony cats gobbled the goodies, the three-legged cat looked sharply at Molly, who, by now had explored most of the nooks and crannies of the woodpile and the colony's crates.

"Who's that?" Theresa demanded.

Molly, who was standing atop the woodpile, looked over her shoulder at Theresa. Unsettled, she toppled backward, landing in a heap on the ground. She jumped up quickly, whirling around to bat at a shriveled piece of orange rind.

"She's one of us, Ma. Maura rescued her up here." Cookie grinned suddenly and added, "She's a bit of a ditz, really. But likeable."

He put a paw on Molly's fluffy tail. "I want you to meet our ma," he said, gently giving her a shove. At this, Lucky leaned closer from her perch on the crate, all the better to hear.

Molly looked up with her huge owl eyes. "Hi, Ma," she said breathlessly, earning a quick wash on the head. She pranced away, purring very softly. Still, the scruffy, multicolored cat had heard her.

"She'll do," Theresa remarked with a smile.

So, even little Molly, now considered part of the family, got her share of soft chin rubs from the colony cats. Lucky sat on the crate, enjoying the reunion.

Then Theresa turned to Cookie, her expression serious. "Now that we're here, is there anything you want us to help you with?" The colony cats had helped to uncover the spy in Connecticut a summer ago.

"I'm glad you came, Ma. We do have another tricky situation here." Cookie quickly outlined what they knew about the mysterious man who visited the old barn in the middle of the night. It left a bad taste in his mouth, this coming and going of the Night Visitor. He had a feeling the man was up to no good, especially since there was a war going on. You never knew! *See something? Say something* was his new motto. He again made a mental note to examine those footprints.

"Lots of people come to the diner, especially men who work at the naval yard," Cookie told his mom. "You can be our eyes and ears. A diner is a great place to hear things, especially when people stand around in the parking lot and gab—you know how they are."

He grinned at his two gray cousins, their pointed ears topped with fluffy rows of fur. "Maybe Smokey or Smokey D can even sneak around, hide, and listen in on conversations." The two cousins leaned forward, their eyes sparkling. How they loved mysteries! Just like Cookie!

"I was also wondering if there might be spies around the naval yard." Cookie was always aware of that possibility, ever since learning that Max, the man who'd sold bait on the Connecticut shore, was really a spy.

Cookie was aware that damaged subs were repaired at the naval yard, thanks to eavesdropping on conversations between Josh and Jim. And where there were warships, there could be spies! It was as simple as that.

Smokey stopped eating and looked up. "Oh, you mean like the spy who killed Bob?"

At the mention of a murder, Molly came to attention. Stopping her investigating, she sat down, suddenly very interested in the conversation. This was unfortunate, as the delightful munchkin was young and thirsty for information. She was always rushing in where others feared to tread. Consequently, Cookie was always putting a restraining paw on her fluffy tail to hold her back. He did not want her to get any crazy ideas.

~

BY THIS TIME, Maura had discussed with Charlie the next dessert she would bake and was sipping a cup of coffee while she wrote a grocery list.

A couple of lumberjacks who worked for the paper mill came in and greeted Gina, and she hurried over, carrying a coffee pot along with two cups.

"Hi, sunshine," one man said. "Bring me the paper, will ya?"

Gina snatched the newspaper from the counter, bringing it to him, and he smiled his thank-you.

He sipped his coffee as he glanced at the headlines. Shaking his head, he leaned over to show it to his buddy, who put down his cup to read the blaring words, Third Monet Watercolor Stolen. Police Have No Leads," he said, giving the paper to his friend. "How do ya suppose, Joey, they're grabbin' these paintings 'thout someone seein' 'em? How could they walk through a museum carryin' a big framed painting 'thout someone noticin'?"

Joey shook his head. "Don't know. Maybe they just pull them out of the frame, roll 'em up, and shove 'em under a shirt. That wouldn't spoil a watercolor like it would a regular painting."

"How do ya figure that?"

"Old oil paintings might crack. They're delicate.   Watercolors aren't."

"No kiddin'." The man motioned for Gina to refill his cup. Like the good waitress that she was, Gina hustled over to refill both cups, knowing the men needed to get to work on time. She got a smile in return.

"Think it's worth much?"

Joey laughed. "Sonny, it's probably more 'an we could make in ten years."

Going to the coat tree near the door, the woodsmen retrieved their red-checkered jackets and shrugged them on. "Maybe I should take up paintin'. I'll paint trees," Sonny said. "With all the trees I've climbed ta hack off branches, I sure as heck know what a tall one looks like, smells like, and feels like." The two went out laughing and hustled down the steps to their truck.

The door closed, leaving Gina to clear the table and wait for new customers. She busied herself making a pot of coffee, thinking how much Mainers loved it and how lucky it was that Charlie—being someone who fed both townspeople and naval men—was allotted an ample supply.

She did have a fleeting fear about what they would do if they couldn't get coffee. But having known Mainers even for a short time, she had come to realize they were a hardy group, used to making their own way. No matter what obstacles lay before them they somehow made do with what they had, or devised something different.

Maura, in the meantime, had finished her coffee. She rose and said, "Going out back now to collect our crew. Are you going to feed the rest?"

"Already did," Gina said. "I'll see you at home."

Maura put on her jacket as she walked to the rear of the diner to collect the cats. The strays didn't run away, as they knew how much she did for them when they lived behind the Connecticut restaurant.

"Well, did you have a good time with your relatives?" she asked, holding the door open so the cats could hop back into the station wagon.

This question elicited a meow chorus of yeses, and when she slid into the driver's seat, Tiggy gave her a heartfelt kiss. "Yes, yes," he mewed loudly, causing Maura to smile.

"Well, I better get us all home to a warm house," she said, determined to scrounge some old sweaters for the colony until she could wheedle Josh into building something that would keep them warmer during the coming winter storms.

Even lower Maine, where they lived, was colder than Connecticut. She was sure she could persuade him to leave some of his repair jobs— such as touching up the paint on the living room walls—until spring to build a sturdier home for the colony.

# Chapter 12

### *Saturday, October 17, 1942*

The twins were helping Rubin with Gertie's newest project. She wanted fresh lettuce in the winter—she dearly loved having salad for lunch—and she'd hounded her husband to build a shed with windows all around and even on the roof. When Rubin complained the greens would freeze, she'd replied, "Well, then, put in a stove, fur heaven's sake! What's so hard 'bout that?"

She'd pestered him so much that in desperation, he'd held up his hands, deciding it was easier to build the small house to grow greens in, than listen to her complain!

"Enough, woman! Stop yar yappin'! I'll build yar damn glass house! But ya know," he'd warned her, "everyone who sees yar glass house, will think ya've lost yar marbles!"

However, being the sensible person that he was, Rubin first studied the situation, deciding to build the building as an addition to the house, so he could open a cellar window to heat it, as he really didn't want to be tied to keeping a stove fired up!

As it was the weekend, as soon as he'd fed the animals, he called on the twins to help him.

First, they built sturdy walls, nailing together a double layer of wood. Next, they fastened a double row of windows to them to minimize the cold. As a finishing touch, Rubin had a roof built with a skylight to let in some of the winter sun, deciding that would be more practical than a roof made entirely of glass.

Inside, Josh built counters to hold the plants and fashioned beds atop the counters. Then he and Rubin dug up dirt to fill them while Jim wired the building for electricity and installed a spotlight, which could be used on a cloudy day to keep the plants happy, which pleased Gertie to no end!

As the men were snugly fitting the door in position, a delighted Gertie rushed inside to call Maura. She asked her to bake some of the extra-gooey brownies that Rubin had a hankering for. Then she sent home a large dinner of roast pork, mashed potatoes, and corn chowder as a thank-you.

However, unknown to her, Rubin had given the twins some extra money for their labors, as it had taken the entire weekend to finish the job. The brothers were happy, as there was still much to repair in their farmhouse.

~

MAURA'S CANNING AND JAMMING was well underway, thanks to an early frost. And with Gertie's helpful instructions, she had just finished canning a bushel basket of tomatoes and slicing the green tomatoes to put into jars of oil. That morning, Gertie had dropped off the last of her tomatoes and some Hubbard squash. She told Maura that because of its hard exterior, the squash would last for up to six months buried in the cellar dirt.

While they were having a cup of coffee, Maude drove up.

The activity drew Cookie's attention, so he moseyed up on the porch as Maura opened the door to greet her.

As Maude climbed up the steps, holding a basket full of turnips, Maura rushed forward to take it from her. But before she could do that, Maude deposited the basket on the porch with a flourish.

"Oh, thanks, Maude," Maura said. warmly. "Elmer's daughter didn't plant any turnips."

"Morning, Maudie," Gertie greeted her, coming out on the porch to peer into the full basket. Then she straightened up and looked Maude in the eye. "Nice of ya, Maudie."

"Just doin' the neighborly thing," the older woman said and left, after declining Maura's offer of a cup of coffee.

"Neighborly thing, my eye." Gertie frowned, watching the retreating car. "Her brother Eric always plants 'em but won't eat many. Maudie's always lookin' fur someone ta give 'em ta. She hates 'em!"

Maura looked curiously down in the basket. "How do you cook them?"

"Potatoes, milk, butter, and a teaspoon of sugar. Makes 'em decent 'nough ta eat." She laughed. "Ya notice, she didn't try ta give 'em ta me!"

Maura took a deep breath as she picked up the basket of curious vegetables. She hoped her crew would like them.

She put the container under the kitchen table, where Cookie had decided to sit, hoping for a stray scrap of food. He was still hungry from breakfast. If this kept up, he might have to try some of that dratted dry cat food that the others seemed to like, even little Molly!

The tomcat peered into the basket. A memory of Lucky popped into his head, causing a slight shiver to run down his back.

In the cottage at the shore, someone had mentioned turnips in jest, and Lucky had looked up with interest. She knew about turnips all that time ago! How did she do that?

"Whatcha lookin' far, Cookie?" Gertie asked, seeing his nose in the basket. "Spies?" She laughed.

The cat looked ruefully up at her. "Of course not!" he meowed. He knew they wouldn't be in a basket. But it didn't hurt to be watchful. Didn't she realize that? He drew his head up and looked sternly at her. "You never know when a spy will pop up and try to kill you!" he meowed. He then sat down and began vigorously washing his silky, gray fur, especially under his tail to show his disdain.

Of course, Gertie didn't understand a word he said. She didn't realize that due to his experience with Max, Cookie was among the advance guard when it came to those evil fellows! Spies could be anywhere, especially with a navy yard close by.

Mulling that over, Cookie sat up suddenly. He should get Tiggy to practice the "right" thing!

He smiled, remembering how he and Tiggy had misunderstood Lucky's direction to "write" a year ago. "You never know when we might need to write another note," he thought. Cookie decided to look for some paper so the marmalade could practice writing capital letters, which he was more proficient at than lowercase letters.

Gertie pulled out a chair and sat down. Maura made a pot of tea and brought the flowered teapot and two cups to the table. She poured a cup for Gertie, mentioning how much she appreciated Maude's unexpected gift.

"Oh, that Maudie's a skinflint! Don't give away a penny 'thout expecting somethin' in return." Gertie slapped her leg, thinking of Maude. "The old biddy will definitely look fur somethin' at Christmas."

Gertie laughed at the expression on Maura's face as she sat down across the table. "Oh, old Maudie is all right," she said. "She was in WLA in the last war."

At Maura's questioning look, she added, "That's Women's Land Army." She took a sip of the tea, remembering. "Maudie lived in Aroostook County. Ya know, potata country up north. Worked the fields durin' her vacation time." She laughed at a faraway mental picture. "Even drove a tractor!"

"Why did she do it?" Maura asked. She couldn't envision the grumpy old lady being young and working the fields.

"With the men off ta war, women were needed ta grow the country's food."

"World War One?" Maura asked.

Cookie sat by their feet, absorbed in the tale. He wondered if they had also had spies during that war. Gertie looked down and chucked him under his chin when she caught him staring up at her.

This caused Lucky issued a warning hiss. Cookie blinked and quickly began to give his stomach a brisk wash.

"Yep," Gertie said. "They called it 'the war ta end all wars.' Boy, were they ever wrong!" She looked wryly into her empty cup, causing Maura to reach for the teapot and refill it.

"Now, all Maudie can do is roll bandages or knit hats fur servicemen ta put under their helmets ta keep them warm." She paused. "I'm sure she misses being out in the fields."

Maude came up a notch in Maura's estimation, and Maura vowed to bake a special dessert to give her as a Christmas gift. She also made a note never to prejudge people without knowing something about them.

Maura smiled to herself, thinking of the jars of jams and jellies she could give as gifts. They filled the shelves in the cellar, along with the newly canned tomatoes. Burlap bags filled with potatoes, onions, and garlic hung from hooks on the wall, while carrots and butternut squash nestled under the dirt in the cellar. She would put Maudie's turnips under the dirt, too. Because of their hard exterior, she now knew they'd last through the winter.

~

WHEN GERTIE LEFT, Maura found herself with time on her hands and not much to do. "Come on, cats," she called as she made her way up the stairs. "Time to explore the attic."

The cats followed—although little Molly raced ahead and sat before the closed attic door. How she loved to explore!

The door creaked as Maura opened it, and a whiff of stale air greeted them, causing Maura to fan herself before pushing forward into the clutter of old chairs, lamps, end tables, and knickknacks of a long-ago, forgotten era. Abundant dust covered everything—even the cobwebs hanging from the ceiling, which were highlighted by the sunlight streaming in the window.

Maura pushed the dust off a small vanity with a long, tall mirror across the back edge and small mirrors on either side. She might want to use it downstairs in the bedroom—or even to store the pouches she'd later fill with dried catnip for the cats' Christmas toys.

While she studied the bureau, noting that the long mirror was in pristine condition, the cats moseyed around, smelling old mouse poop here and there and even finding a dried mouse skeleton off in a corner.

"Achoo!" Lucky sneezed. Then she turned around and headed back down the stairs. "Too dusty! Too crowded!"

Cookie looked around. In the wide expanse of the room, he could only see Maura and the other cats. Maybe, he mused, Lucky meant all the boxes and stuff lying around made the attic feel crowded.

Tiggy sniffed the air. "Stuffy. Moldy."

Maura headed back down behind Lucky, having found some cloth in one of the bureau drawers. She'd wash it; maybe Gina would sew some curtains from it—or even the catnip pouches. Her sister-in-law loved to sew.

Cookie looked at the sun streaming down from the skylight. It illuminated a portion of the attic where an old chest sat. "It *is* a bit stuffy in here. It's been closed up for who knows how long," Cookie mused, catching sight of Molly poking her nose between a trunk and a box. "Could she be on the trail of a live mouse?"

Cookie meandered over to see, and Tiggy moseyed along behind him.

Suddenly, a mist floated up from the old maple chest. Cookie saw it from the corner of his eye and halted. Fear rooted him to the spot.

"What see?" Tiggy asked.

As the mist rose up toward the ceiling, the figure of a lady in a pretty, blue dress appeared. She sat on the chest, and a long, elegant, golden cat sat down beside her.

"Run!" shouted Cookie, racing for the open door with a startled Tiggy hot on his heels. They thundered down the stairs past a surprised Maura.

"What in the world now?" Maura wondered aloud as they streaked past her and disappeared around the corner at the base of the stairs. She peered after them, noticing that Molly wasn't with them. She was puzzled but decided to let the kitten stay for a while—she was certain she'd seen mouse turds. She'd simply leave the attic door ajar.

"Where Molly?" A panting Tiggy asked, once the tomcats were safe under the old couch in the living room, peering out.

"Still there," Cookie said. "But she'll run, too, when she sees what we saw!"

Upstairs in the attic, Molly did indeed spot what the tomcats had seen. "Hi," she to the lady in the whirling mist.

"Ya see me?" the woman asked in surprise.

"Sure!" Molly danced a little jig before plopping down on the dusty floor in front of the chest the lady was sitting on.

"Do you like all cats?" the torti asked, peering through the sunbeam.

"Of course!" The lady patted her lap, and Molly hopped up to sit there, only to sink down to the lid of the wooden chest. There was no lap! She purred contentedly anyway.

The golden cat looked curiously over at Molly, wondering why she wasn't afraid of them. Then, when the lady touched Molly's nose with a wispy finger, even though the torti couldn't feel it, she smiled.

"An old woman used ta come up here once in a while ta keep me company, but I haven't seen her in a long time." She sighed. "I don't know where she is now."

Molly didn't know who that could be, but she didn't want to say so. Instead, she snuggled down and listened to the lady's stories of days gone by. The woman talked of her childhood, so long ago, and how she played hopscotch and ran a large hoop around the yard.

Later, when the kitten jumped down to go to supper, the lady called after her. "Ya'll come back again, won't ya?"

Molly stopped and turned around. "Of course," she said before she ran toward the stairs and through the open doorway, which, being Molly, she would have opened wide enough to slip through had Maura forgotten to leave it ajar.

But Maura knew about Molly's attraction to closed doors. She often found the kitchen cabinets open when she went down in the morning.

The torti finally descended the stairs and crouched down to peer at the two tomcats, who had fallen asleep under the couch.

Cookie sensed a presence and opened an eye. "Are you OK?" he asked, now awake, while Tiggy reached out a tentative paw to touch Molly and make sure she was real.

"Of course I am!" Molly sat down, washing her honey-pot paw clean of a large dust bunny caught there. "Why did you run? The lady let me sit on her hope chest while she told me the most interesting tale. She said the 1860s were something called *turbulent*."

After a pause, Molly added, "She said in war-torn South, times were hard. People everywhere had their own opinions about slavery."

The kitten tilted her head, wondering what that was. Then she dislodged another dust mote from her honey-pot paw.

"The lady said men and boys in both the North and South had very strong opinions about the war and joined whichever army they believed in. She told Molly, 'My John was very adamant that everybody should be free! I remember how handsome he looked in his crisp, blue uniform with its shiny, gold buttons.'" Molly didn't understand most of what she'd just repeated, but she had keenly felt the lady's sadness.

The woman, whom the cats began calling the "Blue Lady" because of her beautiful blue dress, told Molly, "He was so proud in his new uniform, standing there before me. I gave him a lovin' hug and promised him I'd wear my blue wedding gown every day until he returned. But he never came back."

Molly had reached a tiny paw up to wipe away the tear that appeared on the woman's cheek, but the paw went right through her face.

"I still watch fur him every day and night, outta the window," the woman had said, smoothing her blue wedding gown, and Molly had purred and purred to comfort her, finally falling asleep to the woman's soft musings about life in the Maine woods long, long ago.

All of this, Molly recounted to the tomcats. Then she asked, "Why did you run? The lady told me the most interesting stories about her wonderful cat." She put a light paw on Tiggy's cheek. "He looks like you, Tiggy!"

"Cat?" Tiggy never wasted words.

"Yes." Molly sighed. "Leo really misses catching mice. You see, that used to be his job. Now, if he chases them, he runs right through them." She sighed again. "I feel sorry for him. And the lady misses people, too. She can't leave the attic, so I told her I'd visit them often. That is, if Maura leaves the door open."

Molly looked up as the two tomcats emerged from their hiding place. Tiggy stretched out on the braided rug, yawning. "You can visit them too!" she urged.

Cookie shuddered and shook his whole body. "No thanks! Ghosts and I don't get along."

Tiggy looked up. "What's *ghost*?"

Cookie batted the marmalade's ear. "What you just saw upstairs! The lady in the blue dress! Dead people! Not alive! They give me the creeps!" He bit viciously on a nail to underscore his words.

Tiggy was confused. "Blue Lady not real?" He let out a distressed *"EEEOW!"*

This caused Maura to pause in sifting dry ingredients into a bowl. She glanced over to see if Tiggy was all right. Seeing that he was, she concentrated on making a last-minute upside-down cake. Later, she planned to fry some scrambled eggs to mix in with the cats' dry crunchies. She wanted to know if the vet had been right about how to entice Cookie to eat dry food. She leaned over to smell the aromatic pot of chili now bubbling on the stove.

This was something they all liked—with the exception of the cats—as she always added extra chili powder to make it spicy. This pleased the fellows very much, although Gina always complained about it when asking for a second helping, and *that* always caused the fellows to smirk.

"Blue Lady not real," the marmalade repeated as if to convince himself.

In the meantime, Lucky had become interested in their conversation and sat up on the easy chair, her favorite resting place, listening quietly.

"No! Not real!" Cookie yowled. "And if you're smart, not like *some* cats," he said, pointedly looking at Molly, "you'll stay away! I know *I* will."

Tiggy loved having anyone's attention, so he agreed with his brother. "OK."

Then, remembering what the torti had said about the Blue Lady looking out the window day and night, Cookie inquired, "Did she happen to mention if she had seen the Night Visitor?"

Molly had found a beetle crawling across the rose-colored, braided rug and had forgotten what they were discussing.

"Molly!" Cookie put a paw across her fluffy tail to get her attention.

The kitten blinked and tore her eyes away from the bug. "What?"

Cookie huffed. "Did the lady say whether she has ever seen the Night Visitor?"

111

Tiggy waited with interest.

Cookie's big paw still lay on Molly's tail. She gave him a swat and a loud, angry, "*MEEROWWW!*" which caused Maura to stop mixing the cake batter and walk over to find out what was happening.

"Oh, there you are." She was relieved to see Molly. "I thought for a moment I'd have to keep the attic door ajar. On second thought, maybe I ought to. I could swear I saw mouse turds up there." She smiled and went back into the kitchen.

Tiggy wrinkled his nose. He didn't like stepping in mouse turds, either. Besides, they stank! Maybe he'd better stay downstairs with his two favorite women, Lucky, his ladylove; and Maura, his surrogate mom.

"Well?" said Cookie when Maura had returned to the kitchen.

"What?" the kitten replied with a huff. She was already trying to locate the black beetle again. She had forgotten what Cookie wanted.

Cookie sighed. Then he remembered he was dealing with a kitten, whose attention span was very short. "The Blue Lady!" He used Tiggy's description of her. "The window!"

"Oh." Molly smiled at him, making the tomcat shake his head at her foolishness. "I'll ask her the next time I'm there."

Tiggy rewarded her by pushing the black beetle, which he had corralled, toward her, and received a huge smile from the torti in return.

Everybody settled down, and peace descended once more on the house.

Later in the day, Jim ventured upstairs to see the attic for himself. He came down shortly and went into the kitchen, where Maura was making a coconut-cream pie for Fred, the storeowner who had held some of his last shipment of oranges for her—a fair trade for all.

"Maura," Jim said, "we need to buy some mothballs the next time we go to town. The attic is not only covered with cobwebs, but it stinks up there!"

Maura was mixing the cooked pudding with coconut. "Oh, no. We can't do that!" she said. "Molly likes it up there! She might think a mothball is a toy to play with—or even food and eat one!" Maura had spotted a small feather quilt that someone had lovingly sewed in the chest in the attic, and she planned to lay it on top for Molly to use, knowing how much the kitten enjoyed the attic. She'd leave the door ajar. When it became too cold, of course, she'd close the door for the winter. But she'd have to get Josh to install a lock because of Molly's expertise in opening kitchen-cabinet doors.

Jim looked at his sister-in-law for a moment, then shook his head. Maura sure loved those cats. Personally, he and Gina preferred dogs. They were much more predictable.

# Chapter 13

## *Friday, October 30, 1942*

Since all six cats from the colony now lived behind the diner, Gina was responsible for feeding them with food scraps. Charlie had agreed to let them live behind the building after Maura assured him that once the rats were gone, the cats would wander into the woods to hunt and only come back to the diner's woodpile to eat and sleep.

Actually, after seeing how quickly they solved his rat problem, he was happy to have them. His only worry was that a customer would see them and try to shoot them.

But Gina, sensing the kindness of the woodsmen, convinced him that would never happen. "They're powder puffs in disguise," she said. "Once they find out the cats work here and they were brought all the way from Connecticut for the job, they'll respect them." And one thing she'd found out quickly was that in a town as small as Cumberland, a secret never stayed secret very long.

She was wiping the counter after the breakfast rush just a few days later when a big, gruff man with ruddy cheeks called to her.

"Hey, sweetcakes. How about a reorder of hot cakes? Ya know I have a tough job ahead of me, and my stomach still feels empty." He, like so many men seated around him, cut trees for the local paper mill. His red-checkered coat hung on the coat tree just inside the door. The navy men who frequented the diner had come earlier and were now gone.

Gina looked at the plate George had just cleaned. All three pancakes plus fried eggs and sausages were gone. "Where does he put it all?" she wondered, shaking her head. "Another reorder of flats, cackleberries, and some pigs," she called to Charlie. "And rush that order."

Somehow, Gina knew that George would only eat one more of each item and leave the rest. He'd seen her scraping other plates into a small bucket, causing Gina to comment that it was food for the little forest creatures. However, the leftovers were for the cats that Maura thought so much of. It was the least she could do for her sister-in-law, who fed them dry food on the days Gina didn't work.

George looked up at her as she hurried past. "Ya'll have some ta give the local wildlife," he said, winking at his companion.

He'd caught sight of a little gray cat with tufts of fur behind its pointy ears peeking around the corner of the diner one afternoon, and he knew exactly what kind of critters Gina was feeding. "Good for her," he thought, smiling. He had a kind heart, which was why he and some of the other diner patrons had begun to order extra food.

Just then, a boy rode by on a bicycle, and a comeback came to Gina's mind. "Yeah, Georgie, it's called a *re*cycle. That's what I'm doin'. I'm *re*cycling."

Gina was pleased with herself making up a new word. She smiled and did a little dance as she thought, "Wait till I tell Maura tonight about my recycling idea! She'll laugh! I know she will!"

~

MAURA DID LAUGH when Gina told her after supper as they stood at the sink, doing dishes. The twins sat at the kitchen table, reading the newspaper—Jim, the sports section, and his brother, the news, as usual. Josh shook his head after reading a headline on the front page.

"Looks like we lost the *Hornet*," he said, putting the paper down.

Tiggy, who had been dozing on the rose-colored rug, sat up and looked around nervously. "Where bee?"

"No bee, num num," Cookie admonished him. "It's a ship."

"Oh." Relieved, Tiggy lay back down.

Knowing that losing a ship was apparently a bad thing, Cookie wandered into the kitchen, the better to hear.

"Where did it go down?" Maura asked Josh.

"The Solomon Islands. They say the enemy tried to sink the *Hornet*, but it wouldn't go down. Then the Japanese tried unsuccessfully to tow the damaged ship, so our dive-bombers finally sank it. We lost 140 men, but over 2,000 were saved."

Maura sighed. "When will it ever end?"

Josh just shook his head. He had a feeling this was only a beginning.

"We now have a flying unit helping the Chinese," he commented a few minutes later.

"Where, dear?" Maura asked, elbow-deep in soapy water.

"They fly across the Himalayan Mountains, keeping the Burma Road open for supplies to get through. People call them the Flying Tigers." He got up to show her the picture of the planes.

"Painted with that open, toothy mouth, they look more like giant white sharks," Maura said.

Tiggy had been listening to the conversation with one ear. "*EEEOWWW!*" he yowled at the word *shark* and scooted under the couch with his hair standing on end. Hornets were one thing, but tigers and sharks overhead? That was too much!

His yowl brought Maura running in, wiping her soapy hands on her apron. She peeked under the couch. Seeing her, a relieved Tiggy stopped hollering. Crawling out, he erupted in a loud, rumbling purr under Maura's gentle rubbing. He even lay down on the rug and rolled over on his back so she could rub his tummy. Happily, flying tigers and sharks were forgotten. Tiggy could always count on Maura to rescue him.

Cookie shook his head grumpily at his brother's "selective hearing," as Lucky called it. If he paid attention more often, "people words" might stop flummoxing him.

# Chapter 14

## *Friday November 6, 1942*

Smokey D was lying under a bush at the corner of the diner, watching people come and go one cold November afternoon. He remembered what Cookie had said about listening to men exiting the diner, and he knew navy men on weekend leave stopped for coffee and pie before going home in the evening, if family had followed them or lived nearby. The single men among them took their evening meals there as well before going back to rented rooms. He could identify them by their uniforms.

He idly watched as a man wearing a navy-blue pea coat stopped his truck in the parking lot. He and another man stepped out of the truck. As the driver, a red-haired, red-bearded man, bent down to pull up his sock, cigarettes spilled from the pack in his pocket. He frowned at his friend, who was already climbing the steps to the diner.

"Need a hand?" the friend asked.

"No, go on in, Lon. I lost ma smokes outta the package. Order me a stack of cakes, will ya?"

Nodding, the other man opened the door and went in.

However, when the man leaned down to collect his cigarettes, his hair slid to one side. There was a strange design on his bald head.

Looking furtively around and seeing no one, he straightened the hairpiece and scooped up the wayward cigarettes.

Then he hurried inside after his companion, leaving a curious Smokey D wondering what he had just witnessed. Hair didn't just slide off. He'd observed enough humans to know that.

The little gray cat with tufted ears turned and made his way to the rear of the building, where he would tell Theresa, sure that she would tell him to report the incident to Cookie the next time he visited. Unfortunately, by the time he reached the colony's leader, he was so excited by what he had seen that he completely forgot about the strange mark he'd also spotted on the man's head…

~

THE FOLLOWING FRIDAY, Gina looked up to see one of her favorite customers walk in. She had gotten to know many of the locals, especially the men who worked for the navy and the hunters. They loved to tease her, since she teased them right back—especially the men who had huge appetites.

That evening, Mack asked her if she'd been to the Tea Room, a new place on the road to the navy yard. When she said no, he told her that his wife, a welder at the navy yard, had taken to stopping there to unwind when she finished her shift. He then pointed to the morning paper, saying, "Ya haven't been stealing artwork lately, have ya, sweetheart?"

And to Gina's surprise, he went on to read the article aloud "Police said a security guard had seen a woman touching the picture, a Degas, this time, but didn't report it because he thought she might be a little slow, and he didn't want ta embarrass her. The next day, the picture was missing."

Gina laughed and brought him a cup of coffee. "Sure, Mack. It's hanging in the john. You can look the next time you're in there!"

There was a burst of laughter in the diner, and some of the navy men called out funny jibes. In a corner booth, the red-haired man smirked into his coffee cup.

# Chapter 15

## *Saturday, November 7, 1942*

T he next morning, Gina told Maura about the Tea Room, and
Maura decided to check it out. First, however, she had things to
do. Prepping dinner was at the top of the list.
She opened the large cabinet where she kept a variety of tools and
appliances and drew out the grinder. She attached it to the table and
opened the refrigerator, pulling out a hunk of cooked corned beef. She
drained the potatoes that had been cooking on the stove, and then she
began grinding the beef and the potatoes together to make hash,
noticing that the cats were all wandering in, looking for a snack.

She got their dishes out of the cupboard and dropped a hunk of
the ground-up meat and potatoes on each one, smiling as they dove in,
making short work of the treat. Later, for supper, she'd top the fried
hash with poached eggs. It was one of Josh's favorite dinners.

Satiated, the cats wandered into the sunny living room, where they
sat around washing up—Tiggy on the braided rug, Lucky in her easy
chair, Cookie in his usual place on the old couch, and Molly atop the
new couch, where she could look out the front window.

Cookie was still embroiled in the mystery of the Night Visitor. At
his prompting, Molly had asked the Blue Lady about him, and she'd
brought back the information that the Blue Lady had indeed seen the
Night Visitor a few times. But Maura had now closed the attic door for

the duration of the winter, so Cookie's follow-up questions would have to wait. This mystery was so interesting the tomcat couldn't wait to stick his nosey claws into it...

~

RIGHT AFTER LUNCH, Maura went out to start the station wagon and turn on the heat. She let it run while she went back inside to put on a light jacket and herd the cats, who were busy washing up.

"Come on, cats. Let's go for a ride and check out the Tea Room. I'll leave the car running while I go inside." She knew the cats loved to go for a ride and wouldn't mind waiting in the car as long as it was warm and snuggly.

They drove up the road to the fork and took the route to the navy yard. Shortly thereafter, a Quonset hut came into view. You couldn't miss it. It looked like a squat, metal football with a row of small windows, including one next to the front door. Maura noted they wouldn't let in much light.

A sign painted with large, splashy, tropical flowers announced the new business in what had previously been an air raid center—until the town officials decided that it was no longer large enough to accommodate the growing population. Naval yard jobs were attracting many new people to town. The building had been for sale for a while.

Luckily for the present owner, the town had piped gas to the Quonset hut, so it was cozy and warm when Maura went inside.

A spicy, flowery aroma from candles on each small round table in the room greeted her. Pristine white tablecloths covered the tables. The chairs had round seats and doweled backs to relax against. They looked feminine, perfect for the cliental the Tea Room attracted. Fragrant candles provided the muted light in the room, while soft music backed by steel drums flowed from a shortwave radio in the corner.

The warm ambiance of the room made Maura feel at home immediately. She could see why the women who worked nearby would want to relax there before going home. She even felt comfortable standing there alone.

The thought that some people bought black-market coffee flitted through her mind. Then, she remembered that Charlie, the owner of the diner, got additional coffee rations because he served enlisted men and people who help out in the war effort.

Perhaps the owner of the Tea Room was also allowed to buy more coffee, since Gina had said most of her customers were women who worked at the naval yard. Since it was too early for the first shift to be over, the establishment was empty.

Suddenly, the long beads that separated the main room from the kitchen parted, and a very large, smiling woman wearing a flowing, flower-splashed muumuu stood there. Her wide white smile gleamed against chocolate-brown skin. "Welcome. Welcome, lady."

She indicated a nearby table and chair. "Sit. Sit." She swept her hand in the air. "What yo like? A nice pot of tea or, better still, some of me delicious rich, Jamaican coffee?" Her voice reminded Maura of slowly dripping warm caramel. She found it very soothing. "Coffee, please."

"Me get one fo' myself too and will sit and chat a while," the woman murmured.

She turned, her long dress swishing, and walked back through the beads, which made a slight tinkling sound. Maura sat on a chair reminiscent of the ones in the ice cream parlor back in Fair Haven, where they used to go after seeing a movie. It was a perfect setting for women who wanted to feel like ladies even though they were dressed in work pants.

"Put coffee on. We talk while we wait." She set a china plate filled with figs stuffed with goat cheese on the table, and she was about to sit down when she happened to look out the front window. She caught sight of little Molly standing up with her paws on the car window.

"Oh, lady," she sang in her musical voice, her dark eyes twinkling merrily. "There be a precious one in the car. Bring 'er in!" She motioned toward the wooden playpen off in a corner, which Maura had missed seeing. "Me little one would love ta see her."

Maura raised an eyebrow. To take only Molly would cause a grand commotion. "I'd love to," she said, smiling at the small child in the playpen, who was watching her and clutching an island rag doll. "But the rest would be upset if she was the only one invited in."

121

"Oh, wonderful! Bring 'em all in! We be acquainted while they keep 'er entertained!"

Maura immediately like the woman immensely, as an air of friendliness permeated the tiny shop. "I'm Maura," she said, walking to the door.

"I be Cora. It be different in Jamaica, where I come from. But hard ta say. Here, can say Cora." She smiled widely. "I call yo *Me Ma*. Easier fo' me."

Maura opened the door and went outside to get the cats. Cora went into the back room, coming out with two tiny cups of steaming-hot, thick, black, flavorful Jamaican coffee. These she put on a table near the playpen and brought the figs over. She motioned for Maura to join her there, after she'd let the cats inside.

Cora laughed delightedly when the cats stopped short upon spotting her. They were hesitant to approach her, slinking forward in the unfamiliar place. The tomcats sat down in the middle of the room, Tiggy's nose twitching at the candle aroma, and Cookie's ears swiveling back and forth at the thrum of the steel drums.

Lucky, however, went right up to Cora and stared up at her. Cora frowned, then bent down to touch the tuxedo's head.

Maura started to warn Cora against touching her, because you never know how a cat will react to a stranger, much less one like Lucky. But it was not necessary.

"This one be the one they follow," Cora said softly in her musical voice. "She has a regal, all-knowing way 'bout her."

Cookie could have sworn Lucky preened at that comment as she wound herself around Cora's legs. Then she jumped up on another chair, curled up, and drifted off to sleep.

They looked over at the playpen as they heard a cry of "Kitties!" The little girl was delighted by the cat crew, her little arms reaching out through the wooden slats in an effort to touch them.

"Me little one's introducing herself ta kitties." Cora smiled broadly. "Her name Lela. In our language, it mean 'of the mist.'" She smiled at Maura over the rim of her coffee cup. "I be a healer. Perhaps she follow in me footsteps."

Maura smiled too. She really didn't understand what Cora was trying to tell her, but it seemed the island lady was proud of it. It was only later, when Molly got hurt and Cora healed her with incense, chants, and loving hands, that Maura remembered their initial conversation.

She took a sip of the black, flavorful liquid, watching out of the corner of her eye as Tiggy crept forward and sniffed suspiciously at Lela's hands, wondering why she was in a wooden cage.

He rubbed his long body against the wooden slats. "Can't get in!" he complained, as he wanted to get close to the little girl for a pat, which he knew she'd give.

"Jump in," the baby said in a soft, musical voice so like her mother's. She looked directly at him with sea-green eyes and laughed with delight. That stopped Tiggy in his tracks.

Cookie, too, was astounded. Did the baby just understand Tiggy? Lucky also opened her eyes to look over at the playpen.

The Jamaican woman smiled indulgently, turning to Maura. "Now, yo tell me why yo come," she said.

For a fleeting instant, Maura wondered how Cora knew she was more than just a customer. However, before they had begun their conversation, a movement caught their eyes.

Molly, who, up to now, had been standing motionless just inside the door, suddenly made a mad dash forward. "Oh!" she meowed delightedly. "Small, like me!" Sliding easily between the slats, the torti climbed up on the little girl's lap, purring as she snuggled contentedly.

"Soft," the baby murmured, gently stroking the cat's dark, multicolored fur.

Cookie, by this time, had reached the playpen and poked his nose through the slats. "Watch out she doesn't hurt you!" he warned Molly.

The baby looked up from patting Molly and studied Cookie for a moment. "No hurt kitty," she said distinctly, causing Cookie to freeze on the spot.

Tiggy, who was standing beside the playpen, trying to decide how to get in, jerked his head up and stared at her in surprise, his green eyes wide. "Understand us?" Tiggy asked in amazement.

"Understand," she murmured. The baby reached through the slats to touch the thunderstruck butternut cat, whose mouth hung open.

Molly, who didn't understand people talk, tilted her head to look up at the baby.

Lucky, who most certainly did understand people talk, opened an eye and smiled. Then the tuxedo snuggled into a curled, contented position. It felt so good to be in here, out of the cold. They had heat in the car, but it wasn't so warm in the back of the station wagon, where the cats always rode.

Cookie looked around in irritation. "Close your mouth," he hissed at Tiggy, looking in the ladies' direction. "What's your name?" he demanded of the baby.

"Lela," she murmured in that soft, musical voice of hers, putting the emphasis on the long *E* vowel sound.

Cora smiled and put down her cup. She saw Maura was watching the cats' reaction to the baby talking to them.

"Me little one has special talents. Thinks she understands what animals want. Maybe," she said, laughing her musical laugh, "she does understand what they say."

Maura looked sharply at Cora, wondering if she actually believed that, because she had often wondered if the cats understood *her*.

Cookie, meanwhile, had sat down and was scratching away at his ear with a back paw. That ear was fast becoming sore again.

When Cora looked askance at Cookie, Maura reassured her. "He seems to do that now and then. But no matter how many times I comb him with the flea comb, I never find even one flea. Perhaps he only has an allergy of some sort."

"No." Cora picked up her steaming cup, taking a sip of the fragrant liquid. "Somethin' else. Will mull a bit on it. Now, tell me what yo came fo'."

"How did she know I came for more than just the coffee?" Maura wondered. She had come to see if Cora wanted to buy some of the desserts she baked and said so.

Then Cora remarked, "Oh, yo the lady who makes all those sweet nothin's at the diner."

Maura nodded and smiled shyly into her coffee. "Yes. And this is possibly the best cup of coffee I've ever tasted."

"Good. Good!" Cora beamed. "But tell me, Me Ma. Would yo ever sell some ta me fo' small price plus butter and sugar coupons? Me have extra coupons me won't need if yo bake fo' me. Yo can have dem if yo can use dem."

In response to Maura's surprised, "Yes," Cora added, "Yo is welcome ta a free cup a coffee any time yo wish."

Maura smiled broadly. She liked the name Cora preferred to call her, and she was happy with the results of her visit. They could always use some extra money for house repairs, as Elmer's daughter and husband had only used the first floor of the farmhouse, knowing it was only a temporary home for them. The second floor was in dire need of fixing, and some things still needed doing on the first floor, too. So many repairs had gone a long time without someone addressing them...

Maura took another sip of the fragrant coffee. As small as the cup was, she could only take one sip at a time of the thick, dark, liquid. Somehow, Cora saw the question in her eyes.

"Know yo want ta know how me can have so much ta sell."

Maura nodded.

"Have friend who runs skiff between islands and sells ta Boston folk and me. Buy coffee, tea, figs, and spices." She smiled. "He make good money."

Maura had heard about the black market from others.

Cora's finger ran around the edge of the saucer before she continued.

"Yo wonder how me got here."

Maura nodded. She had indeed wondered how the Jamaican woman ended up in Cumberland, Maine.

"Had banana plantation on island. When troops came and needed help fortifying island, workers left. More money doin' that."

She sighed deeply. "Can't make money with no workers." She looked over at the baby.

"When one o' them came back and demanded money ta keep baby safe, I decided time ta leave."

She smiled slyly. "Took all money from safe and put in pillowcase. Tied ta stomach, under dress. Looked fat!" She got a faraway twinkle in her eyes.

125

"Found friend with skiff. Paid good money ta leave island. He smart ta silently slip away in night when U-boats not see." She sighed deeply. "Laughs at Germans. I pray fo' him," she said, shaking her head.

"He brought us ta Boston." She tilted her head. "Got ride here with farmer Rubin, buying new plow. Told me about town selling dis building. Had just enough ta buy."

She looked around the room. "Now need more customers. Have ladies come here. Work in navy yard. Come afta' work ta relax. Have cup o' coffee, pot o' tea, and some dessert fo' they head home. They really don't wanna try and be with men at the diner. Men at work talk rough. Wanna be treated like ladies."

She was silent for a while. Then she leaned forward. "Was thinking if me had time, would like ta stir up some island stew or soup fo' 'em ta bring home so's not have ta cook. Women bring me vegetables. Take money off their bills." She smiled, thinking of her background. "Me can make good island stew!"

"Meals to go?" Maura did not think that idea would ever catch on. Women always did their own cooking—no matter how bad the meal turned out to be.

She finally rose and went outside to start the car and open the door so the cats could jump into the back. Then she went back into the Tea Room. "Come on, cats," she called. Molly reluctantly got off the little one's lap. "Will come back," the torti said.

"Good. Bring friends, too," the baby replied.

To which Cookie began to scratch his ear violently, causing Maura to sigh and shake her head. Tiggy stayed where he was next to the playpen, still trying to figure out how to get in and touch the baby.

Lucky also seemed reluctant to leave. Cora reached down and gently rubbed her fur. "Not ta worry, little one. Me always be here. Live in back room." She motioned to the doorway draped with lengths of rainbow-colored beads. Lucky stood for a moment, looking back there. Cora was standing in the front doorway, and she bent down and whispered to her, "Yo're welcome anytime."

This seemed to satisfy the tuxedo, as she turned and trotted to the car, jumping in and waiting for the others.

"Now, hurry along, me little critters, before all me warmth is gone!" Cora laughed as the butternut-striped cat stayed where he was, still trying to figure how to get inside the playpen.

"Tiggy, come on!" Maura called to the stubborn cat.

Cora saw his reluctance to leave. "Next time yo come, me tiger, will have chair on both sides so's yo can visit with me precious one." Which she did, in the future, whenever the cats visited her.

Cookie saw Tiggy smile as he swaggered out to the car. "He'll never let me forget that she called him a *tiger*!" Cookie muttered. "Ha! Next time, he might even boast he's the greatest spy catcher ever!" Cookie growled the word *spy* as he walked past Cora.

"Spies be everywhere," Cora murmured, causing Cookie to turn and look up at her. She smiled.

Cookie blinked. "Did she just understand what I said? Nah!"

Jumping into the station wagon, he hunkered down, muttering that he didn't need another person in his life like Debbie, Lucky's former housemate, who also seemed to know of things to come.

As Maura was about to close the Tea Room's door, Cora laid an arm across her shoulders.

"Wait, Me Ma. See visions. Bad happenings comin' yo place. Be careful! Very careful!"

Maura turned to look at the island woman. She smiled her thanks, not quite understanding what she had just heard. She hurried to the car, closed the back door, and climbed in.

As she drove slowly away, she wondered what Cora meant by *seeing visions*. "What did Cora mean when she said *bad happenings coming*?" she thought aloud.

Then she dismissed those thoughts, completely missing the sharp look directed her way from the tuxedo in the back seat.

# Chapter 16

### *Sunday, November 15, 1942*

Josh sat at the table, reading the morning paper. Jim sat nearby, finishing off a warm popover. "What's new, Bro?" he asked.

"Another ship went down." Josh took another sip of coffee as Jim waited for him to continue.

"Seems we lost the *Wasp*."

Fortunately, Tiggy was sleeping on the living room rug and didn't get upset over the mention of the *Wasp*, an aircraft carrier. As he tugged at an old nail sheath, the gray tomcat was glad the marmalade hadn't heard the conversation.

However, the next comment caused Tiggy to open an eye.

"The Solomon Islands are still a hot spot for fighting. Guess we were lucky Doolittle got off the *Hornet* before it sank so he could lead the bombing raid on Japan."

The mention of the *Hornet* woke Tiggy fully. He sat up, looking around. Then, finding nothing amiss, he looked into the kitchen to see if Maura was dealing with food, something he was always interested in. And finding her sitting at the table, drinking a cup of coffee and not cooking, he started to wash his expanse of white stomach fur.

And Tiggy being Tiggy, he couldn't resist saying, "Do little?" Do more!" causing a small groan to escape Cookie, which in turn drew a sharp glance from Maura. Seeing he was all right, she relaxed once again.

"Do they ever mention any kind of news besides the war?" asked Jim, taking a sip of coffee and reaching for another popover.

"Yep. Someone stole another painting. This one was by Degas, another famous watercolor painter. Don't know how they're doing it, but someone is getting pretty rich!" Josh read further down the column. "Someone saw a woman standing close to the picture, touching it. Thought she might a bit dense and didn't report it. That night, the painting went missing."

Tiggy opened an eye.

Cookie jumped up on the chair next to Josh. This was interesting! He loved solving puzzles! Nonchalantly leaning over, he peered at the picture of the guard and the woman standing near the painting. "A bit fuzzy," he muttered. "You'd think by now they could take clearer pictures."

Josh, seeing the cat leaning toward him, said, "You want a scratch, Cookie?" Which he gave him, causing the tomcat to give Josh the purr he expected. He'd seen what he'd wanted to see. "Could German spies be involved?" he wondered, and then he lay down to listen to the conversation, deciding he had too much imagination, like Gina's brothers!

"Didn't that happen before? I could swear you read that story to us a month or so ago," Jim said.

"Yep. That, I did. 'Cept this painting was stolen from a different place, an art museum in Boston," Josh said.

"Strange that it happened in two different places," Jim said.

"Hmm. Right," Josh said. "Maybe there's more to these thefts than meets the eye. I'm sure the police are investigating."

Cookie opened an eye at that remark.

Gina had just come downstairs dressed in her uniform and ready to go to work. She frowned, seeing Jim eating the popover. "Let's go." She grabbed her purse, and donning a light jacket, went out to the station wagon. Jim followed, hastily wiping the confectioner's sugar from his hands before grabbing his jacket from the peg by the door.

~

ON THE FOURTH THURSDAY in November, the day that President Roosevelt had declared Thanksgiving, Maura was in the kitchen, as usual, but today, she was preparing the special evening meal. The cats lay in a corner, out of the way, watching her every move.

The stove emitted delicious turkey aroma, as their friend Rubin had delivered a prepared bird as a thank-you for all the help the fellows had given him bringing in the hay and building the glass shed where Gertie could grow her precious greens. He'd already given them some money, which they'd used for needed repairs to their farmhouse.

Maura was especially thankful for the new cellar staircase with its sturdy railing, thanks to that extra money, as she spent a lot of time walking up and down the stairs, what with canning and washing clothes.

She still had to step around the mounds of vegetables hidden beneath the loose dirt on the floor in order to use the washing machine. Jim also had to step around vegetables to stoke the coal fireplace with the shovel with the advent of cooler weather. So, Josh was now busy constructing a walkway around the vegetables so they could easily get around in the cellar.

The smell of turkey cooking in the oven wafted toward the gray tomcat, causing a small bit of drool to drip from his mouth. The cats sat in the archway between the living room and the kitchen, having been scolded by Maura when they tried inching their way closer.

She definitely didn't want them underfoot when she was rushing around, trying to prepare the dinner, but it was too cold to shoo them outside, and she didn't have the heart to lock them in the sewing room. She'd make sure to feed them before Gertie and Rubin arrived.

The effort of being patient was exhausting Tiggy, and he had to lie down. Even Lucky had joined the group, having deserted her usual spot on the easy chair. Molly, however, had other things to occupy her attention. She was batting around a crumpled piece of paper, thanks to Maura, who had noticed that she needed something to play with.

~

MAURA MADE SURE to take care of the cats before the humans sat down at the kitchen table for the turkey dinner. Sated, the felines now reclined in the living room, vigorously washing their faces—especially the torti, who had practically dived into her share of the goodies, smearing food all over her mug.

Now, the two couples were about to dig into their dessert. "I'm so glad Roosevelt fixed it so Thanksgiving will always be on the fourth Thursday in November. Makes it easier to plan the dinner," Maura said, reaching for her glass of white wine, a delightful and unexpected present from her friend, Emma. "And that fresh salad you brought, Gertie, was delicious. Especially this time of year!"

Gertie smiled and blew a kiss to her husband, who smiled. "Maybe," he thought, "it pays to please the little woman!"

"I still can't believe the miners want $8.50 a day," Jim spouted, resurrecting a discussion he'd had with Gina. "Isn't $8.12 enough? Wish we made that much!" Jim drained his own glass of wine and then made a face. "I like beer better. But it costs too much to buy now."

"Never mind that," Josh said, holding up his shoe so Jim could see the hole in the bottom of it. "Put in a new piece of cardboard in this morning. Wish we had the eight dollars to buy a new pair. Maybe they'll give us a raise at the garage!" Both brothers laughed.

Rubin nodded, having just cut a new piece of cardboard for one of his shoes that morning.

"What's the news of the day, Bro?" Jim leaned forward, picking up a lemon bar that Maura had baked that morning. Gina frowned, but got up to get an extra one for Gertie, who'd declared that they were the best she'd even eaten. What Maura wasn't aware of was that her friend, being a no-nonsense person, hadn't much expertise in the baking department. She only cooked the basics! She'd never tasted a lemon bar before!

"They torpedoed a Norwegian tanker and sank it only sixty miles southeast of Montauk Point." Josh answered, shaking his head.

"Isn't that off Connecticut's shore?" Gina asked, leaning back in her chair. Everything had been so delicious that she'd eaten more than she usually did.

"Yep." Jim was more than glad that now they were fishing off the Maine coast rather than in Long Island Sound. They'd put *Big Blue* in a cove near the outlet of the Piscataqua River, close to the naval yard, thanks to Rubin's introduction to Tom, the man who owned the dock where lobstermen docked. Tom knew them all, having been a lobsterman himself until he went into his own business. Besides the dock, he had a small shack in the parking lot where he sold a variety of prepared foods.

"What's *torpedo?*" asked Tiggy, his sensitive ears always picking up new words.

"Big bullets." Came the gray tomcat's answer, causing the marmalade to frown.

Tiggy fervently hoped torpedoes stayed in the water and didn't come on land. He went back to washing his extra-long tail, which had given him a hard time recently. Maura had opened a bureau drawer a few days earlier. He had rubbed against her leg, wanting a quick pat, when, unexpectedly, she slammed the drawer closed, catching his tail in it. "*EEEOW!*" he'd squeaked. With his long tail caught, he couldn't move.

Maura then quickly released it and picked up the poor cat, who struggled to get down. He wasn't one to like being held, as the memory of being hauled from one house into the other, when they lived at the shore, had left a bad taste in his mouth. So Maura released him and simply leaned down to pat his head, while he licked away at his long tail, which, unfortunately, remained sore for quite a while. Since then, the marmalade always made sure to take a wide arc away from any open drawer, no matter how small it was.

"Still can't believe the Cardinals won the World Series. Sure thought the Yankees had it in the bag." Jim twirled his empty wine glass and then rose to get a glass of water, something Gina also wanted. "Isn't it great, Maura, that we now have room to have friends for dinner, instead of having to eat around that little card table?" Gina remarked, looking around at the six chairs clustered around the large mahogany table and noting that they even had room to have two more people at dinner.

"I heard Whirlaway won again," Jim said. "Got ten dollars for the Pimlico Special." He handed a glass of water to Gina and took a sip from his own glass. "Seems he's won over $638 so far. Think we can turn Star into a racehorse?"

The brothers grinned at each other, imagining the stubborn beast that would probably stop to watch the other horses running around the track! Rubin added his own chuckle, as he was well aware of Star's peculiarities.

"Or," Jim added, "would he just faint dead away at seeing the other horses?" Everyone, even the ladies, laughed at that mental picture.

After the dinner dishes were washed, everyone relaxed in the living room with cups of coffee. They listened to music on the radio and enjoyed each other's company. Maura asked Josh to remind her to put her Aunt Sue's letter in the mailbox the next day, as her aunt in Florida loved to often hear from her, being her only living relative.

Just before bedtime, Maura remembered to call Debbie, Lucky's former housemate, in Arizona, which pleased the tuxedo immensely.

~

A WEEK AND A HALF LATER on a cool, bright morning, the cats all felt a desire to be outdoors. They hadn't had much snow yet, which was unusual in Maine, even on the coast, where they now lived.

The felines all walked into the orchard, noticing that most of the apples, pears, and even leaves were absent from the trees. As was their custom, they walked in a line with their tails waving in the air. Even little Molly had hers up, wanting to emulate whatever the others were doing.

While they meandered through the orchard, the brothers were cleaning out Star's stall and checking on the cow, a new addition, thanks to some work they'd done over at Rubin's farm. They also had stocked the barn with enough bales of hay to feed the animals through the winter.

Rubin dropped in to look at Jim's wiring handiwork, something he'd just finished not too long ago. "Hi, fellas," he said. "Just came over ta check out the lights Jim said he wired inside the barn using 'lectricity from the house."

He saw the cow leaning against the horse, peacefully chewing on her cud, and smiled. Star didn't seem to be the least bit disturbed by her presence. In fact, he seemed content with her added warmth. What no one but Lucky knew was that the cow had fallen in love with the horse! She'd decided that Star was definitely a big hunk of bull!

The twins finished their chores and put pails of fresh water in front of the two animals. They'd picked up the other two pails, which had iced up during the cold night, intending to take them up to the house to defrost before bringing them down to the barn the next morning. They all left, with Josh firmly closing the door behind them.

"Bad one comin' soon," Rubin said, glancing up in the eastern sky.

The brothers both looked up, seeing only a drifting of clouds.

"A snowstorm?" Jim asked, wondering why Rubin thought so.

"Ayah. Probably a blizzard." Rubin sniffed the air. "Five or six hours away. Should start easy-like. Smart ta be like most folks 'round here and run a line from yar porch ta the barn, in case it gets real bad, sose ya can get there later on ta tend ta yar livestock."

The twins had come to respect Rubin's comments about weather changes, having helped him bring in hay throughout the summer. This was a knack that farmers hereabouts seemed to have, and Rubin was rarely wrong.

"Don't forget ta get in an extra supply of wood." Rubin looked skyward again. Sure enough, giant, white, puffball clouds were now moving in. "Could be a wicked big one, from the looks of it." He shook his head. "We're due fur one."

Josh was already trying to remember where he'd put the extra clothesline. He could always ask Maura.

"Better hustle now ta fix a line up an' bring in the wood," Rubin said. "Could last a while." He gave Josh instructions about how to fix the line, then he peered up into the thickening clouds as he walked quickly away, muttering, "Ayah. Could last *quite* a while."

"How does Rubin know a bad storm is coming?" Jim asked as he hurried up the pathway alongside his brother.

"Smelled it, I guess." Josh said. "Best to heed Rubin's words."

Jim put a hand on his twin's shoulder to stop him. "Smelled it? Are you serious?"

Josh shrugged and started up the path once more. "Guess these old Mainers have a way of understanding the weather that we don't. Probably born with it."

They saw Rubin getting into his car, driving off, apparently to rush home and take care of his own animals.

Likewise, the twins hustled off to do as he had recommended. Josh found the extra clothesline downstairs in the cellar, and he tied one end to the porch railing and nailed the other end to a two-by-four next to the barn door. That way, he'd have help finding the barn if the storm was long and severe.

He had never seen a blinding snowstorm, but he trusted his friend's advice. After all, Rubin had been born here! And Josh had recently listened to some of the old timers' stories of winters in the north country. "Perhaps," he thought, "they weren't just *tall tales*!"

Meanwhile, Jim brought in a few more loads of wood, making a huge stack on the front porch, where the logs could easily be picked up to burn in the potbellied stove in the kitchen. He found a tarp and was tucking it around and under the pile when Josh rushed up to help him.

"Good thing you hitched that old plow the town was throwing away to our tractor. We can make a pathway to the barn and clean out the driveway so we can get to work, if the storm is a bad as Rubin seems to think it might be," Josh commented. "We should also clean a path from Gus's house to his barn, so he can get in to feed the animals. We might even need to help him with that, as old as he is."

Jim nodded. "I'll go give him a hand bringing in some firewood." At the front house, Jim found Gus running a line from his porch to the corner of the barn.

After they'd finished with their tasks, both twins were more than ready to eat lunch, having worked up an appetite. As they made their way to their porch, Jim glanced up at the sky. "Now, it looks like a bunch of pillows tied together."

Josh laughed. "Doesn't look too threatening to me. Let's go eat." He opened the door.

When they shucked off their jackets, hanging them on a couple of pegs by the front door, Maura greeted them, placing sandwiches on a plate. Jim rushed in, grabbing one before slumping down on a chair.

"Did I see Rubin drive in?" Maura asked, stirring a pot of home-made cocoa on the stove. Josh walked over, sniffing the fragrant aroma while wrapping her in a warm hug. He kissed her lightly on the cheek.

He sat down, picking up the sandwich and taking a bite of it before answering. "Yes," he said. "He wanted to see about the electricity Jim wired in the barn."

He took a sip of the cocoa Maura handed to him before adding, "He also said we're finally in for a good snowstorm."

"How does he know that?" Maura asked. "How soon will it snow?"

The twins just shrugged, concentrating on devouring their sandwiches.

Suddenly, Maura put a hand to her mouth as a troubling thought came to mind. "Have you seen the cats?" She glanced out the kitchen window and then went to the living room, looking out into the front yard. No sign of the cats. But she saw a few large, white flakes floating down.

"Oh, Josh. The snow has started! And the cats aren't in!" She started for the front door, intending to put on her coat to go looking for them. But Josh got up, holding his sandwich in one hand and placing the other on her shoulder.

"I'll go." He handed her the sandwich while he pulled on his jacket. Then he grabbed the sandwich, opening the front door. "They're probably hunting in the meadow. It's their favorite spot." It was. The felines preferred to do their business there, too, even in the cool weather. Maura was aware the cats usually came back when they got too cold, so she usually didn't worry about them. But that day, she did!

Josh stuck a knitted hat on his head—something the brothers had gotten used to wearing, seeing as all the men wore them. "I'll find them and bring them back here in no time flat."

He gave Maura a quick kiss on the cheek and hurried down the porch steps. She kept the door open a moment, watching him, then shut it when a gust of wind blew swirling snow into the room.

~

THE CATS HAD NOTICED that the wind had picked up and the air had gotten colder. Tiggy, looking up at the sky, remarked, "Looks like marshmallow," picturing the white, puffy things that Maura dropped into cups of hot cocoa.

Molly put her tongue out, catching a snowflake. "It's cold!" she said, shaking the snow from her fur.

"Spritzels?" Tiggy asked, looking up.

"No, num-num," Cookie said. "Snowflakes."

Lucky had already started walking back to the farmhouse. "It's a bad one," she said, trotting more quickly across the meadow. "We'd better make a run for it."

Cookie raised an eyebrow. "What exactly do you mean by *a bad one?*" he asked suspiciously, running easily beside her. "Do you mean a blizzard?"

He'd heard Maura mention that possibility the last time it snowed, but he had never seen one, since snow usually melted quickly at the shore, where they used to live.

"Yes, that's exactly what I mean." Lucky had increased her pace to a quick run. The tomcats loped easily beside her. But poor Molly had a hard time keeping up, as the others had longer legs than she did! They reached the barn just as a gust of wind caused a whiteout, making it impossible to see the house. Luckily, Molly had caught up, and she huddled along with the rest. They bunched together against the door, until wind subsided and they could make a run for it.

In the meantime, Josh had come out to look for the cats. Jogging toward the barn and the meadow beyond, he was relieved to see them shaking and licking the snow off their fur as they stood under the roof's extension over the door. "I was wondering when you all would show up," he said, "but I knew Lucky would lead you home safely."

The tuxedo looked up at him for a moment, appreciating the compliment.

Josh picked up Molly, who purred her soft purr as he tucked her close to his body, under his jacket. Taking off at a fast trot, he found he didn't need urge the cats to follow him, as they fell in right behind him. Snow was falling heavily as they reached the front porch. Walking quickly up the steps, he held the door open for them, and a worried Maura rushed off to grab a couple of towels for drying their fur.

"Good!" Josh said, gently putting Molly down on the floor and accepting her loving lick on his hand. "You're all in."

"Where think we'd be?" Tiggy meowed.

"Meatball!" Cookie shook his head. "We could be lost in the storm." He gestured to the window. The air was thick with whiteness. "But thanks to Lucky, we made it home just in time," he said, grudgingly giving her credit.

The tuxedo smiled a Cheshire-cat grin and murmured, "Thank you." Then, after Maura had toweled her dry, jumped up on the easy chair and promptly went to sleep.

Cookie frowned, wondering for the millionth time how Lucky did it. How did she get advance notice of things? How did she know this storm was going to be bad when it had hardly started? Did she have a direct line to the universe, or whatever it was that knew things before they happened? The question was too much for him to comprehend, and he sat down, vigorously scratching behind his ear.

"Thanks goodness you're all in." Maura patted Cookie with the towel, so he'd stop scratching his ear. Tiggy could wait. He didn't mind being wet! And little Molly was already dry, she couldn't see how, until she asked Josh about it later.

Finally satisfied the felines were all safe and dry, she went back to baking, filling the air with the smell of cinnamon rolls, something they all loved, even the cats.

Due to the blizzard, the cats couldn't go outside to do their business. Luckily, the twins had driven down to the shore and put in quite a stockpile of sand. This, they dumped into the litter box in the space under the stairs, which the cats could easily get to, thanks to Josh, who had made a cat door for them. Maura showed the cats where it was and reminded them to use it. Which they grudgingly did, after finding the cat exit on the front door closed against the blowing snow.

~

LATER THAT NIGHT, Gus was standing on his front porch, preparing to relieve himself. He stood there guessing how far his whiz could go in the storm, which was now raging.

Suddenly, a car rolled silently up the snow-covered lane and parked. A man clad in dark clothes emerged, clicked on a dim flashlight, and headed toward the barn, carrying a long, slim cylinder. Oblivious to Gus standing on the porch, thanks to the blowing snow, he ignored the line attached to the corner of the building and pulled the door slowly open, slipping silently inside.

Gus watched as the stranger closed the door behind him. Puzzled, he descended the steps. He judged the snow to be six inches deep already and well over the tops of his slippers, but he ignored this fact and walked purposely toward the barn to investigate.

But before Gus got there, the dark figure emerged from the barn and confronted him. There was a scuffle. Gus's cries were swallowed up by the howling wind as he struggled with the tall figure, fighting valiantly against the long, thin fingers that closed tightly around his throat, cutting off his air supply.

Gus had been a strong man in his prime, but unfortunately, he wasn't anymore. He toppled off the pathway, into a soft mound of snow. With his last breath, Gus reached up, trying in vain to grab hold of the figure just as the fury of the storm increased. *Silence followed...*

Within minutes, the thick barrage of large, white flakes drifted over his body, concealing it. A short time later, the mound of snow became an indistinguishable part of the snowy landscape.

The tall man glanced around to see if anyone had witnessed the struggle. Spotting no one, he hurried back to his car through the swirling snow. The storm muffled the sound of the car as it drove back down the driveway, then turned onto the main road. Once there, the howling wind absorbed the sound of the heavy tire chains clanking against the pavement. Soon, the snow obliterated all tracks.

However, unnoticed by the intruder, two pair of eyes had witnessed the crime. One pair belonged to a creature huddling beneath a bush drooping under the weight of the snow, at the corner of the front barn.

The other pair watched from a small attic window in the back farmhouse, where a translucent, blue curtain wavered in the stillness of the room...

# Chapter 17

## *Sunday, December 6, 1942*

The day dawned eerily silent. The cats looked out the living room windows as Josh cleared the snow from the front porch and steps while Jim hurried to the barn to start the tractor, on which he had fastened the plow he got at work.

The left side of the plow had broken off when a snowplow driver, blinded by blowing snow, had rammed into a stone wall. Unfortunately, even though Josh had welded the blade back together several times, the plow no longer had structural integrity, and the welds didn't hold.

The foreman decided it was unfixable, and he ordered a new plow. When it arrived, he told the men to throw the old one away. Instead, Jim claimed it. Luckily, its present width was a perfect fit for the old farm tractor that Rubin had given them in payment for helping to put a new roof on his cow barn.

Soon, the tractor was putting along, clearing a path down to the barn so they could tend to the animals. Next, Jim plowed a walkway from the rear of the house to the large, covered woodpile, and one to the front barn, so Gus could feed his animals.

He continued clearing the four-foot blanket of snow, down the driveway to the plowed street beyond. As the sun beat down, a glittering crust formed over the snowy landscape.

Meanwhile, the cats ate scrambled eggs and some dry cat food, mixed with gravy. Cookie pawed out the bits of egg, leaving the rest of the mess untouched. He still refused to eat the dry cat food.

Then the cats all scrambled out the now-open cat door, only to come to an abrupt halt on the porch upon seeing the snow-covered landscape.

"Come on! Let's go to the barn!" Cookie said. "It'll be warm in there with all the bales of hay and the cow and horse providing body heat." He hurried to the front door, followed by the rest, and they waited until Maura spotted them sitting there and opened the cat door so they could all go out.

The cats felt they could have a short visit with the animals— especially since the men had finished clearing paths and come in for a quick breakfast before going back out to tend to the livestock. After breakfast, Jim would light the small wood stove in the barn and tend to Star, while Josh milked the cow. Rubin had mentioned they should look into using wood shavings from the nearby paper mill rather than hay to cover the floor of Star's stall—something they might look into, providing it could save them some money.

Once the cats were all outside on the porch, however, they hesitated, as a land of whiteness greeted them. Molly immediately jumped down to the ground and buried her face in the snow. When she came back up, she looked like a miniature snowman!

"Come on!" Cookie growled, not wanting to lose her if she suddenly decided to tunnel beneath the snow. He was well aware how easily the kitten could get into mischief! He knew he'd better keep a close eye on her.

One after the other, the felines walked slowly down the now-cleared stairs and stepped out on the pathway to the barn. First, though, Cookie wanted to walk around a bit.

"Let's visit the chickens and the goat in the front barn," he said. Although that barn belonged to the older couple who lived in the front farmhouse, the cats had discovered that they could sneak in through a broken slat in the door. They visited often, having found the animals, particularly the goat, rather entertaining.

141

Lucky, her yellow eyes growing wider and darker, sniffed the cold air for a moment before following Cookie. She quickly nudged him aside to take her usual spot as the leader.

A slight breeze arose, causing a white haze in the air. Tiggy stopped short. "Spritzels?" That was his favorite word for light snow.

Cookie sighed. "No, meatball! It's just the wind blowing the snow off the trees."

"Oh." Tiggy loped down the path after Lucky, his ladylove, making sure not to stray to the edges of the path, where brushing against the wall of snow could cause some to fall onto the pathway. He also kept a wary eye on the branches overhead that were bending under the weight of snow.

However, little Molly didn't have any snow memory to rely on. Her eyes grew wide as she looked at the mountain of snow before her. And being the inquisitive kitten that she was, she decided she'd jump to the top, where she could look down on the others. How would it feel to be taller than the rest for a change?

With a burst of speed, she raced around the adult cats, skidded, and made a huge leap, landing on the crust of the snow, which easily held her slight weight.

Cookie sighed, shook his head, and sat down to lick the snow from a paw, while keeping an eye on the kitten in case she fell in.

"Wee!" The torti shouted joyously. Standing on the edge of the snowbank, she was taller than the rest. They all looked up at her curiously as she began to dig. Burrowing away, the snow flew behind her onto the pathway.

Some of it landed on Cookie, who shook off the dusting and watched her, an amused smile on his face. "She is such a little ditz!" he thought as he closed his eyes against another barrage of flying snow.

Tiggy, unfortunately, got the brunt of it, as the snow clung to his long, butternut-striped fur. "Hey!" he meowed. "Cut out! Cut out!" He sat down and began to lick the cold flakes vigorously.

Lucky, being the leader of the group, was still walking toward the barn. Suddenly, the tuxedo stopped, as though she had heard something other than the noise everyone was making. She turned around and watched the digging, while her yellow eyes grew wider and darker.

Having brushed the snow from his face as he moved out of the line of fire, Cookie glanced over at Lucky. He grew immediately alert. Something was up! He wasn't sure what, but from the look on Lucky's face, he could tell it wasn't good.

"Come down, Molly!" he yelled, suddenly afraid for her. "Come down *now!*"

"Not yet!" came Molly's muffled cry. "I'm having too much fun!" The digging suddenly slowed, as did the shower of snow on the cats waiting on the pathway.

"Oh!" came Molly's distressed cry. "Oh my!"

Three pairs of eyes turned toward the kitten. Tiggy and Lucky were too heavy to investigate Molly's distress. But not Cookie. Thanks to the dry cat food incident last summer, he was eating less, so he weighed less and was able to jump lightly up on the crust of the snowbank. The snow was densest near the edge, where Jim's plow had thrown it. Standing next to Molly, the gray tomcat only sank down slightly.

He drew in a sharp breath as he gazed down into the hole Molly had made. Then he opened his mouth wide in a Flemish hiss. The smell of death assailed his nose.

"What is?" Tiggy demanded, standing up with his front paws on the edge of the snowbank, trying to see what they saw.

"Hand," Lucky somberly answered.

*"Hand!"* squeaked Tiggy. What on earth was a hand doing buried out here in the snow?

*"Hand!"* shouted Cookie, surprised at Molly's find. "It's a *hand!"*

He knew they should alert someone. And they needed to do it now! He gingerly backed up to the edge of the snowbank. Seeing Jim still working to clear the snow in the lane serving the two farmhouses, he said, "Bro, you need to go and get Josh or Maura! Go now! You're the only one they listen to! Go!"

A surprised Tiggy turned and headed back down the pathway to the house.

"Yell loud!" Cookie called to Tiggy's retreating form. Tiggy, entrusted with such an important message, loped on, completely forgetting the wet clumps of snow still clinging to his butternut-striped back.

Rushing up the porch steps, the marmalade burst through the cat door and came to an abrupt stop. "Where is everyone?" he wondered. He heard the radio in the kitchen and almost followed the music, knowing Maura would be there. But then he heard banging in the living room and hurried there instead. "This," Tiggy thought, "is business for a man to handle."

Sure enough, Josh was hammering a nail into a loose windowsill that had allowed snow to blow in, creating a puddle on the floor.

The marmalade screeched to a stop behind Josh and started howling. Naturally, it came out in his high-pitched squeak. "*EEEOWW!*" he said.

Josh paused in his task and looked curiously at the cat. "Why, Tiggy," he said, placing the hammer on the floor next to his empty coffee cup and reaching over to stroke the marmalade cat. "What's up? What's the matter?"

Tiggy continued to howl, running through the mudroom toward the front door, where he paused to look back at Josh.

Puzzled, Josh followed him and stood over him. Then he bent down to inspect the cat to see if he'd hurt himself. However, before Josh's could touch him, Tiggy loped off, scooting out through the cat door, where he gave another howl before descending the steps. The marmalade then sat down on his rump, waiting until he saw that Josh was following him.

"What the heck?" Josh reached for his jacket on the peg and opened the front door.

Seeing Tiggy sitting there, seemingly waiting for him, he started down the steps as the cat took off down the plowed pathway. Josh followed close behind. "Did one of the cats get stuck in the snow?" he wondered aloud.

Lucky hadn't moved from her spot on the pathway, where she sat watching Molly with great interest. She ignored her cold bottom and looked up as Josh approached.

Cookie sighed in relief. "I knew I could count on you, brother."

Tiggy beamed with pleasure at the compliment and stood up on hind legs once again, his front paws on the edge of the snowbank, trying to peer into the hole Molly had made.

Molly, full of puff at her discovery, danced around the hole, stopping to peer in from different angles.

Cookie reached a paw out to step on her tail before she fell in.

Puzzled, Josh leaned over to see what all the commotion was about. "What do you have here? A woodchuck that came out of his hole too soon and froze?"

His look of amusement turned to shock very quickly. "What the devil! It's a *hand*!"

"A hand?" Cookie said.

"*A hand! A hand!*" Molly twirled away, pleased with her discovery. "I found a *hand!*"

Cookie stood by solemnly. He knew that with a *hand* came a *body*!

Josh knew too. But whose body could be buried there? he wondered. He gulped and pushed his hand through his hair, now covered with snow that was blowing off the trees.

"Stay here!" he ordered the cats. "Don't move till I call the police and find a shovel." He raced away, never once wondering why he'd said that to a bunch of cats who couldn't understand him.

He returned shortly with a shovel and called to Jim, who had stopped the tractor to see what everyone was looking at.

Once Josh told him about seeing the hand and started to shovel a pathway to the body, Jim shooed the cats toward the front of the barn, out of the wind. There, they all huddled together, watching the scene unfold, as the whine of a police siren filled the air.

Soon, the sheriff and his deputy arrived. Taking the shovel from Josh, he began cautiously clearing the snow from the body.

"Why, it's old man Nester wearing only his long johns. What's he doing out here, lying dead in the snow?" the sheriff said. He turned to his deputy. "Go in the house and call the coroner. And fetch Alice. Pronto!"

But by this time, Alice had come out on the porch to see what all the commotion was about. She figured her husband had already dressed and was in the barn, feeding the chickens and milking the goat.

She came slowly down the pathway clad only in her nightgown and a knitted shawl, which she clutched tightly against the cold. Josh started up the pathway to help her, but she held up her hand to stop him. She liked being independent, as old as she was. Coming closer, she spotted her husband. A look of horror spread over her face when she pushed through the snow to her husband's body. As she stood there, stunned, Josh put his arm around her.

The sheriff bent to pick up a slipper lying next to the body. "Looks like Gus heard something in the barn and went out ta check on it," the sheriff said. "Here's his slipper."

He knelt to look at the body again. "Don't know what happened. Gus was old. Maybe he had a heart attack." He straightened up, looking down the main road. "But we'll know later, once the coroner checks into it."

"Gus always went out ta the porch at night ta practice shootin' his whiz over the railing, just like when he was a fireman," murmured Alice, now gathering her wits about her.

She took a deep breath and drew herself up like the tough old Mainer she was. Somehow, life must go on, no matter what. She knew the sheriff would want to question her later.

After a while, she'd have to decide what she was going to do. For instance, how would she be able to stay in that big, old house by herself? "Been here since we married," she murmured, sniffling as a tear rolled down her cheek.

Then, turning, she hobbled back toward the house to brew herself a comforting cup of tea, shrugging off Josh's offer of aid. It was time to move on.

"Yep," the sheriff remarked, leaning on the shovel as he waited for the coroner to arrive. "Old Gus was always the first one ta grab a hose and aim it atta fire." The sheriff was also a former fireman, having worked for years with Gus.

"I'll check out the barn," Jim said, walking away. Josh called to the cats to go back to the farmhouse with him and get out of everyone's way.

"Wait a bit, and I'll go with ya," the sheriff said to Jim as he turned to see the coroner's car coming up the driveway. "I wanna look around." He had a short conversation with the coroner and the two men who came along to help carry Gus's body away. Then he told his deputy to stay there while he accompanied Jim to the barn.

The men were halfway to the barn when Alice turned back and called, "Jim, please milk Marilyn and feed the chickens fur me!" As soon as they took away her husband's body, she'd have to think about what to do with those animals.

Josh picked up little Molly and held her next to his chest as he herded the other cats past the men gathered where the snow had been cleared away and hurried back to the farmhouse. He walked to the porch, where he put Molly down as he waited for the others to catch up before opening the door.

"I found it! I found it," Molly sang in her tiny voice, once they were all in the house. She puffed out her chest and wound around Josh's legs for an appreciative rub, which he gave her, chucking her under the chin.

"So, it was you, my little marbled beauty, who found the body!" he commented, smiling.

Though Molly didn't understand what he said, she thought it must be a compliment, judging by the tone of his voice. She purred and purred when gave her an appreciative squeeze. However, unfortunately or fortunately, although she sang with the vigor of youth, she had a tiny voice that matched her tiny body, and in order to hear it, you had to bend down and place an ear close to her.

"Braggart!" Cookie said. It baffled him that Molly could understand the Blue Lady when she spoke but not people like Maura and Josh—unless maybe the Blue Lady wasn't a people anymore? But secretly, Cookie was proud of Molly. She fit right in with the rest of the crew who had solved the mysterious killing in Connecticut. Molly would be an asset to the investigation if ever another crime took place or a spy appeared.

"*Cats Incorporated*," Cookie mused. "That's what I'd call us. We cats did solve a murder and find the spies who did it. But I guess we don't have a mystery to look into if Gus died from a heart attack."

Luckily, he missed the sharp look from the black-and-white cat, who for some reason, always seemed to know more than he gave her credit for.

"We do have the mystery of the Night Visitor to work on, however," Cookie mused. "But maybe I should think of a different name for the agency—a name without *cats* in it. People might not take us seriously with a name like that.

"Perhaps Tiggy will have a good idea," he thought. Then, shaking off that absurd thought, Cookie changed his mind. "No, Tiggy is too much of a meatball."

He didn't dare ask Lucky. She'd laugh at him and his idea of a detective agency. "Oh well," he decided. "The right name will come to me in good time. Some thoughts just take a while."

Maura was already in the living room, having heard the police siren, and was kneeling on the couch's bolster to look out the front window. She looked up as Josh came inside to take off his galoshes. He shook the snow from his coat and hat, hanging them up in the mudroom, as he told Maura what they had discovered, giving credit to the cats as he did so.

In the meantime, the cats washed up, then visited the litter box. All the excitement made it necessary for them to relieve themselves. Then they jumped up on the couch's bolster to peer out, watching as the sheriff and his deputy scoured the area around Alice and Gus's farmhouse and barn, finding nothing unusual.

They left with no more information than they had when they arrived, puzzled as to how Gus had ended up dead in the snow.

~

JIM HAD TAKEN CARE of the animals, and Alice was grateful for his help. She urged him to take the chickens and goat to his barn, as she wouldn't be able to tend to them.

Jim reluctantly agreed to do so after trying to pay her for them. She refused to take money, saying she was just happy to know they'd be taken care of.

Later, after the coroner took the body away to determine how Gus had died, the twins, along with the nosy cats, walked down to Gus's barn again, this time to take the animals to their own barn.

Unfortunately, Jim didn't have much knowledge about the ways of chickens. He opened the door and tried shooing them out, expecting them to walk peacefully down the pathway past the watching cats. However, the chickens stopped short upon seeing the blanket of white covering the landscape. They began to pick at nonexistent insects on the barn floor in front of the door.

Jim shook his head and grabbed a shovel. "Get!" he yelled, shoving the chickens outside with it. He never expected what happened next.

Immediately, the birds took flight. Jim gaped, while Josh, who was leading the goat, stopped abruptly behind him, seeing feathers and chickens flying everywhere. The birds landed on the snowbanks, taking immediately flight once more, completely muddled and squawking incessantly.

Jim dropped the shovel and ran after them, shouting, only to trip and fall face first into the snow! Feathers floated down around him as he struggled to get up, spitting out a mouthful of snow.

The commotion drew Maura outdoors. She stood on the porch, leaning over the railing. "Oh, my goodness!" she cried, laughing at the ridiculous sight, which added to the uproar.

The chaos so unnerved Tiggy that he opened his mouth wide, and a huge howl erupted. *"EEEOW! Enough! Stop!"* he meowed in his high-pitched squeal.

Immediately, the fowls' flying and flopping ceased. They looked over at Tiggy.

Lucky looked on with great interest to see what would happen next. She didn't have long to wait.

To everyone's amazement, the hens made their way to the edge of the snowbanks. One by one, they jumped lightly down on the cleared path and walked toward to the marmalade, where, clucking contentedly, they milled around him.

"Do they think he's a rooster?" Cookie meowed to Lucky, who simply smiled in response. Molly sat next to her, watching the scene, her sea-green eyes as wide as saucers.

Satisfied that he'd stopped the chaos, Tiggy turned, and with a line of contentedly clucking chickens trailing him, marched smartly down the pathway to the barn in the rear. There, the marmalade led the clucking hens through the open doorway.

He loped in and sat down on his haunches, watching the chickens make themselves at home. Some flew up to find new nests in the sweet-smelling hay. Others pecked away at the tray of chicken mash Jim delivered, happily filling their bellies.

Jim looked around in amazement! "Well, Tigs," he said, leaning down to give the cat a rub, "who knew you were going to be our own Pied Piper?"

He didn't quite understand why the chickens had acted that way until he talked to Alice about it. She just scratched her head at his ignorance. "Everyone knows those stupid clucks hate ta get their feet cold. They never walk out in the snow!"

Josh came in after Jim, leading the goat, with Lucky and Cookie trailing.

Maura also walked in, holding the kitten, who had a habit of wandering, and smiled at Tiggy. She shook her head as she bent to rub his back, sending the marmalade into a series of loud purrs, which increased in volume when Cookie came over to rub against his brother's cheek. "Great going, Sherlock," he said.

Even though Tiggy didn't know who Sherlock was, compliments from his brother were few and far between, and he purred longer—especially when his ladylove gave him a quick kiss in passing.

Tiggy was the hero of the day, and his accomplishment was happily recounted to every visitor to the house. Even Maura's friend, Emma, hearing the story the next day, congratulated him with a quick rub under the chin. This was something she rarely did, for she'd been bitten by a friend's dog when she was a child and shied away from all animals, even the kitten.

Eventually, though, she grew to like the cats, thanks to Tiggy's and Molly's loving natures, and she even brought cat treats whenever she visited, making her one of their favorite Mainers.

Maura was well aware that her wishes had all come true since they'd moved to Maine. She had a house of her own, where all the cats could live with her. She had a vegetable garden and fruit trees. Now, though she was sad that Gus had died, she had chickens to complete the list. Sometimes, she decided, wishes do come true.

# Chapter 18

## *Monday, December 7, 1942*

The next day found the sheriff knocking on the door. Maura let him in. "The fellows are at work, Sheriff. Come in and have a hot cup of coffee and some sugar buns I just baked."
The sheriff smiled, taking off his jacket and hanging it on one of the pegs by the front door. Sitting at the kitchen table, he gratefully accepted a cup of coffee, taking a long sip of it as Maura sat down opposite him with a plate of warm sugar buns.

The cats were all lounging in the living room, having had their morning run and snack. Washing his paw, Cookie looked curiously at the uniformed man sipping nervously at his coffee as though debating what to say. The cat flicked an ear in his direction. "What," he wondered, "is the sheriff doing here again? Didn't he look around the place yesterday?"

Putting his cup down, the sheriff hesitated, almost as though he regretted what he was about to say. "The coroner's report just came back," he said. "Gus was strangled."

Maura gasped.

"He was murdered," he added.

Cookie was instantly alert. A murder! There was a mystery to solve! He scratched his ear as he puzzled over what he was hearing.

"Oh, my goodness!" Maura cried. "Who on earth would want to do such a thing? Gus wouldn't hurt a flea." She glanced ruefully at Cookie, who was scratching his ear.

"That's what's so strange," the sheriff said. He took a bite of the steaming sugar bun Maura had just removed from the oven, murmuring, "Ahh," and making a mental note to ask Maura if she'd bake some for the deputies at work. They would sure like that! "Even Alice told me there wasn't a soul who didn't like Gus," he said.

They talked for a while, after which the sheriff left to look around the front house again for clues he might have missed,

Now, Cookie was certain he should activate *Cats Incorporated*, which is what he would call the feline detective agency after all. When they began to solve mysteries, people would take them seriously.

He needed to go to the diner to enlist the aid of his relatives in finding Gus's killer. They had helped solve the mystery back home in Connecticut, and he knew he could count on them here.

~

COOKIE GOT HIS WISH a week later, when a warm front came through, prompting Maura to take the cats to visit their relatives.

Someone had cleared a path from the parking lot around to the back of the diner, and Gina used it to feed the cat colony. As soon as Maura opened the car door, Cookie was off like a flash, racing to the rear of the restaurant. "Must have a hurry call," Maura said, walking up the diner's steps.

Soon, the gray cat was talking earnestly to his mom about the new mystery.

"So, Ma," he said. "As long as you're listening for clues about the Night Visitor, you need to keep an ear out for clues about who would want to kill Gus."

His mom gave him a loving lick. She could tell that he was all jazzed up about this new mystery.

When Maura came out to gather the cats up again, Tiggy rushed forward to grab his loving lick before they had to leave. With the weather, who knew when they'd be able to visit the colony cats again.

~

AT HOME, MAURA let the cats out of the car and decided to let them roam a bit. The snow was slow to melt, but the temperature wasn't bitterly cold. Jim had cleared paths so they could run around outside, and as soon as they moved Star to the back barn, Josh had made a cat entrance in the barn door, knowing the cats would want to visit— because just like Maura, they were a curious lot.

Presently, the felines made a beeline for the barn. As soon as their eyes adjusted to the semidark interior, Cookie saw Lucky jump up on a sweet-smelling bale of hay. The goat was blatting at them, and Lucky studied the animal with her head cocked to one side.

"Marilyn's a funny name for a goat," Cookie remarked, getting a sharp look from the tuxedo.

"Billie's her real name," Lucky said. "Her name is Billie."

Cookie just stared at the tuxedo. He would like to ask her how she knew that, but she would probably say the goat had told her! He hated it when she had all the answers!

Tiggy stayed close to his brother. Since his success herding the chickens, Tiggy had been fascinated by them. One day, however, he went too close to a hen who was busy laying an egg. Unfortunately, the indignant hen pecked him on the paw for being so curious. From then on, the marmalade watched the chickens from a safe distance away.

The goat blatted once more in Lucky's direction.

"What say?" Tiggy asked, perfectly comfortable with the tuxedo's ability to talk to various animals.

"Yes. What did she say?" Cookie mumbled. He'd only recently come to grips with Lucky's talent for understanding what other animals said. This time, her reply floored him.

"Billie said she saw the Night Visitor come into the barn the night Gus died."

Cookie stared at her. It didn't take too much imagination to connect the dots. Could the Night Visitor be Gus's killer?

The gray tomcat wasn't aware of any witnesses to the terrible crime. It was all still a giant puzzle to him. Why would anyone kill a poor, defenseless, old man?

But given this new tidbit of information, Cooke knew it was time for Tiggy to practice writing letters with his dexterous double paws. The gray tomcat vowed to find some paper for that task. He had already kicked one of Maura's pencils under the couch for safekeeping.

Back in Connecticut, they'd used Tiggy's talent for penmanship to write a note to Uncle Jack, who was a local police officer, naming the man who'd killed their friend Bob. Cookie had pointed to letters while Tiggy practiced writing them until they had the words they needed for the note, much to Lucky's approval. They discovered the marmalade had better success writing capital letters; lowercase letters were more difficult for him.

A piece of the new puzzle had just fallen into place. It was time for *Cats Incorporated* to swing into action again. When they solved Gus's murder, Cookie would figure out some way to give a note to the police. Too bad Maura's uncle wasn't part of the police force here, like he was in Connecticut.

# Chapter 19

## *Saturday, December 19, 1942*

As Maura looked out the front window, she noticed a figure wobbling up the driveway. "Josh, go help Alice. She's headed here and looks like she might need help walking." Like Gertie and Emma, the family had been helping Alice with whatever she needed since Gus died. Maura had taken coffee cake or muffins over many times, and each time, Alice had tried to give her some of her household furnishings. Maura had finally selected an old, oval mirror with gold edging, and she'd hung it in the hall, where Gina, in particular, could check her appearance before going out.

Josh rose, taking his jacket off the peg and shrugging it on as he went outside to meet the old woman and help her up the steps.

Once Alice was inside, sitting at the kitchen table with a cup of hot tea and a piece of warm, apple coffee cake, she got right to the point. "Just wanted ya ta be the first ta know," she said. "I'm movin' out. No sense in staying in that big, old house all alone."

She took a bite of the cake, smiling at its taste. "Delicious." Then, sighing, she pointed out the front window, where a car had just driven up. A man got out, holding a FOR SALE sign, which he proceeded to hammer into the frozen ground.

"Gonna live with ma niece in Portland," Alice said. "She has a big house, so it's gonna be OK."

Maura would be sad to see Alice go, but she agreed with her decision. When Alice got up to leave, Maura asked Josh to walk her home.

After they left, the phone rang. "Hello, Uncle Jack!" Maura loved to hear from him, as she missed his visits.

Jack had called to say he'd be retiring from the police force the first of the year, stating he'd put in his time and was ready for something new.

Before she hung up, Maura offhandedly mentioned that Alice was putting the front house on the market. She wished Uncle Jack and her aunt would move up to Maine, so she'd see them again. "It would certainly be nice," she thought.

Sighing deeply, she went back to washing dishes. "If wishes were fishes…"

On the rose-colored rug where he was dozing in a spot of sunlight, Tiggy licked his lips at the mention of fishes.

~

THE NEXT DAY, Maura announced that she'd be running a chocolate pie to the diner, and the cats were welcome to ride with her. The sky was cloudy, but there was a slightly warmer feel to the air. They were delighted to scoot behind the building for a fast visit with their relatives while Maura went inside with the pie to find out what desserts Charlie required before he shut down for the holiday. The diner was open every day of the year except Christmas and New Year's Day, something the townspeople appreciated. He even cooked turkeys on Thanksgiving for those left behind by the war effort.

The cats hustled down the pathway, which was almost devoid of snow; the sun had melted it. But Cookie had heard Josh and Jim say there would be more snowstorms. "Who knows when we will see Ma next?" the gray tomcat said, eager to know if his relatives had discovered any information on the Night Visitor.

Behind the diner, the colony exited the new dwelling Josh had made for them against the building, where warmth seeped out of the tiny holes gnawed by wood rats. The colony cats were proud no new holes had been chewed since they arrived.

Theresa hobbled on her three legs into the clearing Gina had made for them so they could easily eat from their bowls. "Hello, everybody!" she greeted them.

Lucky drew back diplomatically so the tomcats could talk with their mother. However, Molly, being Molly, decided to investigate the new dwelling, and slid inside the door, only to encounter a sleeping Grandma. The old cat woke up when the torti nosed her cheek to see if she was all right, and she gave the kitten a light lick on her soft coat. Satisfied that all was well, Molly slid out again to listen to the conversation.

When Cookie asked if the outdoor cats had any news, Smokey D. excitedly came forward to tell him about the red-bearded man's hair slipping to one side.

Unfortunately, just as Cookie tried to make sense of that story, Maura appeared around the corner of the diner carrying a plate. "Come on, cats!"

The cats smelled bacon and rushed toward her, Cookie vowing to ask his ma about sliding hair the next time they visited. But as they hurried after Maura, he forgot all about Smokey D's news. And by the time he was eating the bacon scraps she laid out on the ground next to the car, he had forgotten to remember to talk to his ma.

~

WINTER DRAGGED ON. There was, indeed, more snow, and with each new layer to the white blanket covering the earth, the cats—Cookie especially—felt more constrained.

Josh had learned to milk the goat. However, nobody wanted to try to drink the strong-flavored milk. He hated to waste it, so he gave all the creamy liquid to the cats, who very quickly acquired a taste for it. Similarly, the humans had sampled the gift of turnips from Maude and discovered they didn't like them. To their amusement, however, the goat found them very tasty.

Lucky occasionally joined the tomcats in the barn, venturing from her usual spot on the easy chair to watch in amusement the doings of the barn dwellers. She would perch on a fresh-smelling hay bale, from which she could pay attention to any animal that uttered a noise.

The only unhappy animal at the farm was the snowshoe hare, whose snack of clover was gone. His fur was completely white now to blend in with snowy landscape. With all the action going on in the vicinity of the barn, due to Gus's death, the hare had decided to move to the meadow and had taken up residence under an old door leaning against a black cherry tree, which offered him shelter as well as a spot to tunnel under the snow to nibble on scrub grass and bark.

Even his relative, Mickey, the chipmunk, had gone underground into the cozy den filled with grassy weeds he'd gathered for his little family.

As for the attic, shortly before the blizzard, Maura had firmly closed the attic door, commenting to the cats, "There's not enough heat to go up that far." She even had Josh install a lock to deter Molly, who had a penchant for opening doors. The adult cats weren't interested in going to the attic, but poor Molly was disappointed to lose access to her friend, the Blue Lady. She spent a good deal of time on the back of the living room couch, looking out the window and wondering how the Blue Lady was.

~

IT WAS MONDAY December 21, the shortest day of the year. Maura had just finished baking scones for the Tea Room and cranberry muffins for the diner when she decided to go up to the attic to look for cloth that Gina could make into little pouches for the cats' catnip Christmas presents. She also needed fabric to make curtains for the upstairs rooms and thought there might be some in the old chest. She planned to knit scarves for both fellows—blue for Josh and green for Jim—and she had just knitted a cute red hat for Gina to match her red boots.

Molly tried to follow her up the stairs, but Maura shooed her away. The torti joined the tomcats in the living room. They had enjoyed a quick run outside and a visit with the animals in the barn. All this activity had tired them out, and they were now preparing to take a nice nap after a good bath. They loved to keep their coats gleaming.

Lucky saw Molly's ears droop in disappointment and made room for her on the easy chair. After a quick wash, the torti snuggled in and closed her eyes, but the tuxedo kept her eyes on the stairway, as though waiting for something.

~

IN THE MEANTIME, Maura pushed cobwebs away as she moved to the wooden chest in the musty attic. She had already seen to it that Josh and Jim carried the one item she desired downstairs. It was an old vanity—two bureaus, one on either side of a knee well, connected by a tabletop with a lovely old mirror mounted behind it. She had installed it in her bedroom, along with a chair with a needlepointed seat, so she could sit in front of the mirror. She delighted in the old piece of feminine furniture. She would muse about the women who had used it over the years when she sat there every morning, combing her hair.

Now, she opened the chest, finding an album containing old black-and-white pictures atop an elegant, blue dress with yellowed lace ringing the collar and wrists. It looked special. She sighed, wondering whom it had belonged to long ago.

Maura looked around for discarded curtains, which she found in a box in a corner. They didn't look too old, and once she washed them, they would probably look like new material.

Tucking the album and curtains under one arm and leaving the dress in the chest, she closed the lid and descended the stairs. Walking into the living room, Maura dropped the curtains on one of the couches and sat down on the other, next to Cookie. He opened a sleepy eye and became instantly alert when she opened the album. There, on the first page was a black-and-white photograph of a woman wearing a fancy dress with a lace collar and cuffs and holding a large, elegant cat on her lap.

"Look, Tiggy," Maura said, holding the book open to the marmalade, who was stretched out in his favorite spot on the braided, rose-colored rug.

"Looks like me," Tiggy said.

Molly trotted over and peered down at the photo. "Yes, his name is Leo, and he is golden like you," she meowed softly, gently touching the picture with her paw, which caused Cookie to look up at her sharply.

"How know?" Tiggy demanded.

159

"Because she told me so." Molly smiled, continuing to gaze at the photograph. "And that's her wedding dress."

Cookie frowned and immediately began to scratch his ear vigorously, causing Maura to look up at him. "Must find that flea comb before we're infested with fleas," she said. "It's funny, though. I never seem to find any." Cookie immediately stopped scratching and sighed when Lucky smirked at him. Would Maura never learn that he scratches in response to hearing something unusual or upsetting?

Cookie put his head down on his paws when Maura got up to look for the flea comb. But Tiggy grinned. He'd line up to get his share of combing, because it sure felt good!

However, she came back empty-handed and sat down once more. Placing the photograph album next to her on the couch, Maura moved the pillow behind her. She retrieved her knitting and went to work on the scarf she was making for Josh for Christmas. This, she could only do when he was off at work. She had to work fast, though, because she planned to make one for Jim, too. She'd been the lucky recipient of Emma's old yarn when Emma was cleaning house.

Her friend had taught her how to knit in return for her help on the quilt that ladies of the sewing circle would soon auction off at the church's Christmas bazaar. Now, whenever Emma came to visit, the two would sit together knitting while they talked, Emma making small caps for children and Maura working on a larger hat.

For practice, Maura had knitted some small blankets, including one for Molly, which she'd put on the chest in the attic when she finally opened the door. She felt sure the cats wouldn't mind all the dropped stitches.

Later that day, Maura washed the old curtains she had found in the attic and left them on the sewing machine for Gina to make the little pouches that she would fill at the last minute with the dried catnip hanging from the clothesline in the cellar.

Then she decided which jars of jam and jelly and wine she would give to whom, wrapping everything in the colored, Sunday funny papers she'd been saving for just that purpose. Oh, and she must remind Jim and Josh to cut a fir tree on Rubin's land, as he had offered to give them one. Rubin was a wonderful neighbor. The twins normally tended to the animals in the morning before they went to work and when they came home. But Rubin pitched in when they worked longer hours during snowstorms.

Christmas was bearing down on them, and Maura still needed to make time to cut out figures from the cardboard she'd gotten from the store. She'd already put aside a box of tinfoil to cover them with, and she'd bought popcorn to cook and string for the tree. She'd enlist Gina's help with that. Plus, she'd already asked Gertie for some of her daughter's construction paper. She'd cut strips and glue the ends together to make a chain of colorful rings to drape around the tree. If they made a long enough chain, she thought, they could use some of it to decorate other rooms, too.

Maura wrote a long letter to Adele, Gina's mother, and one to her Aunt Sue in Florida. Plus, she made sure to mail the promised photos of Lucky to her friend, Debbie. And, of course, she baked and baked for the holidays.

Maura loved baking all kinds of Christmas cookies and topping them with sweet, bright-colored frosting, which was possible, thanks to the sugar coupons her friends had given to her. However, noticing how quickly a plate of frosted cookies would disappear when Jim was around, Maura took to hiding them in the old wooden icebox sitting next to the cellar door. Fortunately, Jim never discovered that hiding place.

~

SNOW FELL LIGHTLY on Christmas Eve, refreshing the coating already on the ground. Earlier, when the cats had gone outside to do their business and visit with their new barn friends, they'd noticed footprints in the new snow, crossing the driveway leading toward Gus's old barn and then away from it.

However, before they could investigate, Josh and Jim caught their attention by dragging a large, newly cut fir tree to the house. They were home early that afternoon, having only a half day of work. Once on the porch, they shook the tree to dislodge the snow clinging to its branches.

161

The cats loped across the melting snow, interested to see why a tree was going into the house and completely forgetting to investigate the new set of prints.

Maura held the door open for the fellows and then, noticing the trailing cats, kept it open for them too.

The fellows stopped by the front door in the mud room and leaned the tree against the wall while they unfastened the hooks on their galoshes and tugged them off. Galoshes—boots they could slip over their shoes to keep them dry—were something all Mainers wore in the deep snow. Then, grabbing hold of the tree, everyone, even the cats, trooped into the living room.

Gina peered in from kitchen table, where she was busily smoothing tinfoil over cut-out cardboard decorations. She got up and moved over to watch as the twins stuck the tree's trunk into a bucket of water instead of nailing a wooden $X$ to the bottom.

Rubin said this would keep the needles from falling off longer, and they were willing to try that helpful hint. "Maybe these Mainers know something we don't," Jim said.

While the cats licked the snow from their paws on the living room floor, Gina, Josh, and Jim decorated the fir tree. Much to Gina's delight, it was ten feet tall and had plenty of branches to decorate.

First, they draped long strings of construction-paper rings around the tree. Next, they added strings of cranberries and popcorn and hung a handful of tinfoil-covered decorations. The older cats, who were especially fascinated by the tinsel, were content to watch. But Molly wanted a more active role and periodically got under everybody's feet.

Maura was busy in the kitchen, stirring hot cocoa on the stove, while the delicious aroma of baking gingerbread filled the air. She had whipped up some lemon sauce to drench it with, and that was now simmering in a pot.

The cats had already partaken of bologna scraps, thanks to Maura.

Christmas carols on the radio added to the festive mood. Gina sang along, urging everyone to join her, as she danced around, decorating the tree.

When they were finished and stood back, admiring their artistry, Molly made a mad dash, scrambling up to the very top of the tree, flinging decorations to the floor. Everyone's laughter made the scene even more festive.

~

CHRISTMAS DAY found the couples opening gifts around the tree after stoking the potbellied stove and the coal furnace. They sat around, drinking coffee and watching the cats' antics with their catnip toys. The felines had appeared drunk after inhaling the dried catnip, and now they lay about in exhausted ecstasy. Cookie glanced ruefully over at Tiggy, lying upside down on the braided rug, the catnip bag clutched tightly against his upturned tummy, a silly grin on his face as he purred mightily in his sleep.

Josh and Jim were happy with their knitted scarves, hanging them over their jackets by the door, and they put on the new shirts Gina had sewed for them. Much to Maura's delight, Gina tried on her knitted hat and refused to take it off all day.

Maura now stood in front of the new mirror in the hall, a gift from Alice, turning round and round in front of it to view the flowered, burlap apron Gina had sewn for her from some old feed bags she'd found in the cellar and washed. She was thankful for Alice's gift and made a note to call her the next day at her niece's house and see how she was.

The fellows had pooled their money to buy Gina a bolt of bright-blue cloth she'd admired in the local store, after she said she wished she had the money to buy it.

Much to her surprise, Maura received a variety of new baking pans, something she intended to put to good use the very next day.

Later, after a supper of roasted chicken, Maura brought out her famous chocolate brownies topped with wild raspberries.

"How in the world did you ever find raspberries this time of the year?" Gina asked between bites of the gooey chocolate treat.

"I didn't!" Maura smiled, reaching for one. "I found a patch of berries late in the fall and left them outside in the cold to freeze. I simply defrosted them." She smiled at Gina's obvious delight with her favorite treat. She was glad, now, that she'd put in the extra effort to please her sister-in-law.

The telephone rang, bringing Debbie's voice to Lucky and perfectly finishing off her day. Maura put the phone receiver down on the floor for the cat and opened the box of ribbon candy, a gift from Maude, which she passed around.

In the meantime, Cookie smelled the brownies and closed his eye again, knowing it wasn't anything cats could eat. Purring softly, he murmured that Maine was indeed peaceful, being so far away from anything having to do with war.

However, a low, warning growl from Lucky jerked him upright and left him with an unsettled feeling in his stomach...

# Chapter 20

## *Friday, January 1, 1943*

Everyone was off from work, even Gina, with the diner closed for the holiday. Jim was in the barn tending to the horse. Josh planned to join him as soon as he finished reading the newspaper, and Gina was busy sewing something from her new cloth.

"Another Monet was stolen," Josh said, incredulous.

"How many does that make?" Maura asked.

"Six so far. Funny; the thieves only steal watercolors, even though other paintings are worth more on the black market," he said, reading a comment from an art expert.

"Was this theft in Boston or New York?" Maura asked.

"Neither. The painting was stolen from an art museum in Chicago," Josh said. "Go figure."

Maura was washing her new pans when the phone rang. "Hi, Uncle Jack. Happy New Year!" she said, happy that he had called. Then a surprised look washed over her face.

"You bought Alice's house?" She held the receiver away from her ear and called out, "Josh! Guess what? Uncle Jack and Aunt Sarah just bought Alice's house!"

Cookie looked up from washing his face. "Perfect!" he thought. "Now if we do solve Gus's murder, we'll have someone to give a note to!" After all, Uncle Jack was a policeman! He'd know what to do with a note!

Unfortunately though, all Cookie had, were *pieces* of the mystery. Gus had been killed. But by whom? A "Night Visitor" came now and then to the front barn. Did he have anything to do with Gus's murder? Cookie simply didn't know. Still, he decided, "I definitely have to find something for Tiggy to practice writing on."

At that moment, Maura looked out the front window as a car drove up. A man got out and hung a SOLD sign from the bottom of the FOR SALE sign next door. Maura still held the phone away from her ear, so Josh could also hear her conversation with Uncle Jack.

Josh smiled broadly when Jack said he wanted the twins to repair Alice's old farmhouse during the winter, and when the repairs were finished, they'd move up.

This would be a new source of income for the twins. They might even earn enough money to buy lumber for a much-needed garage in which to park the truck, the tractor, and possibly, even *Big Blue*!

While they were talking on the phone, Cookie pushed the ad section of the newspaper, which Josh always put to one side because he was not interested in it, behind the old couch, where he'd stashed a pencil weeks ago. It was the perfect place to have the marmalade practice his letters.

~

A BULLDOZER CAME a few weeks later to push Alice and Gus's outhouse over, smashing it and breaking through the frost to cover the hole. In late March, as the thaw set in, a well digger arrived. He pounded away until he found water for the front house. Jack wanted all the new conveniences in the house: electricity, running water, and a flush toilet. The furnace man came and installed a new furnace, while Josh worked at restoring and painting the interior of the farmhouse. Jim completely rewired the house for electricity.

By late March, the house was habitable enough for Jack and his wife to move in, much to the delight everyone, especially the cats—all but Molly, who didn't yet understand the importance of Jack's presence.

Jack was a policeman! He'd know what to do with the note they'd write when they solved the case, wouldn't he? Or would he? Cookie felt unsure about the whole thing.

First, they needed to find out who had killed Gus. Next, they had to discover why. Then they'd need to find a way to get a finished note to the police. Cookie felt they'd somehow figure it out, when the time was right.

~

ONE MORNING, everyone except Gina, who was working, piled into the station wagon and went to the navy yard. Rubin had informed the twins that due to an increase in enlistees in the service, the navy had posted "help wanted" ads.

They turned into the parking lot and drove up to a small wooden guard shack. A red-haired man came and stood behind the bright-red gate that was lowered to keep cars and people out. He leaned over the gate to ask what they wanted. The fellows got out to talk to him, and the cats, seeing nothing interesting, lay down to have a good morning wash.

The navy man, his puffy cheeks red from the cool breeze, motioned for the men to slide under the gate and pointed to the building where they should apply for jobs.

Then he walked over to the car window and leaned over to tell Maura to move the car. "Yeh need ta pahrk the carer o'er terr, ann get out of the rudd," he said, his Irish brogue on top of a Maine accent confusing her until he pointed to a parking space away from the gate. Finally getting the gist of his statement, she drove the car into the space he had indicated while he moved back to the gate. She figured the man had been inducted, but once the naval officers heard his thick accent, they decided not to send him overseas, but to put him to work in the naval yard.

Another car approached, and the man questioned that driver too. At that precise time, Molly woke up and hooked her claws into the fabric on the back of the seat to stand up. She peered out at the guard, whose attention had turned away from them.

"Look, look!" the little kitten said, hopping up and down. "His beard slipped."

"Beard slipped?" Tiggy asked, opening a green eye.

"Beard slipped," she repeated, poking Cookie with her paw to wake him up.

"Beards don't slip," he reprimanded, putting his paws over his eyes.

"Did so slip," muttered Molly, sitting down next to Lucky. "Beard slipped!"

Her insistence caused the tuxedo to sit up and look curiously out the window.

Cookie reluctantly got up and looked where Molly pointed.

"I saw it!" Molly insisted. "That man's beard slipped down when he leaned forward to talk to that car."

After watching the man, now engrossed in conversation with the new arrival, and seeing nothing amiss, Tiggy smiled indulgently at the kitten. "Good imagination," he commented, receiving a light swat from the torti.

Cookie curled up again. As he drifted off to sleep, however, the gray tomcat remembered his cousin's tale of hair slipping. "Hair and beards don't slip, do they?" he wondered. Then, deciding these unlikely happenings probably didn't mean anything important, he let go of the thought and began lightly snoring.

The tomcats and Lucky slept until the fellows returned with the news that they had both gotten jobs and would start working at the naval yard after giving the town garage notice. Town work was bound to slow down now that the warmer weather was melting the snow. It was a happy group that drove away—all but the torti, who was still grumbling because no one believed her.

~

THE FOLLOWING WEEK, Maura saw a late-model car turn onto their lane and park outside Alice's farmhouse. Maura moved to look out the front window and then cried in delight, "Oh, look! Uncle Jack and Aunt Sarah are here!"

She went outside to greet them, followed by the cats.

"Hello," Uncle Jack said, bending down to pick up a purring Molly. "Who do we have here?"

Maura quickly filled him in as they all entered Maura's house and sat down at the kitchen table to have something to eat and drink. The tomcats slunk behind the couch to continue practice writing. They had two words now: *Gus* and *killed*. It was a start, but Tiggy was having difficulty forming the letter *G* in *Gus*. Lucky looked on from her easy chair, content that a piece of a puzzle would soon be in helpful hands, now that Jack was here.

"It's so nice that you moved next door," Maura said.

"Yep. Next week, I start my new job as a sheriff, and I'll get an official car," Jack said. Cookie blinked, holding the paw he was washing in midair. Jack! A policeman again? Perfect! Now they had the perfect person to give the note to! It could not have worked out any better if Cookie had planned it himself!

Maura glanced at Aunt Sarah, who rolled her eyes as if to say, "You're right, Maura. Jack will never truly retire."

Cookie started washing his paw again. "This just gets better and better," he murmured. Now that Jack was here, they could get back to business. And that was solving mysteries! The tomcat decided that now the well digger had finished digging, they could investigate those dusty footprints in Gus's barn—something he'd forgotten about until then.

~

LATE ONE AFTERNOON, after the twins had been working at the naval yard for a few days, Josh drove back to the yard to get a thermos he'd left behind. The cats, always up for a ride in the car, accompanied him. This time, a different guard was at the gate. Josh rolled down the window to state the purpose of his visit.

"OK!" the guard said, lifting the gate so he could drive in.

Josh went into the building where he and Jim worked and retrieved his thermos. Driving out, Josh stopped at the guard house again.

"Ya'll need a name tag next week before ya can get in," the guard told him.

"Yep," Josh said, nodding. Jim had ridiculed the idea when the twins learned they'd have to wear badges with their pictures on them. "Tough times when you need to advertise who you are," he'd said.

Josh held a brown paper bag through the open window. "Present from Maura, Dave."

Raising his eyebrows, the man took the bag. When he opened it, he smiled. "Ahh! Maura's chocolate-chip cookies. Just the thing ta eat while I read the latest Superman comic an' wait fur the night man ta come on."

Josh laughed and started to drive away, but Dave held up his hand to stop. "Wait a minute, Josh. I've got somethin' fur ya."

Rushing into the small building, he came out with a handful of posters depicting a man with a gray beard and wearing a tall, striped hat. The man was pointing his finger. "Uncle Sam Wants You" was printed below in bold letters.

"Put these up around town, wud ya?" He handed them into Josh, who turned and tossed them onto the back seat next to the cats.

Delighted, Cookie quickly snagged one with his paw and then another, shoving them both under the corner of a blanket. Tiggy looked questioningly at him.

"Practice." Cookie smiled, meowing softly. "Write."

Later, he planned to snatch the papers in his teeth and somehow manage to shove them, one by one through the open cat door in order to hide them behind the couch.

Hearing that interesting word, the Tiggy smiled, showing his dagger-like teeth. "Right!" he meowed softly in return. "Write!"

Those two words no longer confused Tiggy, thanks to his ladylove's clarification...

# Chapter 21

## *Saturday, March 27, 1943*

At the end of the month, Maura decided to give the guard another gift of chocolate-chip cookies, as he kept telling Josh how much he'd enjoyed the first batch.

Naturally, the cats all piled into the back of the car, delighted to go for a ride. Josh even cracked the window open to let the warm breeze waft in.

At the shipyard, Josh parked the station wagon in the last vacant space and locked it, as he didn't want the cats wandering outside, now that he knew of Tiggy's ability to open car doors. He and Maura walked toward the guard shack, Maura carrying a small package.

The felines peered out the windows, watching the humans move away. Tiggy wanted out. So he did what was natural for him and put his large paw on the door handle. To his amazement, the door stayed shut.

Lucky looked on in interest, as did the others.

"Door won't open!" grumbled the frustrated marmalade. He stretched up to put his paws on the window and then proceeded to slide down, through no fault of his own, dragging his claws on the glass with an irritating screech that earned him a dark look from Lucky. But he continued sliding, unwittingly shifting the position of the door lock and then dropping the weight of his upper body onto the door handle. It moved down, and the door opened slightly.

Delighted, the marmalade pushed it open further, and all cats except Lucky exited the car. She curled up for a nap.

The others wandered down the bank to look at the river.

Molly jumped up on a long steel beam resting across two sawhorses, while Cookie and Tiggy nosed the ground, smelling forest critters' scents.

Unnoticed by all was a red-haired man bending down on the wooden dock, fastening a line to a small boat. He straightened up and noticed Molly, and then his gaze fell on Cookie and Tiggy. His eyes widened in surprise. *"Verdammt katzen!"* he yelled and ran at them, sprinting up the bank toward Molly, who was closest.

Startled, Cookie and Tiggy instinctively bolted in different directions and hid. *"Katzen?"* Cookie thought when he was confident of his safety in a thorny thicket nearby. "Where have I heard that word before?" Suddenly, it dawned on him. *Max* used that word! The killer from the Connecticut shore!

But this man was not Max. Max was bald, and he walked hunched over with a hump on his back. This man was straight and tall and had red hair and a red beard.

"Holy cats! A red beard and red hair!" Hadn't he heard recently about both of them slipping? Cautiously, Cookie crawled out from under the branches to warn Tiggy and saw that the man was quickly closing the distance to the kitten perched on the metal beam.

"Max! It's Max!" he yowled and raced toward the kitten. "Run, Molly! Run!"

Tiggy looked back at the sawhorses from his new vantage point and saw the confused torti turn her head at Cookie's loud meowing. This caused her to teeter uncertainly atop the beam. Then, to Tiggy's horror, the man snatched Molly and heaved her into the wide, deep Piscataqua—a river deep enough for submarines to navigate.

Molly landed with a splash, immediately sinking beneath the surface, only to rise a moment later, sputtering, flailing her paws, and mewing pitifully.

Terrified, Cookie and Tiggy rushed down to the dock as the red-haired man ran past them and slipped into the utility shed near the parking lot. Suddenly, from the group's parked car, a loud, piercing howl erupted, renting the quiet.

Ignoring it, Cookie kept an eye on Molly and shouted, "Quick, Tigs! Run! Get Josh! Yell loud!"

The stunned, wide-eyed marmalade took off at a fast pace, loping toward the car, which was rocking with Lucky's shrill howls.

Cookie leaned over the end of the dock. "Hang on, Molly!" he howled to the frightened torti. He desperately wished he had hands so he could help her. "Hurry, Tig!" he yowled over his shoulder. "Hurry!"

Tiggy raced toward Josh and Maura, who were now running across the parking lot to see why Lucky's mournful cries were filling the air.

Reaching the car, Tiggy looked up at Josh and Maura and added his high-pitched squeaks to Lucky's cries.

Josh was leaning in to see what could be wrong with the tuxedo, when Cookie's yowl echoed from the riverbank. Maura turned to look in his direction and spotted the splashing of a small creature the river by the dock.

"It's Molly!" she screamed, grabbing her husband's arm. "Oh my God, Josh! It's Molly! She fell in the water! Hurry! Run!"

As Josh ran down to the river, Maura looked inside at Lucky, who continued to howl—something she'd never done before. Tiggy continued to howl too, adding to Maura's panic.

Meanwhile, Cookie, who had spotted Josh approaching, stopped yelling at the top of his lungs and turned to comfort the kitten. "Hang on, Molly," he urged as she desperately tried to claw her way up on the dock with her tiny, delicate claws, only to slip back into the water. "Josh is coming!"

With Maura watching in horror, Josh thundered down on the dock, jetted past the tomcat, and reached for the frightened torti, grabbing her by the scruff of her neck. Everyone breathed a sigh of relief when he held the dripping kitten up for Maura to see. The marmalade stopped howling, and silence emanated from the car's interior.

With her tiny claws, Molly clung to Josh as he and Cookie ran back to the car. Lucky stopped pacing when they all got in, and Maura reached for Molly. She cradled the kitten, immobile and barely breathing, on her lap.

"We'll take her to Dr. K. Good thing he's the vet now," Josh said, hurriedly backing up.

"No, Josh. Wait!" Maura took hold of his arm, and he braked, looking quizzically at her.

"Dr. K's not there now. He's off at the sanctuary, extracting teeth from a moose. I called him this morning to ask him about Cookie and his ear scratching."

"Well, what can we do?" Josh looked at Molly's limp body, suspecting the worst.

Suddenly, Maura brightened. She remembered what Cora told her the first time she went to the Tea Room. *"I be a healer."*

"The Tea Room, Josh! Go to the Tea Room!" She pointed in that direction. Josh drove off quickly, while Maura stared out the window, hoping Cora could help. She rubbed her hand over the torti's wet fur, getting the faintest of purrs in return.

None of them saw the bearded man slip out of the utility shed, climb to the top of the riverbank, and stare after them...

~

WITH A SCREECH OF TIRES, Josh pulled up in front of the Tea Room as Maura opened her door, telling everyone to stay in the car, including Josh.

Cora heard the commotion and opened the front door. Seeing Maura holding Molly in her arms, her welcoming smile faded. "Come in, Me Ma. Come in."

Maura rushed in, while the cats clung to the fabric on the back of the seat, looking anxiously through the Tea Room's front window.

Cora gently took Molly and headed for the back room. "Stay here, Me Ma. Pray," she mumbled.

Sitting uncomfortably on the edge of a seat, Maura worriedly looked through the beads covering the doorway and saw the Jamaican woman lightly running her hands over the limp feline she had placed on her bed. Soft humming filled the room as time hung by a thread.

Outside in the parked car, Josh and the cats waited anxiously for any word of her condition. Presently, to everyone's relief, Cora opened the front door, smiling widely. "Come in! Come in, everybody!"

Josh and the cats rushed in, only to stop short at the sight of Molly hungrily slurping tidbits from a small bowl. Three other bowls of food sat in a line on the floor next to her, and soon all the cats were happily munching. Once again, life was good.

Satisfied that the kitten was now fine, the humans sat at a table, enjoying the dark, thick, Jamaican coffee and some lemon bars that Maura had made.

Cora had once more placed a chair inside the playpen and another one outside the playpen so that a satisfied marmalade could visit with Lela. The baby sang softly, holding Tiggy, who was finally content when he had her all to himself.

"Kitten safe now," Lela commented, causing Cookie to look up from licking his paw. He glanced at Lucky, who had curled up on a chair. Her eyes remained closed. All was well in their world. For now.

# Chapter 22

## *Early Spring 1943*

Snowstorms deposited a few inches now and then throughout the month, but the warming of the sun quickly melted those layers. Since his hole was beneath the tree, the chipmunk was not bothered by the spring snows. And one morning, the hare, wearing his warm-weather coat of motley gray, made his way back across the meadow and stopped at Mickey's hole to chat a bit. They traded the news they'd collected over the long winter, and then the hare took up residence nearby, under a prickly bush in Maura's backyard that had new growth to munch on.

In a nod to the warming weather, Maura was doing some spring cleaning indoors, and she opened the door to the attic, much to the torti's delight. Molly immediately went up to visit her friend, the Blue Lady, and not long after, she came racing downstairs with some startling information; the Blue Lady saw the Night Visitor kill Gus!

Lucky confirmed this tale during a long-overdue visit to the chipmunk, who told her that his cousin, the hare, had told him much the same thing.

Now, Cookie had something to chew on. The threads of the mystery were coming together. Here, at last, were two witnesses to the murder. And both fingered the Night Visitor. "But who *is* this Night Visitor?" Cookie wondered.

At his urging, Tiggy practiced his capital letters by tracing newspaper headlines again. And he worked on the wording of the note they would write to police as soon as they cracked the case.

~

THAT EVENING, WHEN THE CATS RETIRED to living room for the night, Cookie was amazed to see Lucky hop up on his favorite cushion on the old couch instead of retiring to her usual spot on the easy chair.

"Hmm," he thought, "I wonder why she did that? She never goes there. Oh well, I'll sleep on the new couch." He lay down on a cushion, giving Molly a look. She was perched in her usual spot on the bolster above him, swishing her tail back and forth and gazing out at the night, interested in any critters that might wander by.

After giving his mug a halfhearted wash, Cookie ignored the kitten's ever-moving tail and drifted off to sleep. He woke a short time later, when Molly jumped down from her perch and poked him. "The Night Visitor is here!" she said and then hopped back up on the bolster.

*The Night Visitor!* Wide awake now, Cookie jumped up next to her, and they both peered into the night. Clouds were drifting over the full moon, allowing them only a glimpse of a man walking to the barn. Opening the door, he paused for a moment to look around. Then he slipped inside, closing the door quietly behind him.

Watching intently, the tomcat had a fleeting thought. "Is this why Lucky changed her sleeping habits? Is this something she wanted me to see?"

The clouds had vanished by the time the Night Visitor emerged with a long, slim canister under his arm, enabling Cookie to see that the man had red hair.

"Red hair?" Cookie thought. "Where have I seen someone like that before?"

Just then, Molly let out a small, growling hiss, jogging his memory.

He suddenly remembered the unfortunate episode at the water's edge. That man had called the cats *katzen*, and he had run at them, just as the spy at the Connecticut shore had done.

"Max! The Nigh Visitor is Max!" he said, glancing over at the torti, who was still hissing. She'd *never* forget the man who threw her in the river! She almost drowned!

Both Harry Hare and the Blue Lady had reported seeing the Night Visitor kill Gus. And they'd just identified the Night Visitor. Max! *It was Max who'd killed Gus!*

Cookie smiled. Pieces of the puzzle were falling into place!

Molly's growls woke Tiggy, who quickly jumped up next to them to peer out the window. Sure enough, Tiggy confirmed the Night Visitor's identity. "Max," he muttered with a growl.

They watched intently as the man walked back and forth from the barn to the car, each time depositing another oblong roll behind the driver's seat.

Cookie was gleeful. They still needed to find out what was in Max's long, slim containers and why he'd killed Gus. But they had their man! In the meantime, he would have Tiggy practice his letters so they could write an informative note to the police.

The staff of *Cats Incorporated* would have to keep their eyes open— especially the ones who lived behind the diner. Something would come up; Cookie just knew it.

Lucky simply sat up, peacefully washing her snow-white bib, content that she had done her share of the business, such as it was.

The three cats watched as the figure retrieved five long canisters before getting into his car and driving away.

Only then did Cookie sit down to consider what he'd just seen. The cats hadn't been able to investigate the front barn with all the construction going on at Uncle Jack's farmhouse. Who wanted to venture close to a well driller or a machine big enough to push over an outhouse?

Not he, for one! All that commotion had put on hold Cookie's investigation of the footprints in the dust around the moldy bale of hay. Well, that along with his forgetting about those footprints, although Cookie would never admit that to anyone. "Maybe tomorrow we'll be able to investigate. Although," he thought wryly, "all the clues might be gone now that the Night Visitor has taken away what he'd been hiding there." Or, so the gray tomcat thought...

## Chapter 23

*Monday, March 29, 1943*

Thanks to a warming wind blowing from the south, Monday dawned bright. While the cats were patiently sitting beneath the kitchen table, waiting for the snack they knew would be forthcoming, Josh came in and sat down. He opened the newspaper only to exclaim, "Now they've stolen another Degas!"

"What? *What?* Let me see!" Maura said, bringing him a cup of coffee.

She shook her head as she looked at the photo, and then she went back to the stove and cracked some eggs into a frying pan. "How many does that make now?"

"Seven, all told." Josh sipped his coffee. "They must be smuggling them out of the country and selling them overseas. No one here would buy them; the stories have been all over the papers. Wonder how they're doing it?"

"They've got some *chutzpah!*" Jim said, yawning as he poured himself a cup of coffee and sat down. This caused the cats to move to the archway, where they'd be safe from his ever-moving feet but still be able to see what was going on.

Maura shook her head, busy with making breakfast for the humans and the cats.

Gina ran a hand through her unkempt red curls and plunked down for a moment before getting up to pour herself a cup of coffee, seeing Maura was busy.

"One of the navy men just came back from the front," she said. "As I was pouring him a cup of coffee, he told his friend that he'd picked up the diary of a fallen German on the battlefield."

She paused, looking up. "A doctor's ID badge fell out of the diary, along with a picture of the man's wife and children. And when the navy man got a buddy to translate the diary for him, he learned that the German had written, 'If I don't make it, tell my wife I love her.'"

Tears came to Gina's eyes. "Makes me realize the Germans are just like us. They're just regular people with wives and kids and dreams."

She fell silent, wiping her eyes as Jim got up and put his arms around her. "War is hell, Gi! Let's hope this one's over quickly."

Jim's comment drew a sharp look from Lucky, which, fortunately, the other cats missed, since they were all eating their scrambled eggs.

The cats ate quickly and rushed out the cat door as soon as Maura opened it. She stood there, watching them, slightly amused.

"Boy, look at them run. I thought they had to do their business. But I guess what they really need is to run with the wind." She grinned, going back to the sink to wash the dishes as Gina and the men left for work.

~

THE CATS QUICKLY did their business behind the old barn, which had remained untouched since Gus died. Jack was considering renovating it into a garage, but not until the house was finished. The door still had its large crack, enabling the cats to slip inside, even Tiggy and Lucky. Weak light filtered down through the skylight, highlighting the dangling cobwebs. The cats looked around, finally meandering over to the moldy bale of hay.

Lucky sat down in a patch of sunlight to lick off a cobweb, while Tiggy was distracted, finding a trail of mouse turds. His sensitive nose twitched as he followed the mousey smells.

Cookie, however, was studying the different footprints that had caught his eye way back before the snows came. His attention was drawn by the new footprints superimposed on top of the old ones. He sneezed at the new layer of dust that had accumulated.

Molly raced forward, jumping onto the old, moldy bale. Prancing lightly on it, she leaned forward, then disappeared over the back of the bale.

Cookie shook his head and stifled a smile. Molly was a stitch, as Gina would say.

"Ooh! Ooh!" Molly called in a muffled voice. "Pretty! Pretty!"

"What? Let me see!" Cookie demanded as she backed out from behind the dusty bale, her whiskers draped with cobwebs.

Cookie inched forward, taking her place behind the bale. A long, cylindrical tube lay on the floor with its cap lying close by. A roll of paper had been pulled out, and he could tell that a rat had been gnawing on one corner. Cookie stepped on the edge of the paper and used his other front paw to unroll it a bit. Large flowers were splashed in bright watercolors across the paper.

"What see?" Tiggy asked, his nose still exploring a mouse hole.

"This could be one of the paintings that Josh was reading about in the paper this morning!" Cookie's astonished reply was muffled as he inched back out from behind the hay bale. He sneezed violently. "It's been here a while." He sneezed again, dislodging the cobweb hanging from his nose. He blinked when he saw Lucky staring at him—almost egging him on with his deductions.

"That's what Max was doing here last night!" Cookie said. "He had to be collecting the paintings! The ones that were still good!"

"Five tubes," Tiggy said, reminding his brother of what they'd seen.

"And one ruined one is left," Cookie said, nodding. "But that's only six. Josh said seven paintings were stolen."

Tiggy shrugged.

"Maybe we didn't see him come for the other one," Cookie mused.

Lucky rose then, came over, and licked him on the cheek, as though to congratulate him on his deductions. Cookie turned a deep shade of red, which fortunately, was hidden by his dark fur. Hoping no one had seen him blush, he looked up to see the other two cats staring at him. Darn.

"We need to put this in the note," he meowed, as he made his way to the door. But first, there were cat things to do. They were so happy to find another piece of the puzzle that they raced to the meadow, chasing anything that moved. "Now," Cookie thought, "all we need to find out is how Max plans to smuggle the paintings out of the country."

~

THE NEXT DAY, once the men were off to work and the cats were napping in the living room, Maura heard a rap at the door. She moved to the front door, and seeing a man in a crisp, white navy uniform, she smiled and opened it.

"Hi," the man said. "I'm Howard, Elmer's son-in-law."

"Oh, come in. Come in." Maura held the door open. They went into the kitchen, where she offered him some newly cooked apple fritter with a cool glass of iced tea. "I came ta see how yar making out with Star," he said, causing a flutter in Maura's heart. She knew how proud Jim was of tending to the horse, now that someone had taught him the proper way to ride.

"I'm assigned ta the hospital ship, now docked at Portsmouth Naval Yard. We put in fur slight repairs and ta pick up additional supplies fur the hospital bay. We might even need ta replace our head nurse, as she's 'bout ready ta have her little one! So, I thought I'd come an' talk ta ya 'bout Star. We'd like ta see if ya'd like ta keep him permanently."

He went on to explain that his wife would be moving frequently until he finished his hitch in the navy. "So, ya see," he continued, "she won't be in a position ta take Star." He leaned down to scratch Tiggy under the chin.

"If yar not interested, we can always sell 'im," Howard said reluctantly. "But we'd really like keep 'im here, where he's used ta livin'. And we'd keep sending money fur his upkeep ta the farrier who tends ta his feet an' horseshoes and ta the horse doc. Plus, ya'd have a runnin' credit at the feed store."

"Oh, you mean like a pal who pays?" Maura grinned, taking a sip of her cool drink. She could tell he really didn't want to have Star go to someone else.

He smiled. "Star can be a bit of a wimp when ya tighten his girth."

Maura nodded in agreement. They'd discovered that.

"We found that if ya offer him a carrot, he'll let ya do most anythin'," Elmer's son-in-law said.

This helpful hint along with the news that they could keep the horse would please Jim, who had grown quite fond of him.

And so, it was settled with a simple handshake. Star would stay. Jim would be in seventh heaven when he came home and heard the news.

Maura wondered if Jim and Josh had seen the hospital ship arrive while they were at work. She could hardly wait until they came home.

Cookie had listened with half an ear to the conversation, drifting in and out of sleep. He did catch the news about the hospital ship being in port, but it didn't interest him. Unfortunately, he missed seeing Lucky jump from her easy chair, wander into the kitchen, and sit under the table, looking up with great interest at Elmer's son-in-law as he talked.

# Chapter 24

## *Saturday, April 3, 1943*

Maura was at the sink washing breakfast dishes when she turned to Josh, sitting at the large kitchen table. "Where's your thermos, Josh?"

Josh put down his cup and slapped his forehead. "Darn! I forgot it again! I was welding a piece of the ship's rudder on a sawhorse, and I took a coffee break…but then I put the thermos on the ground. Never noticed it when I left."

He got up and moved to the front door, taking his light jacket from a wooden peg on the wall. His name badge was pinned to the pocket. "I'll take a ride over there and grab it."

Tiggy, hearing the word *ride* rose and followed him to the door.

"Take the cats!" Maura called, smiling as she saw the marmalade walking after him. "They all love to ride in the car."

"Sure. Come on, cats," Josh called, holding open the front door until they all trotted out and piled into the car.

Arriving at the naval yard, Josh showed his badge, and when the guard lifted the gate, he drove slowly down the road leading to the dock. A huge white ship lay at anchor next to the loading dock.

"*X*'s tilted," Tiggy commented as they drew closer.

Cookie, never having seen a hospital ship with the giant red crosses painted on it, remained silent.

Molly stood up, peering with wide eyes at the huge ship.

Josh got out of the car and walked over to the sawhorses to retrieve his thermos. As he did so, a man exited the shed carrying a large cardboard box toward the dock. The ease with which he carried it made it look very light, despite its bulk.

As he came closer, the small torti let out a rolling growl that startled Cookie.

The man walked past them, the box making it difficult for him to see the cats. However, they could easily see his red hair and beard, along with the large black letters on the side of the box that read "gauze."

"Max!" shouted Cookie as the man trod away, onto the gangplank carrying the large box. "That box could hold the stolen artworks, unrolled at the bottom," the tomcat surmised. "So *that's* how he's getting them out of the country!"

Josh came back with his thermos and opened the car door to a barrage of caterwauling. *Max is here! He killed Gus! He has the stolen artwork! It must be in the big box!* the cats yowled.

"Good grief!" Josh said, turning the car around and motoring up the road again. "What on earth is the matter with all you cats? Haven't you seen a big boat before?" Unfortunately, Josh had never gotten the hang of cat language, so they were all howling in vain!

When they left the naval yard, the cats all sat down, tired from their meowing. Molly was panting from the exertion; Tiggy was wide eyed; and Lucky was frowning but kept her thoughts to herself. Cookie, however, was already thinking of what they now knew about the mystery of Gus's murder.

"I think we have the final piece of the puzzle," murmured Cookie. He put a paw on Tiggy's paw. "We can  finish the note now." He realized it was urgent to get it to the police before the big ship left port.

If Cookie's theory was correct, Max planned to sail with the ship, which was bound overseas, and he must have a contact who would meet the boat. He'd probably help bring wounded aboard and then smuggle the watercolors out to be sold to the highest bidder. And if Cookie knew anything about Max, he knew he'd use the proceeds to buy guns and bullets for the Germans. Max was a *spy*!

~

ONCE HOME, THE CATS scrambled out, hurriedly did their business, and rushed inside to scoot behind the couch.

"You must have pooped the cats out," Maura said, chuckling as she smoothed the top of a cake with green Kool-Aid frosting. "They usually run in here and check to see if I have any snacks for them." She laid the spatula down and walked toward the living room to check on them.

Lucky heard her footsteps coming and turned halfway around to walk toward the kitchen, nosing the kitten in that direction, too. This seemed to satisfy Maura, who returned to frosting the cake.

Now that she had had success in diverting Maura's attention, Lucky licked a slightly confused kitten, who was not yet used to subterfuge, something the tuxedo was very good at, for some unexplained reason.

Meanwhile, the unfinished note had been pawed out from under the old couch, and Tiggy had snatched up the pencil. He juggled it for a moment before getting a firm grip on it.

"What write, Bro?" he inquired.

Cookie thought for a moment and snagged the front page of the morning's newspaper. Cookie smiled in satisfaction as he looked at a photo of the hospital ship.

He studied what Tiggy had written so far.

The note said: MAX HERE. HAS RED HAR IN NAVY. KILLED GUS.

"Add these words," he murmured, finding the first one in the headlines. He lucked out with most of them and then guessed at the spelling of a very important one.

After writing the words, Tiggy sat back and admired his work. He demanded to know what they said.

Lucky smiled when she saw them, but she decided not to correct Cookie's spelling. "ART IN GAZ BOX," Cookie read to his brother.

"We finished, Bro?" Tiggy asked.

His brother puzzled for a moment before speaking. They had to be as specific as possible, but they also needed to hurry up and deliver the note, not knowing when the ship would sail. The police needed to know *now!*

So, Cookie decided to only use the letter *H* for the ship. He couldn't find the word in the headlines. "Surely," he thought, "the cops will be able to figure out what that word is supposed to be."

Pointing to the words they needed to finish the note, Cookie noticed Lucky smiling at all their labors. Even Molly lay close by, not understanding the words, but sensing the excitement at finishing the note.

Tiggy sat back on his haunches when he finished writing, "IN H. SHIP." The cats still did not know why Max killed Gus, but they would trust Uncle Jack to figure out his motive.

Meanwhile, the torti thought, "Maybe someday I'll discover I have some sort of special talent." It was something she could wish for.

When the note was finished, Cookie peered out from behind the couch. Maura had finished the cake and was now frosting cupcakes with tart, green Kool-Aid icing.

He knew she would be delivering them first thing the next morning so Charlie could sell them to the early church crowd. Like Harry Hare, he kicked with his back feet to scrunch the note into a tangled pile. Then he had Tiggy sit on it several times to flatten the pile and make it smaller.

Then, while Maura was still busy in the kitchen, he grabbed the crumpled paper with his teeth and sneaked it out to the car, stuffing it behind a tire. In the morning, he'd make sure to be up early to ride to the diner with her while the others slept.

# Chapter 25

## *Sunday, April 4, 1943*

The next day, Maura was surprised at first to see the tomcat trotting alongside her when she went out to the car to deposit the cake on floor in front of the passenger seat. But she shrugged and decided the cat just wanted a ride. She opened the back door for Cookie to jump in. After he'd gotten in, she closed it and went back to the kitchen for the cupcakes.

As soon as she turned her back, Cookie jumped over the front seat, careful not to step on the cake, and bolted out the door she'd left open. Unnoticed, he retrieved the note from under the car. Quickly hopping back in and over the front seat with the note in his mouth, he shoved it under the towel Maura always left there for cats to sit on. He was peacefully sitting on the towel, waiting for her, when she returned with the cupcakes.

A short while later, parking in front of the closed diner, Maura inadvertently left the car door open after grabbing the cupcakes. She climbed the steps and knocked at the door, so Charlie would let her in. When she felt something nudge her leg, she looked down, dismayed to see the cat, sitting there by her feet.

"Cookie!" she cried. "How did you get out?"

"How indeed!" thought the smug cat, scooting past her when Charlie opened the door. "Houdini Jr., they call me." He needed to scope out a place to hide the note where it would be found by the right people.

"Cookie!" Maura went to grab him, but Charlie stopped her.

"Leave him," the owner said, propping the door open with a wooden wedge. "Bring in the cake and then stay for a cup of coffee. This cat keeps me company. I'm thinking of making him the official diner cat because the customers like him so much." Charlie bent down and patted Cookie's head. Spotting a leftover scrap of bacon next to the griddle, he gave it to the cat.

Cookie rewarded him with a rolling "*MERRR*" as he scoffed down the treat. Then he dashed out through the propped-open front door and jumped into the car while Maura was still talking to Charlie.

Grabbing the note, the tomcat dropped it on the ground under a bush by the front steps and waited until Maura left the building again to get the cake from the car. Then the cat snagged the paper with his teeth and scooted back up the steps and into the diner.

Charlie was busy in the kitchen, making a pot of coffee, so Cookie trotted over to the clothes rack, where customers hung their coats and hats. He scampered behind a pair of galoshes and dropped the note on the floor.

The boots had been there since winter, when their owner was inducted into the army. Unfortunately, the man would never come back to claim them. Charlie had left them there as a reminder that, as he said, "Some give up their own dreams so that others might have theirs."

Charlie had just put some fresh bacon on to fry, and smelling this, the tomcat went to the kitchen and sat down next to him. Chuckling at the tomcat, Charlie snagged a whole, freshly fried strip and gave it to him, furtively looking around to see if Maura had noticed.

She hadn't. She was only now walking in, carefully holding the cake that she slid  onto the counter.  Then she helped herself to a cup of fresh coffee and  sat on one of the red-vinyl stools, sniffing the steaming cup appreciatively.

This allowed the cat, sitting behind the counter and out of her view, to take his time munching the delicious, fragrant strip of bacon. He smiled, knowing full well Tiggy would question him later, as his mouth definitely smelled of bacon.

While he was chomping away, Uncle Jack and his deputy stopped for a cup of coffee before going to work. Seeing Maura at the counter, they walked over. Jack gave his niece a hug, and both men took seats at the counter, next to her.

"You're working on a weekend, Uncle Jack?" Maura wanted to know.

"Yes," Jack replied, sighing. "We usually don't work on weekends, but we have been lately because of the murder. We're trying to figure out who did it."

He lowered his voice and looked around before going on. "People in town are scared. They don't like the idea of a killer running loose. And personally, I don't either."

He sighed. "We have to go over some of the information on Gus's death to see if we missed something." They talked for a while, and then Maura got up to leave.

"Leave the cat here. Come back for him later," Charlie said, putting a plate stacked high with pancakes on the counter for the weekend waitress, who had just arrived, to take to Jack and his deputy when they moved to a booth. He knew the men wouldn't refuse them, and so did Cookie.

Before sitting down in a booth, Jack walked over to the coat rack and deposited his briefcase behind the galoshes, much to the cat's delight.

Cookie nonchalantly strolled over. Then, when no one was looking, he moved past the boots and knocked the satchel over, happy to see some important papers spill out. Grabbing the note that he'd dropped on the floor, the tomcat shoved it into the now-open top of the briefcase. Unfortunately, his teeth left a series of small, damp, bacon-smelling holes.

When the cat trotted out from behind the boots with a satisfied smile on his face, Charlie spotted him. "Whatcha lookin' for, Cookie? Spies?"

The cat went over to wind around Charlie's legs. "Yes," he meowed, showing his teeth in a huge smile.

Charlie reached over to break off another small piece of bacon for the tomcat. "You're my kind of cat!" He laughed, thinking of customers' smiles when they patted Cookie. His presence seemed to give them some peace of mind. "You're a real patriot!"

"If only you knew," meowed Cookie, crunching the bacon while he watched Jack rise and retrieve his briefcase, shoving the spilled papers back inside. "If only you knew."

Cookie trotted over to the door, where he'd wait for someone to let him out. He would visit with the cat colony until Maura was ready to leave.

He could hardly wait to tell his ma that they had solved another mystery and passed the information to the police! He was content that the information was in the right hands. Now, all they had to do was sit back and wait, confident that they would eventually see the results of their hard work, thanks to Uncle Jack's unwitting involvement in *Cats Incorporated*!

Once again, the cats had solved a murder, although they would be the only ones who would know it...

# Chapter 26

## *Tuesday, April 13, 1943*

The day President Roosevelt dedicated the Jefferson Memorial as a "shrine to freedom," the hospital ship finally left the dock at Portsmouth Naval Yard, having been detained by the FBI until then. Speculation was running rampant in town, as the FBI investigation was hush-hush. Everyone was talking about it. Signs reading "Loose lips sink ships!" appeared around town. The navy brass stayed closed-mouthed, leaving everyone but the cats to wonder what was going on.

Unfortunately, their informants, Harry Hare, Billie Goat, and even Mickey, the chipmunk, remained uninformed of the happenings. Lucky wished they could all understand her to share in the cats' satisfaction. But since they couldn't, she sidled up to each one to rub against them—even the goat—as way of thanking them.

However, the Blue Lady was informed of the note's delivery and its contents, thanks to the young torti's ability to visit the attic. But the humans living in the farmhouse were left in the dark until Uncle Jack arrived that evening, when everyone was home from work, to tell them the news.

"Sit down, Uncle Jack. Sit down," Maura urged, although, she, like the others, couldn't wait to hear what he had to say. He'd tell them the latest news, knowing they wouldn't spread it around.

Maura offered him a cup of coffee and a piece of nut bread, and they all sat down at the kitchen table. Even the cats were clustered in the archway, listening.

Noticing this, Maura cut them each a bit of bologna, assuming that's what they were waiting for. She was wrong, of course, but they were happy to get the snack anyway. So, they sat nearby, nibbling, all ears turned toward Jack.

After eating the nut bread, which Maura had spread with cream cheese, Jack took a sip of coffee and told them about finding the note.

"Thanks to that informant, we stopped the shipment of those valuable paintings before the hospital ship left the dock." He took another sip and then said, "I don't need to tell you all that this information is to go no further than this room."

Cookie paused in licking the bottom of his paw. He knew Lucky wished she could pass the information to all their informants and congratulate them on their part in solving the mystery of who killed Gus.

Lucky walked over to Cookie and gave him a slight nudge and a wink before wandering to their bowl for a drink of water. Actually, she wanted to get closer to Jack. The tomcat began to lick his paw again.

The purring cats knew that all was now well in their corner of Cumberland, and they would no longer see the Night Visitor at Gus's barn.

"We just had a meeting with the FBI. They told us that a certain security guard had worked at all the museums where paintings were stolen. He was a young man who couldn't enlist because he was deaf in one ear, and he told his employers that he had an interest in keeping American treasures safe. That's why they hired him. Now, the FBI suspects the Germans purposely made him deaf by detonating a hand grenade next to his ear so he wouldn't be able to enlist—but he *would* be able to get jobs vacated by men who had joined the service."

He motioned for Maura to refill his cup, which she quickly did so he would continue.

"They can't prove it, but they suspect the 'woman' who was seen touching the paintings—who nobody bothered with, thinking she was senile—was really one of the spies we encountered back in

Connecticut," Uncle Jack said. "The one we call the Master of Disguises."

"Max and the driver of the white truck!" meowed Cookie, making everyone look at him.

"They strongly suspect that these were the same two spies who stole guns from the New Haven factory, and stealing the paintings was another Nazi plot to raise money for arms." He looked at Maura, and she hurried to cut him another piece of nut bread and slather it with cream cheese. She knew her uncle very well.

"You mean the Nazis made that guy deaf just so he could infiltrate American workplaces?" Jim asked, disbelief in his voice.

Uncle Jack nodded. "It's not as farfetched as it sounds. Spies are everywhere, especially during wartime." He took a bite of nut bread and chewed thoughtfully before adding, "Unfortunately, the two disappeared before the FBI could nab them. Hopefully, they've gone back to Germany."

Lucky snorted at this pronouncement, causing Maura to jump up and stand over her, asking, "You aren't going to throw up, are you, Lucky?" Jack moved his foot away from Lucky.

Tiggy just looked at her. He knew his ladylove well enough to know that she disagreed with Uncle Jack's statement that the spies were gone.

Even so, everyone, including the cats, was glad that the plot to sell famous paintings to buy war supplies for the Germans had been foiled.

# Chapter 27

## *Saturday, April 17, 1943*

The diner was busy when Jack and Dan, his deputy, stopped in for a snack before lunch. They had just left the navy yard, where they'd had a second, private meeting with the FBI. Nothing had changed. The spies were gone.

However, they had been questioned repeatedly about the identity of their snitch and how he managed to enlighten them about what was going on. Unfortunately, Jack and Dan didn't have that information. They simply didn't know the identity of the informant. They'd also been grilled again about their roles in the whole affair.

"Strange doings," Jack said, slipping into the only empty booth. He asked the waitress for a cup of coffee and a couple of Maura's applesauce cupcakes. Dan indicated he'd have the same.

Maura had just dropped off that dessert, having come with her cat crew. By this time, Cookie had officially become the diner cat. "The customers love him," Charlie told Maura every time Cookie came in with her. "Leave him."

Tiggy didn't want to go into the diner. "People step on tail," he complained, which was true, due to his tail's extra length.

So, Cookie asked the marmalade to keep an eye on Molly. Tiggy didn't mind doing that as long as he could talk to his ma, whom he dearly loved. He was thrilled to be able to visit her, now that the colony had moved up to Maine.

Lucky also preferred to visit the colony rather than venture into the diner. Humans, she knew, could be a big puzzle sometimes, and the colony cats kept tabs on the ones who frequented the diner.

And so, when Maura delivered the desserts, the cats always rode along, with Cookie rushing in for his scraps of bacon.

Maura made sure Charlie knew that the pieces of bacon should be small, although now and then, when she wasn't looking, he slipped the tomcat a large piece, much to the cat's delight.

Cookie held up his part of the bargain, moseying over to customers and letting them pet him.

That day, Uncle Jack sat back after eating the two cupcakes. "Can't stop thinking about the notes I've gotten, one in Connecticut and one here," he said to Dan.

He shook his head, leaning forward and lowering his voice. "Look around you. Lots of people. Navy, townspeople, and some just moving through on their way somewhere else. What are the chances someone stuffed a note into my briefcase here and my raincoat pocket at the shore in Connecticut?"

"Yeah," Dan said. "How could the snitch be in both places?"

Uncle Jack thought for a moment. He didn't have the informant's notes now. The FBI had taken them. But he remembered them vividly. "The first note looked like a kid had written it. The letters were a bit wobbly, especially the *O*'s. In the second note, the handwriting was better, although the snitch tried to throw us off by being a poor speller."

Cookie was sitting behind the counter, munching on the tidbit of bacon Charlie had slipped to him. He perked up his ears. He remembered the paper bag on which they'd written that note. It had faintly smelled of shellfish because it had held crabs for the fishermen. Now he strolled over to the booth to greet Uncle Jack—and to position himself to better hear the conversation.

"Hey, Cookie. I see you're now the diner cat." Uncle Jack held out his hand, and the cat rubbed against it, acknowledging his presence, while Maura watched from her stool.

Jack turned back to Dan and picked up his cup. "The first note had a faint smell, and we never did figure out what it was. There was a small bite mark on the corner, almost like a rat bit it." Jack sighed, remembering. "The informant apparently stuffed it into my raincoat pocket when I stopped at the diner for coffee and pie."

Under their table, Cookie smirked.

"This latest note smelled of bacon and definitely had bite marks on it," Jack added.

"But how could you get a note in both places?" Dan asked. "It just doesn't make sense!"

Jack frowned, agreeing with him. The front door swung open and Jack looked over as Dr. K came in—something he did every Saturday at noon, after he closed his veterinary office. The vet wasn't married and hated to cook. Uncle Jack and Dan had often seen him in the diner at suppertime, sitting at the counter eating the special of the night, when they stopped after a long day of work.

Now he was standing by the cash register, waiting for a cup of soup and a hamburger to go.

"Hi, Dr. K," Jack called.

When the vet received his burger in a paper bag, along with a cup of soup, he walked over to say hello to the police officers.

Jack had a thoughtful look on his face as the vet approached their booth. "Hey, Dr. K," he said. "Maura's really happy you decided to move up here."

"Yes." Dr. K put the paper bag and cup of soup on their table.

"You eat at the diner often?" Jack inquired, getting a curious look from Dan.

"Yes. All the time." The vet sighed. "Sometimes it makes me think I should look around for a wife."

Dan laughed. But Jack kept on with his questioning, almost as if he were interrogating a crook!

"I didn't go to the diner often back in Momauguin," Jack said. "Did you visit that one, too, to get your meals?"

"Yes. All the time." The vet picked up his soup and sandwich and told them good-bye. "Have to get home and eat this while it's still hot."

"Yeah. See you, Doc." Jack smiled.

Dan leaned across the table as Dr. K went out the door. "You look like the cat who just ate the canary. What gives?"

"Well, I just solved the mystery of who wrote the notes."

"Who?" Dan was baffled.

"Dr. K," Jack said with a smile.

"*What?*" Cookie blurted.

Hearing the startled meow, Dan looked down at the cat, frowning.

Cookie pretended to be tugging at a nail sheath, but he rose and repositioned himself under an empty table, still close enough to eavesdrop on the conversation. He couldn't wait to hear how Jack arrived at that conclusion.

"How did you deduce that?" Dan asked. What had he missed?

Jack motioned for another cup of coffee. "Who do we know who lived in both places and who frequented the diners where I got both notes?" Jack asked.

"Dr. K, I guess," said an incredulous Dan.

"Yep. Mystery solved," Jack said triumphantly.

Maura came over to their booth to say good-bye and pick up Cookie, but as she reached under the table, the gray cat scooted away. He definitely wasn't going anywhere until he heard the rest of what Jack had to say.

"OK, Cookie." Maura shook her head. "I'll corral the rest and give them their snacks and then come back for you." At the door, she turned and shook her finger at him. "But, Mister, you'd better be ready!"

The tomcat smiled at Maura. He intended to comply, provided Jack finished his tale first.

The men laughed at Cookie huddling under the table, so he started to wash, making sure he could hear their conversation.

"He tried to throw us off by misspelling words," Jack said. "But I know better. He still writes like a little kid." Jack laughed. "And he tried to throw us off by having an animal, probably a cat or a rat, chew on the notes." He finished his coffee and stood up. "This time, he added the smell of bacon to confuse us. He'll probably do it again, if he has to write another note, thinking he's confused us."

The two men started for the door as Maura walked back in. She held the door open for them.

"But he didn't confuse us, of course," Jack went on, starting down the steps. "We're too smart for that!"

Cookie meekly followed Maura to the car. And as soon as he joined the others in the back seat, he told them what he'd overheard.

Maura glanced in the rearview mirror at the cats as she drove home. She couldn't understand why they were all meowing delightedly.

*Cats Incorporated* had done it again. They'd solved a murder mystery *and* had a cover story if ever they needed to deliver another note! Cookie could hardly wait to return to the diner and tell his ma and the colony that last bit. Plus, he'd tell Theresa that now, even though he didn't know it, Uncle Jack was part of their organization.

# Chapter 28

*Sunday, April 18, 1943*

M aura and the cats had just arrived at the diner. She loved trying new desserts, and she'd made something called cannolis, hard pastry shells filled with chocolate pudding.

As she opened the car door to let the cats out, she smiled at a woman parked near the diner steps who was herding a toddler and a slightly older child into her car.

*Someday*…Maura thought as she walked around to the passenger side of the car and reached in for the long cookie pan covered with tinfoil.

Cookie, meanwhile, had made a beeline for the diner door and slipped inside on the heels of a customer. Tiggy, who now had the job of keeping an eye on Molly, loped beside the kitten as she trotted toward the beckoning forest behind the building. The torti loved to roam the woods, with its many intriguing smells.

Lucky, just waking from her nap, rose, stretched, and moved to the open door to sniff the air. She was about to jump out when a movement caught her eye. She hesitated, watching, and her eyes grew wide as the scene unfolded.

Maura was still leaning into the car, lifting a corner of the foil to make sure her cannolis were all right, when suddenly, a man's anguished cry filled the air.

Maura stood up and looked over her shoulder. "Oh, my God!" she cried. "Someone just got run over!" She dropped the tray on the seat and ran toward the knot of people forming near the diner steps, cannolis and cats forgotten.

Maura did not see the tuxedo jump out of the car and turn deliberately away from the noise. At the corner of the diner, Lucky glanced once more at the human hubbub. Then, she trotted purposefully down the path to the rear of the building.

Lucky was on a mission…

# A Peek at Book 3: *A Tale of Five Tall Tails*

It's 1943, and the war in Europe has spread around the globe. American troops are fighting abroad, and factories and shipyards are humming at home.

In their farmhouse in Maine, Josh, Maura, Jim, and Gina are dealing with rationing in addition to making new friends, while the cats are becoming acquainted with a bloodhound who often gets lost and needs rescuing, a bear with an itchy butt, and a hermit who makes moonshine.

Then a rare and unsettling earthquake leaves a truck containing the body of a missing navy man bobbing in a nearby lake. Suddenly, the cats have a new case to unravel.

With the aid of fairies, the sleuths tug on the threads of a mystery that grows to involve a code walker, a ghost army, sheep dropped by parachute, and cookies that go BOOM!

# About the Author

Adrienne E. Schabel spent her early years on her grandparents' Connecticut farm and in a cottage in Momauguin, a village on the shore of Long Island Sound. She began writing at age twelve, when she penned a mystery in which she killed off all her classmates except the boy she liked. Her husband, Al, claims he has always taken a back seat to the many cats she's rescued and insists that in his next life, he will come back with a long tail.

Made in United States
North Haven, CT
16 December 2023

45910152R00126